Smith's
MONTHLY

Every Month Original
Novels, Stories, and Articles

USA Today Bestselling Writer
Dean Wesley Smith

TABLE OF CONTENTS

SHORT STORIES

Skiing the Graveyard of Souls	6
Eyes On My Cards	
A Doc Hill Story	20
Bryant Street	40
Captain Bob	
The End of the World as We Know It	50
The Songs of Memory	
A Jukebox Story	54

FULL NOVEL

Heaven Painted as a Poker Chip	
A Ghost of a Chance Novel	66

SERIAL STORIES

The Life and Times of Buffalo Jimmy	30
Chapters 28-30	
The Adventures of Hawk	44
Chapters 28-30	

NONFICTION

Introduction:	
The Memory of a Really Fun Idea	3

POEMS

Plane Crash Lover	29
Jukebox Memories	162

Smith's Monthly Issue #10

The Writings and Opinions of

Dean Wesley Smith

Introduction
The Memory
of a Really Fun Idea

IN WHAT SEEMS like a land far, far away and long, long ago, I wrote a novel I really liked. I wrote it in the writing method and style that I would eventually adopt to write well over a hundred other novels along the way.

The novel was my fourth written novel ever. The year was 1987. The place was my small apartment in Eugene, Oregon.

My first two written novels had been lost in a fire two years before. My third written novel, started in 1986 and finished in early 1987 became my first published novel, *Laying the Music To Rest.*

But the fourth novel never saw the light of day. I ran into some confidence problems with it among other things (like making the mistake of having a workshop look at it).

I wrote the novel on an electric typewriter and never had a computer file for it. As I lost confidence in the book, I put the original draft of the novel and a few other copies of the manuscript into a box and tossed it in storage.

And that's where that book still sits, never to come to the light of day.

That book was called *Heaven Painted as a Condominium.*

As the decades went past, my memory of the book turned the sour experience into a good one, and my memory, never good in the best of times, remembered the book fondly, but not in detail.

In other words, I remembered the basic idea for the book but nothing more past the opening few chapters.

So this last month, I finally decided to bring the idea back.

That happened one evening as I was starting to doze off for a quick nap in a chair in our living room.

Suddenly the idea of the *Heaven Painted* book came roaring back and

Thanks for the Support

Dean Wesley Smith

smashed into another world and I knew I had a brand new series.

The *Ghost of a Chance* series.

I sprang from the chair, which at my age is something to behold, and made notes, and then a few days later I started writing the book.

That book, *Heaven Painted as a Poker Chip,* is in this issue. I'm very happy with it. It is nothing at all like the first one (or my memory of the first one) from 1987. I never bothered to even try to find that old manuscript. (Honestly, not really sure where it's at.)

So a memory of a very old, unpublished book triggered the writing of this book twenty-seven years later.

So with this relook at the past, I decided to find another turning point story for me. That story is called "Bryant Street" and I sold it way back in the late 1980s to a small magazine called *2 A.M. Magazine.* It was published in 1990, but I wrote the story years before that. I doubt more than a few hundred people saw the story the first time out. If that many.

Early on I wrote a lot of stories set in homes along Bryant Street. I still do.

I've had one or two "Bryant Street" stories in this magazine so far. At one point, since I have a degree in architecture, I designed the entire subdivision around Bryant Street and just started down the street writing stories. The Garden Lounge, where my Jukebox stories are set, is at one end of Bryant Street.

Most of those early Bryant Street stories were also lost in the fire. But because the story "Bryant Street" was out in submission to a magazine at the time, I didn't lose it. A copy of the story came back to me.

So since I had brought the Heaven Painted idea to the present, wrote it fresh, and gave it a new life, I figured this would be a good issue to put "Bryant Street" in. Sort of an old home week of story ideas.

Then, in a continuing effort to pull back from extinction a few other fun and old stories, I have included a really silly and somewhat goofy story about Captain Bob. That story was first published in a very, very tiny regional sf magazine called *Sirius Visions*. I think exactly twelve people saw it on first publication.

Also in this issue, I am including a Jukebox story that I published in the small paperback and electronic standalone form. The subscribers to my short stories saw it, but not many others.

The reason that I am including "The Songs of Memory" is that the story is the start of the linking stories between the Jukebox world and the Thunder Mountain series.

I hope in the next few months to write a few more linking stories and the first jukebox novel, so I wanted to get this story back into awareness, at least in my own mind.

There are five stories total in this issue, plus the full novel, plus the two serials and some poems. As with every issue, I'm proud of these stories and novels.

Ten issues down and still going strong. And I'm still having fun, which is the most important thing for me.

I hope you enjoy the stories and the brand new novel, the first of a brand new series.

And thank you all for the support. It means a great deal to me.

Dean Wesley Smith
June 8, 2014
Lincoln City, Oregon

Coming Next Issue in Smith's Monthly
A Return to the Seeders Universe
in a brand new novel THE HIGH EDGE

USA *Today* Bestselling Writer

DEAN WESLEY SMITH

SKIING THE GRAVEYARD OF SOULS

I used to waterski early in the morning when the surface of the lake seemed like a mirror. Looking down into the water as the boat pulled me across the calm waters, all I could see was a reflection of myself flashing over the surface.

But to me, there always seemed to be something beyond, behind, deeper than just my own reflection. Those moments cutting over the water felt magical.

So years later, remembering those times, I wrote this story about Benny, who needed something special in his life, who needed to do something special with his life.

Benny's father found the magic before he died. Could Benny stand to face his own life, his own reflection, as he skied?

Or would his own soul join the graveyard flashing past below him? That's a question we all face at one point or another.

SKIING
THE GRAVEYARD OF SOULS

One

"HIT IT!" the vagrant stood near the front entrance shouted to nothing in particular, then went back to staring out the window at the city spread out below the Penthouse Bar.

His words brought a faint ripple of a memory, but I ignored it and glanced over at my only two "real" customers, a guy about thirty and a younger-looking blonde with, from what I could tell, a real driver's license saying she was twenty-four. They huddled over their strawberry daiquiris and talked in lovers' whispers. Nothing short of this twenty-story building tipping over was going to bother them.

The bar had everything, from plush dark-leather seats in all the booths, the tables, and on the couches to one side of the small dance floor. Dark oak bar and pillars accented everything else with a tan carpet that helped ground the place along with the indirect lights tucked along the walls and in panels in the low ceiling. And around three sides of the room there was more glass looking out over the city than I could ever imagine trying to wash.

The huge room's lights were kept low everywhere except the center circular bar so that customers could enjoy the fantastic view of Boise spread out below them. That's why everything was dark wood and leather, to not distract from the view. I didn't much notice the view anymore. But everyone who came in from the elevators sure did.

The room could hold two hundred people, but at this late hour on a Tuesday night, there were only the two lovers, the vagrant, and me on the entire top floor high over the city.

The vagrant stood, moved over closer to the window and eased himself down into the ten-person booth. Behind him was a wall that divided the big room from the back area and restrooms. It was covered with autographed pictures of famous stars who had visited the hotel.

Somehow it felt odd to have him sitting there. How he had gotten past the hotel security I would never know.

I studied him while he stared out over the lights.

His hands looked red, stained by the cold night air. He wore a rolled up blue stocking cap, a dark blue, naval-style coat, and shin-high mud-waders over the tops of the cuffs of his pants.

He kept his eyes averted as if not looking at me would keep me from throwing him back out into the cold.

Maybe it would. I didn't much care at this point. I had slowly come to hate this job, the snobby college kids who thought this place was their own world, and the businessmen and women who didn't even notice the "help" as I was called.

One more person snapped their fingers at me and I would be gone. There had to be more to making a living than dealing with these people.

I went back to restocking the beer and pretended to ignore him.

He kept gazing out the window and didn't say another word.

Twenty minutes later I had finished all the stocking and was cleaning the well when he decided to break his silence. He stood and moved closer to the bar.

"You ever water ski?" he asked without taking his gaze away from the city, standing with the side of his head in my direction. His voice was hard and deep, but his words were clear over the soft, background music.

I wiped off my hands and studied the strands of brown hair jutting from the side of his stocking cap. "Sure."

"Ever single ski?"

"Sure. My dad taught me."

He nodded, but still didn't turn around to actually look at me directly.

I glanced out over the city with all its lights sparkling in the cold winter air. I couldn't see anything in particular he was staring at.

Why the hell was this guy talking about water skiing in the middle of February? Maybe thinking of warm things was one of the ways he kept himself warm.

More likely he was completely nuts.

"You ever ski early in the morning," he asked, "right after sunrise, when the water is glassy smooth, undisturbed by wind and the waves of boats? So smooth that you can see your own reflection?"

The memory of those mornings flooded back.

I could feel the rope pulling me through the crisp morning air.

Back and forth, back and forth, my cuts across the waveless surface so effortless it felt like flying. The difference between water and sky a line I crossed at will.

I had skied those early morning runs many times.

Every year, on the last day of our week long vacation to Driscoll Head Lake, Dad would wake me up real early. It would be barely light and the dew would still be on the pines and the path down to the dock. I always complained.

Then he'd fire up the boat, toss me the rope and life jacket, and in a few quick minutes I would be out on the lake making wide, deep slashes across the mirror-like water.

Then I'd remember why Dad loved it so much.

Every year Dad let me go first and we'd go north up the lake. I always skied hard, at times my shoulder almost skimmed the surface. Then I'd take Dad on a long run down the lake to water I hadn't disturbed.

He'd make his long, lazy swings behind the boat and I'd watch him smile like I never saw him do any other time.

Looking back now, I think Dad put up with Mother's constant bitching about vacationing in the same place every year because he wanted to make that one run. Maybe making that one run was what kept him going during those long graveyard shifts at the plant.

The summer of his last year, when he was so sick, he wanted me to take someone up to the lake and make that early morning run for him.

And for me.

He said I should do it every year. It would give my life balance.

I had promised him I would. But I never had.

Not once.

I had always been too busy.

But I still remembered the silence of those early morning runs, the feeling of something so special that a crazy vagrant's question triggered ten-year-old memories at two a.m. in a smoky lounge.

I shook my head to clear it as the vagrant slowly turned and moved the few steps to the bar.

His face was as red and weather-beaten as his hands, but his eyes were deep blue and as clear as any spring water.

He stuck out his hand. "My name's Craig. Edward Craig."

I took his rough hand and tried to match his strong grip. "Ben Hodges. Benny to everyone here."

The vagrant nodded and seemed to laugh. "It's nice meeting someone who knows. Would you like to make a run? I'll steer for you if you'll steer for me."

This guy was totally nuts. Of that I had no doubt. I was suddenly very annoyed at myself for not calling security and getting him out of here when I had the chance.

"I'd love to," I said. "But I don't have a boat and it's February." I shrugged and gave him my best bartender "You're-out-of-luck-so-go-the-fuck-away" look.

The vagrant smiled and for a moment I thought he might laugh out loud. His gaze held me and I could tell he wasn't laughing at me, more enjoying the moment with a deep understanding, like a parent watching a child open presents on Christmas morning.

"Look at this city," he said, waving his hand at the windows. "Imagine it as a lake. During the daylight hours it's choppy with human activity. Rough. Hard to stay on the surface. But in the late-night hours everyone is asleep and the souls of the world are smooth like a surface of lake at sunrise. Wouldn't you like to ski that?"

He looked at me as if I should understand his ravings. Hell, I wouldn't know what he was talking about if he stuck it up in neon.

I glanced out at the city and then back at him. My favorite time was between two and six in the morning. No one around, no waiting in lines, no stupid drivers, no loud noises.

But I had no idea what he meant by skiing it.

"So just how do we go about doing that?"

Again the vagrant smiled as if explaining an obvious answer to a child. And after a bitch of a long, slow night bartending, I didn't much feel like being treated as a child.

"Benny," the vagrant said. "If you simply stood on a water ski, you would sink. Correct?"

"Of course. If a jetliner stops in mid-air, it falls. I know the physics involved with lift. What's that got to do with skiing on a city?"

"Right now," the vagrant said, indicating the bar around him. "You and I are stopped. We are, for lack of a better way of putting it, dead in the water. We can't even see the surface. But it's there."

"Yeah, so?" I said. For some reason this guy had me so irritated, I wanted nothing more than to show him how stupid he was being. "And what kind of boat floats on this surface of yours? And what kind of engine are we going to use?"

This time he actually laughed. "We don't need much of a boat to ski among the souls. In fact, this stool will do nicely." He dropped onto the bar stool, adjusted himself, and continued.

"For power we use the mind and the force of change. But as with flying, it is the movement that is important. Remember that. The movement is the critical part. Now, are you ready?"

"For what?"

"Why, to take the first run. I'll steer for you and then you steer for me. What will it hurt to try?"

Now I was beyond irritated and starting to get damn mad. "This is nuts, you know that? And your scam isn't going to work. You're not going to get a free drink just by spouting a wild story about skiing."

The vagrant's smile disappeared and his eyes dimmed, as if he had aged ten years in a fraction of a second. He shook his head slowly. "He said you wouldn't believe."

"Believe what, for God's sake?"

He shrugged, the coat draping like a huge weight over his shoulders. "It doesn't matter. Your father warned me—"

"You knew my father?" I must have shouted it at him because the two daiquiri customers looked over at the bar and then went back to whispering.

"Of course," the vagrant said, his voice barely carrying over the soft music. "We worked every night together for thirty years. For the last fifteen of those we skied the graveyard of souls. That is, until your father died."

My head was spinning. "What was my dad's name? Where did he work?"

The vagrant sighed. "Carl Hodges and he worked at the Lane Lumber Mill. You see, I never had a son and I wanted to show someone what we used to do. But your dad said you'd never be a skier. He said he'd tried to show you every summer, but you'd never let yourself believe, just like some don't let themselves believe that a plane can stay in the air."

Some of the strange things my dad had said while getting ready those early summer mornings came flowing back.

"The surface of that lake, Benny, is no different than the surface of life."

"Benny, to do anything, you must first believe you can do it."

Then I remembered even more of his words.

"Don't fight the surface, Benny. Move along it. Feel it. Always remember there is more than one surface."

My dad's voice echoed in my head as the vagrant said, "I think I'll be going now."

"Wait," I found myself saying.

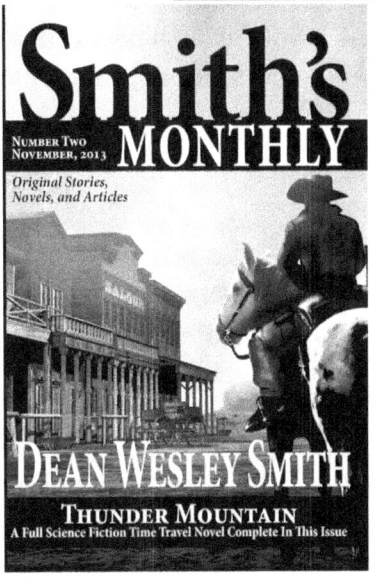

The vagrant looked up at me and I could tell the hope and some of the life was gone from his eyes. I struggled for a question to ask. Anything. I didn't believe the water-skiing bit, but he obviously had known my dad. For some reason I wanted to hold on to that. Besides, he had found me.

"How did you know where I was?"

"That was easy. Your dad told me. It's not important, really. I was being foolish."

"I've only been here seven months. My dad has been dead for ten years. So I don't think that's exactly possible. Why don't you just tell me what you really came here for?"

The vagrant closed his eyes and sighed. "When you look out those windows, you see buildings and lights. Am I right?"

I nodded and motioned for him to go on.

"When I look out there I see a graveyard of souls. Oh, the people all still walk, talk, eat, and sleep. But a surprisingly large number of them are dead. People who haven't taken a chance or done something really new in years. And who never will. They are content to sit and watch life, without ever touching. They are dead souls whose bodies haven't stopped yet."

Again I motioned for him to go on, even though my anger was slowly returning.

"Twenty years ago your dad and I were both dead. Oh, we worked and we ate and we did all the things we were supposed to do. But, in reality, we weren't alive. Then one night, when you were still fairly young, your father came back from his vacation and started talking about that special morning run. He described it over and over and we began pretending on the

really boring nights that we were skiing over the city, on the surface of the dead souls. We'd describe it to each other, the colors, the feelings, while one steered and the other skied."

The vagrant laughed and looked up at me. "And you know, one night we found that we really were skiing. We had found the surface of the dead souls and enough motion to stay on top of it."

"Motion?" I asked.

"The power we used wasn't an engine, but more our belief that we were alive and could see the surface and ski it without falling into it and being lost. After that we skied every night until your dad died."

I shook my head, finally having enough again. "Come on, you really don't expect me to buy all this shit?"

"Your father was right," the vagrant said. "At this moment you are as dead as most of the souls of this city. You are afraid to believe in anything beyond the shallow surface of your own reality. I was wrong to come, to think that you might be able to ski with me."

The vagrant stood, turned, and walked down the hall toward the elevators. I wanted to shout out for him to stop, but somehow I was frozen by his words until the elevator doors closed behind him.

Two

"THIS IS STUPID, you know?" Carla said. She carefully picked her way down the dew-slick path that led to the dock through the tall pine trees.

The morning air was crisp, almost too cold for a July day, even though the temperature would reach the eighties by noon. But it smelled wonderful. Clean and crisp, with that hint of pine filling up everything.

Carla wore her down ski parka, tight Levis and tennis shoes. Her long blonde hair was pulled back tight and it was the first time in the four months we had been going out that I had seen her without make-up.

"I warned you I wanted to do this every morning," I said. "And it won't take long, I promise."

Carla didn't answer. She reached and crossed the narrow beach, dropped the life jacket on the wooden dock and stood there shivering, hands jammed in her coat pockets, staring out over the smooth water.

The sun wasn't quite above the ridge of mountains and the lake was as glassy as any mirror. Clouds of mist hugged the blue-black surface and in the distance a bird broke the morning silence with a sharp, echoing call.

Everything was exactly as I had remembered it when Dad and I skied. Only this time I carried the ski and Carla did the bitching.

I jumped down into the boat, dropped the engine into the water and fired it up, just like Dad used to do. So powerful was the silence of the mountain morning that it dampened even the sound of the engine.

I made sure the yellow ski rope was hooked up right, then tossed the coil up on the dock and got out. "I'm going to jump start off the dock, so do exactly what you did yesterday afternoon. Okay?"

Carla nodded and got in the boat without a word.

She'd been all fun yesterday when the sun was hot and she could lie on the dock in her bikini. She had found it exciting to learn how to drive a boat. She even

wanted to learn to ski because it looked like so much fun. But she hated it at this moment.

I remembered how she felt.

I unhooked the lines holding the boat and nudged it away from the dock. "Head down the lake and watch for my signals."

Carla nodded and kicked the boat quickly in and out of gear so that it drifted slowly away from the dock as I had taught her.

As Dad had taught me.

I pulled off my sweater and put on the life jacket, then dipped the ski in the water, laid it flat on the dock, and stepped into the cold shoe.

I'd been waiting for this moment since Edward Craig had disappeared into the elevator of the bar in February. I'd tried to find him in the lobby, but no one down there had seen him.

And for the past five months I had looked for him in records and in shelters and everywhere.

I found out very little.

The day my father died Edward had quit his job and simply disappeared. No one had seen or heard from him since.

I had no better luck.

I grabbed the slowly uncoiling ski rope, made sure the handles were untangled, and moved to the edge of the dock.

"Get ready!" I shouted to Carla. She sat up on the back of the driver's seat and nodded, her hand poised on the throttle.

I watched and waited as the drifting boat gradually pulled the rope closer and closer to the right amount of slack. The cool morning air gave me goose-bumps.

The fear that I wouldn't make the jump right twisted my stomach.

The anticipation of cutting back and forth across that smooth surface, scattering the morning mists with my body, doing what very few others had ever done, made me feel alive.

More alive than I had felt in years.

Was that what my dad and Edward Craig had meant?

The rope was at the right length.

It was time to start finding out.

It was time to really start living.

"Hit it!" I shouted, and stepped out on the smooth surface of the water.

Three

EDWARD CRAIG was waiting on the dock as Carla swung the boat in close enough for me to drop off.

I had pushed the run a little too long.

My arms ached, my legs were made of rubber, and my face stung from the cold wind.

But I was alive.

I had tried to memorize every detail of the run, every sensation, every thought.

By the time I motioned for Carla to turn around and head back up the lake toward the dock, I understood a lot more of what Dad and Edward Craig had been talking about.

But I was still surprised to see him standing there.

He was dressed exactly the same as he had been the night five months earlier. And he looked just as out of place on the dock at five in the morning as he did in the plush bar at two a.m.

He nodded to me as I sank slowly into the water beside the dock.

I pulled off the ski, stood on the sandy bottom, and handed the ski up to him. "You have this knack for finding me. How'd you know I was here?"

He laid the ski carefully on the dock and then smiled as I waded the last few yards to shore. He handed me a towel without a word and then we both watched as fifty yards off shore Carla finished winding in the rope and putting it on the back seat.

"Well?" I said.

His soft laugh seemed to carry up into the pine trees. "I hoped you might have heard some of what I said. This was the week your father always took his vacation. And this was the place he always skied. I took a chance you might come back here to try to discover for yourself. Nothing more. You ski very well, I might add."

"Thanks," I said. "It seems you hit it on the nose."

Again I felt angry at him. Who was he to spoil my perfect morning? Who was he to read me so easily?

Carla swung the boat in a little too fast toward the dock and it took both Edward and me to stop it from hitting hard. Carla looked Edward over with obvious distaste as she jumped out of the boat.

"Are we done?" she asked me.

I nodded.

"Good. I'm going back to bed. Excuse me."

She brushed past Edward and crossed the beach toward the path to the cabin.

"She doesn't ski, I take it," Edward said.

I laughed. "Not hardly."

"What does she do, then?"

I watched as she climbed the path and disappeared in among the trees. "She works for a dentist. Beyond that I'm not really sure."

Edward nodded, took the bow rope from its hook and expertly tied the boat to the dock.

Four

CARLA WAS FRIENDLIER after a few more hours sleep and after I told her that Edward was an eccentric millionaire who didn't talk about his money.

Edward spent the morning telling me of his times with my dad at the plant and in the bars. Not once did he mention skiing or the graveyard of souls.

I cooked us a huge lunch of trout I had caught the night before, then Carla headed off to sun on the dock while Edward and I moved out to chairs in the shade of the pines.

It wasn't until we were both settled that I finally broke the silence about skiing. "So explain to me again exactly how you and my dad started skiing the graveyard of souls."

He laughed and went back over exactly what he had told me the first night in the bar. It had started with my dad coming back from vacation and explaining to Edward what it was like to really feel alive and had progressed to them skiing the surface of the dead souls of the people who inhabit the city.

"So did you actually leave the plant?"

Edward shook his head. "Not really. We would sit in the break room. We'd take short runs because while we were skiing our bodies would be frozen, like statues."

He laughed. "Got kind of embarrassing the few times someone walked in while we were skiing."

I shook my head in an effort to try to clear it. "You mean there was actually a physical effect involved?"

"Sure was," Edward said. "I suppose you were too young to remember the night your dad was sent home with what they thought was a gas poisoning?"

I vaguely remembered it. "Something about a leak that got into the lunch room and a few people were hurt."

Edward laughed. "We were skiing and old man Bridges came in and saw us. By the time we got back, they had your dad's body out on the floor giving him mouth to mouth and they were about to start on me, too. Gave your dad quite a start, let me tell you."

Edward's eyes glazed as he drifted back along the memory, smiling.

I gave him a moment, then asked my next question. "So what exactly did you ski on?"

Edward shrugged. "Just an old piece of pine your dad cut one night. Whichever one of us was skiing would put the board under our feet. Made us keep a mental picture of a ski and made the skiing seem easier."

I shook my head and looked around at the pine trees and the rough lake beyond, ruffled by a slight wind and a lot of boats crossing back and forth.

I couldn't believe all this. Here was a guy making a great case for the fact that my dad was an A-1 looney. And I was letting him, even helping him. It wasn't right for someone to make Dad sound so nutty.

"I have to be going, now," Edward said, and stood. "Got some things to do and I can see you need time to think about all this."

"Are you coming back?" I tried to keep my voice even and hold back the feeling of panic that was growing in my stomach. I wanted to be mad at this guy, not have him stick around. Yet I couldn't stand the thought of him going away for good like Dad had done.

"You planning on skiing tomorrow morning?"

I nodded.

"From the looks of it, you might need some help."

I glanced in the direction of the beach where Carla was sun bathing. "You're right about that. You want to drive the boat?"

Edward laughed. "I'd love to steer for you. But only if you'll promise me one thing. Tomorrow, while you're skiing, look down."

"Into the water?" I asked. "It's like a mirror."

"I know," he said, "Just look. I'll see you in the morning."

He turned and ambled past the cabin and toward the road.

Five

EDWARD WAS WAITING on the dock as I picked my way down the dew-wet path at shortly before five a.m. Carla was still tucked under the blankets and had made it very clear she wanted no part of skiing before the sun came up.

Again this morning the lake was like a picture off a postcard, glassy smooth, with little wisps of clouds hovering along the surface. The air was crisp and cold and smelled of wet sand and pine.

Edward was dressed exactly as before.

"Morning," he said.

I nodded, laid the ski down, and looked out over the lake. "It's beautiful, isn't it?"

Edward sighed. "Yes, incredibly so."

We both stood for a moment gazing around at the pine-covered mountains reflected off the misty surface of the lake. Again this morning I could feel my heart pounding as I slowly came alive. The smell of the pines seemed sharper than any smell before.

The crisp taste of the air seemed more fresh than anything I had tasted.

The cold of the morning felt good against my face. I had never been alive all those years working in bars. I had experienced nothing sitting in front of my television. Was that what Dad and Edward Craig had meant? Part of me said it was. But I knew there was something more. Something I was missing.

I turned to Edward. "Would you like to go first?"

He laughed. "I'm afraid I never learned how to ski on water. But I can drive a boat. Are you ready?"

I nodded, pulled off my coat and put on the life jacket. Edward eased himself down into the boat, found the way to drop the engine in the water, and then tossed me the yellow rope.

I told him how to start the boat, then untied it from the dock and gave it a little shove. I was ready, with the ski on, poised at the end of the dock by the time he had the boat warmed up and in position.

He wore the biggest grin I had seen in years when I gave him the thumbs up sign and yelled, "Hit it!"

My jump off the dock onto the surface of the lake was smooth, even though my stomach clamped up in fear that I would go headfirst into the water.

I gave the boat time to get completely up to speed before I made my first cut to the right out onto the mirror-smooth water. Edward's smile never left his face as I cut back and forth, loosening up the tight muscles, letting the bite of the cold air and the spray numb my face.

It felt as if I was skiing over velvet, almost flying.

After a long minute, I finally let myself really look down into the water.

I had been thinking about what I might see since Edward had made me promise to look. And I had come up with no expectations. At this point I was willing to try to understand anything.

But there was nothing there.

No magic.

No sights.

Nothing.

Oh, I could see myself, blurred only slightly in the dark surface. And I could see the sky and the mountains above me.

But there was nothing else.

I held my position to the right of the boat and looked up at Edward.

He pointed down, indicating clearly that I should keep looking. So I went back to staring at myself in the reflection of the water as the surface slid past my ski too fast for me to focus on it.

Maybe it wasn't the surface Edward wanted me to see.

Maybe it was something down in the water.

I tried to stare beyond and behind my reflection, down into the black depths.

And as I did, blurred images formed.

I wanted to shout to Edward that I saw something, but I didn't.

Instead I kept staring as faint lights and dark shapes came into view. As I struggled to bring them into focus, buildings and streets and lights formed below me.

I was flying over them at a height far above the Penthouse Bar. Yet close enough to see the details.

Then, suddenly, there were colors. Rainbows of colors, in all shapes, flowing, merging into one another like the colors gasoline makes on water.

The lines of colors flowed in and around the buildings and over the streets, heavy and thick in some areas, light and airy in others.

Part of me wanted to discount what I was seeing, to look up at the boat and focus on the trees and the lake I knew.

But instead I let myself go, let myself ski back and forth and back and forth over the tops of the buildings, over the colors and the lights, staring down into the souls of the people.

And, as in the water, I again saw my reflection in the mirror-like surface of the dead souls. Only this time I knew it was a reflection of what I might have been had I let myself completely die.

My face was blank, my eyes empty and afraid.

The reflection cut at my breath, twisted my stomach. It was a reflection I had seen many times in the morning mirror over the last few years and it scared me.

I forced myself to look beyond it, deeper, until I found myself closer to the buildings and the streets, again skiing a new surface of souls, sleeping souls of people who were alive, people who enjoyed living and trying new and different things.

This time my reflection was smiling.

Behind and below the reflection I could see many surfaces left to ski and explore. Surfaces that I could only guess at what they were.

But for now I felt content to be alive, so I skied the rainbow colors until my arms began to ache and my legs felt weak and limp.

The end of the run was coming.

I desperately tried to memorize the feelings, the power of the run so that I could return. As the rope started to go slack and my speed dropped, I took a deep breath and looked up, following the line of the rope toward Edward.

I expected to see the boat, the lake, and the mountains beyond.

Instead, I saw the inside of the Penthouse Bar.

My dad was perched on a bar stool next to Edward and the wall of celebrity photographs was behind them. The yellow rope hung between us. They both held it.

And both were smiling the biggest damn grins I had ever seen.

I could feel my speed dropping. The rope between us almost touched the carpet.

"Nice run," Dad said. "Keep practicing. Keep searching."

Edward nodded in agreement.

The rope touched the floor and I sank into the cold water of the lake.

Six

THE BOAT WAS empty and idling in neutral.

I looked around, trying to figure out where I was. It looked as if I was about a mile down the lake from the cabin. I swam toward the boat, pushing the ski along the surface of the water in front of me.

"Edward," I called out, as I tossed the ski into the back of the boat and pulled myself over the side.

But the boat was empty, as I had half expected it would be.

The lake around me completely smooth, as if the boat had not crossed it, as if I had not skied it.

I stood in the back of the boat, feeling alive, gazing out over the mirror-like water and the reflections of the mountains and morning sky.

Dad had been right all those years ago. There was always more than one surface.

All I had to do was look for them.

I dropped into the driver's seat and turned the boat toward the cabin, letting it cut slowly through the mirror waters, just enjoying the moment and the memory of skiing over the city.

And enjoying the feeling of really being alive.

Now Available
from all your favorite booksellers in trade paper and electronic editions.

DEAN WESLEY SMITH

EYES ON MY CARDS

A DOC HILL SHORT STORY

Way back in 2005 I wrote a thriller with the name Dead Money. *It starred Doc Hill, a professional poker player. I had every intention when I wrote the thriller to continue to write more Doc Hill stories, but because of the strangeness of publishing at the time, I put the novel in a drawer and pretty much forgot about it.*

Fast-forward to 2013 and a meeting with the publisher of WMG Publishing, Allyson Longueira, and my wife, Kristine Kathryn Rusch. Kris brought up Dead Money, *the long-stored thriller, and suggested I take it out, dust it off, and sell it to WMG Publishing.*

After rereading Dead Money *and coming to remember and like the characters again, I decided to write a new Doc Hill story for* Fiction River Special Edition: Crime. *This story is the first of many to come.*

EYES ON MY CARDS
A Doc Hill Short Story

One

I PUSHED BACK from the table and stood, disgusted.

I needed a break.

I left my chips in my spot indicating to the dealer I would be back. I wasn't down any of the five hundred I had bought in for, but I sure wasn't up either.

But for a change, winning money wasn't the reason I was at that table.

Around me the noise and lights of the Grand Casino and Hotel on the Las Vegas strip seemed muted and flavored by the slight smell of popcorn, like I was walking in a carnival instead of a casino. I moved between the empty poker tables, away from the no-limit game, and toward the larger part of the casino and the gaming tables.

To my right three tourists in shorts and bright shirts stood, laughing at something, and beyond them Webster stood in his dark silk suit, his hands crossed over his chest, his eyes missing nothing on the gaming floor around him.

B. B. Webster, the head of Grand Casino operations was the man who had hired me. He was the reason I was sitting in this mid-level no-limit game in his casino. He had asked a favor and I had agreed to help.

He had a suspected cheater working his poker room, a guy in a dark golf shirt and Reds' baseball cap. Webster wanted me to tell him how the guy was doing it.

And after an hour at the table with the cheater, I had no idea.

Not one, which had me totally frustrated. I had spent all that time at the table and couldn't spot a thing. Yet I too was convinced he was cheating.

I walked past Webster without even a nod and headed to the left of the gaming tables and toward the huge, ornate front lobby of the hotel and casino. Giant marble pillars dominated the lobby and it never seemed to be empty or quiet, no matter the time of day. And the popcorn smell faded in the big space as well, replaced by the faint smell of lilacs. Over the sounds of the people talking I could hear the fountains that lined two walls, water flowing over rocks and into pools.

A dozen tourists stood along the large front desk on the left, talking with smiling front desk clerks, clearly checking in. Suitcases were scattered behind them like deer droppings along a trail in a forest.

Right now it was just after midnight on a Thursday night.

As I went around the corner to my left and out of sight of the poker room, Annie Lott joined me, tucking her arm in mine and matching me stride for stride.

She had on a black pants suit with an open-neck white blouse and low heels that clicked lightly on the marble floor.

Her long brown hair was pulled up tight on her head. She looked stunning and just having her walk with me, her steps matching mine perfectly, made me calm down a little.

We had been together now for over a year, living together for the last six months, and I had loved every minute of it.

And sometimes, like tonight, we worked cases together as favors for friends. She had been a former Las Vegas detective before becoming a full-time poker player. I saw things on poker tables she didn't see. But she saw things in the real world I never noticed. It was one of the many reasons we made such a good team.

Since our first meeting while investigating the death of my father, we had become known for being able to figure out some darned strange crimes in and around casinos. We didn't take every request for help that came our way, but if the friend really needed help, or the problem was weird enough to get our attention, we would try to help out.

"He's cheating all right," Annie said. "I can see that from beyond the rail. You figure out how?"

I shook my head. "Not a clue and it's driving me nuts."

"Yeah, me too," she said.

Poker was a difficult game to cheat at in a monitored casino. But it did happen, usually with some sort of collusion between a dealer and a player. This guy clearly wasn't working with any of the MGM dealers, since three dealers had gone through the table in the hour I had been there. And Webster had made sure the dealers tonight hadn't worked or dealt to the guy last night.

And two of the dealers had actually looked at the guy funny a couple of times, as if they were picking up on something being wrong as well.

We walked in silence past the front desk and down a very wide hallway that headed toward the parking garage. A few paces down the hall we went through an unmarked door on the left and into a reception area with a large desk.

We moved toward a lounge area on the right that had bottled water and soft drinks in a fridge and tea and coffee on a counter. The room was comfortable, with three overstuffed couches on three walls that seemed to be from an earlier MGM Grand décor. A very red one, including strange red paintings of desert landscapes on the walls. It seemed like it would have been too much, but oddly, I found the room comfortable.

I grabbed a bottle of water and dropped onto one couch and Annie worked to make herself a cup of black tea.

We didn't say anything. There was nothing to say until one of us came up with an idea as to how this guy was cheating.

The door opened and my childhood friend and business partner, Fleetwood Korte, entered, followed by Webster. Fleet's silk suit rivaled Webster's and together they looked like they belonged on Wall Street, not in a Vegas casino.

At six-two, Fleet was two inches taller than me and thicker around the waist than I was. His hair had thinned since our college days ten years earlier, but he made up for that with a huge handlebar moustache. Every time I kidded him about how Carol, his wife, liked his moustache, he would just smile and nod, a distant look in his eyes that told me far, far more information than I actually wanted to know.

"You got anything, Doc?" Webster asked, his voice deeper and filled with a sound like gravel being washed together. He clearly had smoked far, far too many cigarettes in his day.

"He's cheating all right," I said.

"That much is clear," Annie said as she moved over beside me and sat down

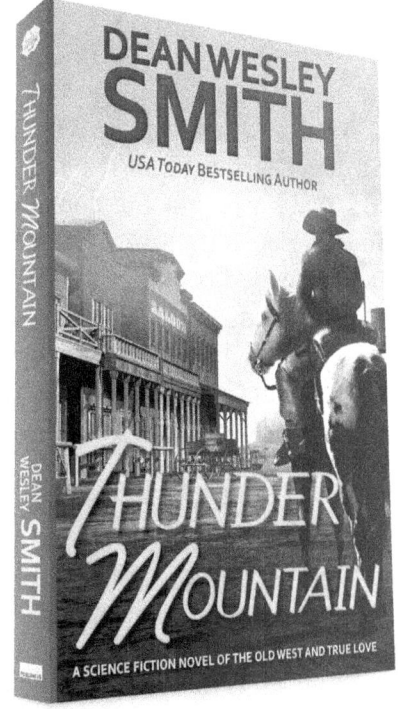

with her tea. "I could see that just watching from a distance."

Fleet took a bottle of water and sat on another couch while Webster sort of stared at the three of us.

"Doc, I think he's got spotters," Fleet said.

I glanced at Fleet and nodded. I had thought the guy had spotters as well, but I hadn't been sure. That's why both Annie and Fleet were here, to scout around the table and the poker room area. "Guy in the blue tee-shirt who is pacing the hall?"

Fleet nodded.

"What about the woman in the green sun dress and long black hair," Annie asked, "sitting in the room to the back reading?"

"Possible," I said. "But she came in with the big guy who called himself Big Ed two seats to the right of our target."

"And what good is a spotter going to do him?" Webster asked. "They can't see your cards or anyone else's cards. I've watched some security videos and everyone is playing down on the felt, no flashing at all."

I shrugged, because I honestly didn't know.

Webster shook his head at our silence. "Strangest damn thing I have ever seen. And that's going some considering how long I've been in this damn business."

He headed back out the door and left the three of us sitting and thinking.

Finally, I broke the silence. "Let me lay out what I've got and see if we can put any theories together before we go back in there."

Fleet and Annie nodded, so I went on.

"He's a decent player. Nothing fancy, like he has played a lot of hours in a low-level casino somewhere in a three-six game."

"He doesn't know how to bet in a no-limit game," Annie added.

"That's right," I said. "But somehow he knows the cards in other player's hands."

"Or he's manipulating his own cards to make sure his cards are the best," Fleet said.

"He's not a mechanic," I said, shaking my head. Beside me Annie shook her head as well as she sipped her tea.

I went on. "The guy can barely hold his cards at times. And he's not playing hands when he doesn't have the best cards. But when he does play, he almost always wins. Or drops when his hand gets beat on the last card."

"Maybe he can read minds," Fleet said, shrugging.

"That would explain a ton of things," Annie said, laughing. "But my guess is that this is some sort of very ornate scam we just can't see yet."

"I agree," I said, the frustration coming back. "The guy played for five hours last night and didn't lose a hand he played to the end. And tonight he has kept that streak up, at least for the hour we've been watching."

"You know, if he were better at hiding what he was doing," Annie said, "Webster or any of the rest of us would never have picked up on this."

I glanced at Annie and smiled. "I think you might have given us a clue. He's a mid-level poker player, so this winning and high-stakes game is unusual to him. He flat doesn't know how to hide what he's doing yet."

Fleet shook his head. "And that's going to help us how?"

I ticked off three items on my fingers. "He can't manipulate cards, he isn't working with dealers, and he isn't used to these levels of games. What's left?"

Both Annie and Fleet shrugged.

"Mechanical," I said. I pointed at the ceiling.

"He can't be working with anyone in the security room," Annie said. "I doubt that would be possible. And Webster would have checked that first, before even calling us."

"The guy's not working with anyone in the casino staff," I said, standing. "I'm sure of that now. But I've got an idea how to take this guy and expose him."

"And how are you going to do that?" Annie asked, as she stood to join me.

"If he's not used to this level," I said, smiling, "I bet he's never dealt with a blind player."

Annie laughed, the sound wonderful to my ears while Fleet just looked puzzled.

"I'll show you," I said to my best friend. "You just keep on eye on the spotters. Especially that black-haired woman in the back."

"Got it," Fleet said, looking even more puzzled. "I think."

Two

I WAITED UNTIL Annie and Fleet got back into positions so they could see the table, then I joined it again.

The cheater with the Reds' baseball cap had a stack of chips in front of him that looked to be a few thousand large and there were two new players in the game.

I glanced at my cards a few times, tossing away garbage, then when the button came around to me, I decided it was time to really see what was happening.

One guy in early position made a slight raise, the cheater called, and I re-raised just enough to not scare anyone.

Big Ed folded quickly as did others.

I had not looked at my cards at all. In fact, I hadn't even touched them.

And I knew for a fact that the cheater hadn't noticed I hadn't looked at them.

The guy in early position called my raise, but the cheater was looking puzzled, shaking his head slowly.

Finally he folded.

The flop came and I pretended to look at my cards again, then folded to another bet from the player in early position.

The next hand the cheater limped in again with just a call and I raised. Again I had not looked at my cards. I was playing blind.

By the time the other players folded around to him, he looked very, very confused. Since I had not looked at my hand, he didn't know what I had either.

This sort of made sense if he was reading minds, but I doubted that was what he was doing.

Finally he again folded and I knew I had him.

As the dealer was washing the deck and putting the cards in the shuffling machine imbedded in the table, I pretended to play with my chips as I felt the underside of the rail in front of me. It took me a moment to find them, but I did.

Very slight bumps just under the rail in the leather.

My guess was that they were very, very tiny cameras, no larger than the size of pins stuck into the leather of the rail.

I looked around at the other seats. I honestly couldn't see the tiny camera heads at all, they blended in so well on the underside of the edge of the table.

I was impressed.

In major tournaments there were what were called "button cameras" to allow television viewers to follow along with the play. This guy and his team had cameras so small and perfectly matched with the table that they couldn't even be seen. At least three per spot to make sure that no matter where a player looked at their cards, the camera would pick it up.

This must have taken him and his partners a long time to set up. Days carefully installing the tiny pin cameras without seeming to do anything strange at the table.

Webster would have to go back over a lot of footage to catch the people who had installed the little pin cameras.

I just shook my head in disgust. Even a monkey could win at poker if he knew what everyone else held for cards. The idiot in the Reds' baseball cap was worse. I hated cheaters, almost more than anything else.

I made myself calm down and sit back and try to think. I had found the cameras, but how was this guy getting the information relayed to him?

I played the next hand normal, looking at my cards and playing them like a normal mid-level player. When I did that the cheater seemed to relax again and I studied his face when he didn't know I was watching.

I couldn't see a thing.

I could read the best players in the business and this guy was a blank slate. I doubted he had a good poker face. He just didn't think he needed to hide anything from anyone.

In other words, this guy was not trained well and I was starting to doubt he was in charge of this.

It took someone smart to figure out how to do all this.

People had always tried to cheat casinos. Over the years, people had put in signals in their shoes, small electrodes on their arms, and so on to help them count cards in blackjack or get information from spotters. But this guy didn't seem to have any of that and the Grand Casino's normal security systems were designed to block most electronic signals, or at least spot odd ones.

And from what little I knew about tiny cameras like these, they didn't have a very large broadcast range. In fact, they were so tiny, I couldn't imagine them broadcasting much beyond the edge of the table, which would guarantee that the signals from that many small cameras would not be picked up by casino electronic scanning.

The dealer took the cards out of the shuffling machine, cut and started to deal.

I glanced over at the woman with the long black hair sitting in the back of the room. She was reading on some sort of tablet and she had it turned so no camera over her could see what she was reading.

Suddenly I knew I had it figured out. And I had a sinking feeling it was a lot larger cheating scam than anyone had first figured. A lot more than one bad player winning too many hands.

I mucked my cards without looking at them and stood up. "Back in a second," I said to the dealer.

Then I again turned and headed out of the poker area and toward the casino. Again the popcorn smell filled the air and shouting from the direction of the craps table seemed to cover almost everything.

Out of sight of the table, Fleet and Annie and Webster caught up with me.

"So that's playing blind, huh?" Fleet asked as we stopped near the hotel lobby.

Annie laughed. "Doc drives people crazy doing that in tournaments when he spots someone who really cares too much."

"He drives a lot of us crazy like that," Fleet said, shaking his head.

"Well, Doc?" Webster asked.

"I got him," I said, smiling. "When did you switch out those shuffling machines?"

Webster looked puzzled. "A month or so ago, if I remember right. But they are carefully checked."

"I know," I said, nodding. "That's why this is so amazing, more than likely there's more teams involved in this working other casinos right now."

"Oh, crap," Webster said.

Annie squeezed my arm and smiled.

Fleet just shook his head as he often did when I said outrageous things.

I just smiled. "Get security to surround the entire area and hold that woman in the back with the tablet as well. She's the spotter, so you had better take that tablet away from her quickly before she erases anything. And my sense is that the guy who calls himself Big Ed is also in this, since he never played against the guy in the cap. He's just a better player is all and harder to notice."

"You're sure about all this?" Webster asked, his voice sounding even more full of gravel than normal.

"Positive," I said, smiling at the frown on the casino manager's face. "I'll show you. It's actually pretty damn smart system. Just get your people in place and keep a lid on this until you can warn other casinos."

Three

IT TOOK WEBSTER five minutes to carefully put his men into position around the poker room without anyone seeming to notice. His guys were good.

"Introduce me when we walk up to the table would you? I want to see their faces."

He laughed. "Gladly."

"Just make sure your guy gets that tablet quickly."

Webster nodded at his guy standing behind the woman and I smiled. She wouldn't even see that guy coming.

Fleet and Annie followed us a few steps back.

As we neared the table, Webster signaled for the dealer to stop play.

"Folks, I'd like to introduce you to Doc Hill, the top ranked Texas Hold'em player on the planet."

I did a slight bow, smiling at how the guy in the Reds' baseball cap had gulped and his face had gone white.

The guy named Big Ed just shook his head and muttered something about how he thought he recognized me.

Webster's man had taken the woman's tablet and was holding it and blocking her escape.

"I asked Doc to join this table," Webster said, "because it felt like something was wrong with the play."

I reached forward, under the edge of the leather near my chips, and pulled out a tiny pin and held it up.

"Camera. Three at each spot," I said to the table. "Pretty nifty, huh?"

All the regular players except Big Ed and the guy in the Reds' cap started feeling under the edge of the table in front of them and pulling out camera pins.

"The cameras all relayed their data to a small device inside the shuffling box," I said.

With that the dealer looked shocked and actually moved back from the box like it might bite him.

"The shuffler then sent the image of all our cards as a phone signal to the woman in long hair sitting back there."

Everyone looked around at her and she just sneered.

I went on. "She would then relay the information about the cards to our two friends here also by phone signal, which is not blocked in a casino or monitored."

I turned to Webster. "You'll find tiny ear bugs in their ears set to receive the phone signal from the woman's tablet."

"You can't prove that," the idiot in the baseball cap said.

Webster only snorted and motioned for the guards to take them away. Then he had the dealer split the cheater's chips among those of us at the table and broke the game.

"You had better be informing the other rooms around town and up in Reno," I said to Webster.

"I'm going to, as soon as I take that box apart and figure out how we missed the phone device in there. But I know you are right. This is a big ring and these three are going to suddenly vanish into some deep parts of this casino for a short time so that we don't alert everyone else."

He stuck out his hand. "Thanks, Doc. Fleet. Annie."

"Check's in the mail?" Fleet asked.

Webster snorted. "Not so much a check, but a lot of free dinners from here and I'm betting other casinos in town."

"Sounds even better," Fleet said, laughing.

"Come to think of it," I said. "I am hungry. That popcorn smell has been driving me crazy."

"It does that," Webster said.

"Steak?" Annie asked.

"I love steak," Fleet said, smiling at Webster.

"Maybe I should write you a check. Might be cheaper."

Then in his gravelly voice he laughed. "Head on over to the steak house and I'll tell them you're coming."

He turned and walked away.

The three of us laughed as I tossed the small pin camera on the table and racked up my chips. Then we turned and headed for a late meal.

It felt great to help protect the game I loved. Poker is a game of skill, but there will always be those who look for shortcuts in anything that takes skill.

I just hoped Webster kept these three "lost" for a very long time before turning them over to the police.

And that thought just made me laugh, so I told my friends what I hoped Webster would do and they laughed as well as we headed for dinner.

Even Annie, the former Las Vegas detective.

"In Vegas," she said, "casino justice can be much worse than police justice. Always has been, always will be."

"Especially for cheaters," I added and they both laughed again.

~

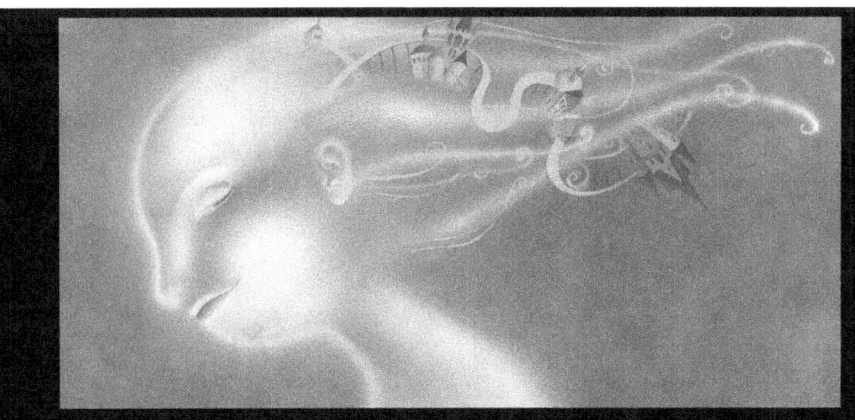

Poems by DEAN WESLEY SMITH

Plane Crash Lover

She is by herself... sitting at a bar.
Makes you wonder why.

Is she lover proof?
Or maybe she lost her lover
in the great plane crash of '04.
147 people died.

I sip condolences,
mixing Bloody Mary taste
with left love.
She runs endless corridors
to miss the plane
as I step aboard her flight.

Sitting on my bar stool
as a window seat,
I gaze quietly through scratched glass
down the distance of the bar at her lost stare.

My thoughts move to comfort her
but my feet refuse to carry me
from my doomed flight.
Another Bloody Mary appears.
We taxi apart
without touching.

USA *Today* Bestselling Writer

DEAN WESLEY SMITH

THE LIFE AND TIMES OF BUFFALO JIMMY

Chapters 28-30

What Came Before…

Nineteen-year-old Boston native Jimmy Gray had been traveling with his parents and older brother, Luke, headed west to find a new home and new riches. Before even reaching Independence, they were attacked and robbed by Jake Benson and his gang. Jimmy's parents were killed, his brother wounded.

In one of the wildest towns in all of American history, Jimmy Gray, a sheltered, educated son of a banker from Boston suddenly finds himself very, very much alone. But then through some luck, he finds other young men about his age and down on their luck who might be able to help him.

Together, the five of them head west after Benson. They end up hunting buffalo as he always dreamed of doing, but then they are hit with a massive flash flood and Jimmy is left alone, his friends more than likely dead. Luckily, they all meet up again and are all safe. So they continue west, knowing that Benson is just ahead of them.

Suddenly they come upon Benson and his men killing a farm family. They manage to get one of the men separated from the others, but in a fall he accidently dies. So they scatter to meet up later at a camp. They managed that but found a survivor of the killings. So one of them had to go back with the kid while the others followed Benson.

They caught him once again terrorizing a small wagon train and managed to scare him and his men off. But then they had to cross the forty-mile desert. And right from the start, things started off deadly. Then, in the middle of the worst part of the desert, they find a wagon train, horses stolen, water gone, only women and children left to die. But what can they do? If they try to take them along, everyone will die.

THE LIFE AND TIMES OF BUFFALO JIMMY

Part Twenty-Eight
TOUGH DECISION

"**CAN WE JUST** rest here in the shade of the wagons until the sun goes down and make a run for it?" Truitt asked as all six of them gathered together.

Jimmy had been wondering the same thing.

Long, C.J. and Josh all shook their heads.

"The heat on this desert would drain all of our water, even if we were resting," Josh said.

"Look what three hours did to the women and children," C.J. said. "And that was what one of them told me was their plan."

"We would never make it to the river without water," Josh said, "even at night."

Long agreed. In his steady voice he said simply, "We can't stop. We must press on and soon."

"How many are there?" Zach asked.

"Eight women still alive and all claim they are able to walk," Truitt said. "A dozen children, six of them too young to walk in this deep sand."

Jimmy turned to Long. "How much water do we have?"

"After what we have given to the women and children, we will be out of water before we get to the river, even if we went without them."

That made all of them stand in silence in the hot desert sun, just thinking about the huge risk they would take if they continued to help this wagon company.

Jimmy nodded, then looked around at his friends. "Is everyone agreed that we try to save these woman and children? I vote that we do."

All five of his friends nodded as one.

Jimmy laughed. "You know, we're all crazy."

"That seems clear simply by where we are standing," Truitt said.

Everyone laughed, but it was worried laughs. Jimmy was scared at the idea of what they were about to do. He knew the rest of them were as well.

"Everyone take a small drink," Jimmy said, "then give a small drink to

the horses as well. After that, get the six kids who can't walk tied onto the horses so if they pass out, they won't fall off. We need to get moving."

Jimmy glanced in the direction of the hot sun as everyone spread out. It couldn't be much past nine in the morning. They had the hottest part of the day still hours ahead of them, and fifteen to twenty miles of sand to wade through.

And nowhere near enough water to get six of them, eight women, seven horses, and a dozen children to the Truckee River.

But they were going to try.

And with luck not die in the attempt.

Part Twenty-Nine
AN ATTEMPT

THE NEXT TWO hours went slowly as the sun climbed higher and higher in the sky, sucking every bit of moisture from anything alive.

Long led the group, leading the only pack horse. The strongest woman among the survivors was leading Long's horse right behind him. A young boy was tied to the saddle, his head and back covered by a light shirt.

Jimmy, with a young girl on his horse, followed. A girl about Jimmy' age named Caroline walked with him, or behind him, as they tried to stay in the wagon wheel tracks to make the walking easier. It was Caroline's younger sister who was on Jimmy' horse.

Caroline was a blonde with flashing blue eyes. Her light skin was blistered by the sun, even though she wore a wide-brimmed hat. Her once blue dress was tattered, faded, and dirty. Jimmy liked her at once, but he wasn't sure why.

She seemed strong and was able to keep up. They didn't speak hardly at all, since that would have taken too much energy. But Jimmy found himself enjoying her company as much as it was possible in these circumstances. And thinking about her and wondering what she was like certainly kept his mind off of the heat and the deep sand.

After two hours, Long gave a little water to each horse, then had each of them take a very shallow drink. Jimmy had put him in charge of the water and told everyone to not drink unless Long told them to.

Jimmy was trusting Long to know when they had to drink to keep them going. Josh was also making a few suggestions to Long from things that he had read, and Long was sometimes following his suggestions.

Again, it was taking all of them and all their skills to survive this.

They didn't stop for longer than a few minutes at any point. There was just no point in resting. Every minute stopped was one minute longer it would take them to reach the river.

Before the next quick stop, Zach shouted from the end of the procession and Jimmy looked around.

A woman had fallen face first into the sand and two other women were not able to move her. It was the woman that Jimmy had given a drink to under the wagon.

Jimmy had Caroline hold his horse and he went back to see what could be done. But by the time he waded through the sand to where she was, C.J. was standing up shaking his head. "She's dead."

Two other women were still kneeling in the sand beside the dead woman.

Jimmy looked at the dead woman for a moment, the thoughts of his own mother filling his mind. Benson would pay for this.

For everything he had done.

Jimmy turned his back on the dead woman. "Let's get moving."

He knew his voice sounded cold and mean, but he didn't dare allow himself to look back at her body just laying there beside the trail with all the other bones of travelers and horses and oxen.

They weren't crossing just a desert. They were crossing a graveyard.

An hour later, they were slugging up a low ridge. The sand was so deep, that even staying in the wagon wheel tracks from companies that had gone before, the horses sank up to their knees in the sand.

Every step for Jimmy seemed like torture.

Long stopped them halfway up the impossible slope and had them all drink tiny sips of the water they had left. Now they were completely out of water, and the sun was still high in the sky, baking them.

Jimmy just hoped there wasn't far to go. He could tell his energy was draining quickly, and beside him, Caroline was stumbling far more often than she had when they started out. He wasn't sure how many more miles any of them could go.

Over an hour later, they crested over the top of hill. The wagon trail went downward with a much harder base sand between some thin sagebrush. The going was easier, a relief since they were going downhill and not wading in such deep sand.

In the distance, in the bottom of the valley below them, there was a tall stand of cottonwood trees that seemed to curve off into the distance toward the mountains beyond. Jimmy had learned that distances out west were very hard to judge. He had no idea if those trees were just a mile away, or ten miles away.

But what those tall trees meant was water. The river was there, under those trees.

They just had to get to them.

Part Thirty
THE RIVER

AS C.J. CAME over the ridge behind Jimmy and saw the trees, he shouted, "Three miles left! Just three miles!"

Caroline looked back at C.J., then ahead at the trees. "Can he be right?"

Jimmy smiled. "When it comes to this trail and where we are, C.J. and Josh are always right. They've read everything about this trip that has ever been written. I have a hunch that Josh will eventually write his own book about all this as well."

"Three miles," Caroline said, her voice cracking in what sounded like a sigh. "I can make three miles."

She was right. Jimmy knew he could as well.

They walked on side-by-side in silence through the baking heat.

Long kept their pace steady and didn't speed up at all, even though it was downhill and they could see in the distance their goal. Jimmy knew that they could still lose people and horses in these three miles.

Three miles was a very long distance in this kind of heat.

But Long also didn't call a rest break half way down the gentle slope. At this point, there was no point in resting. They had no water left. They either made the last few miles, or they died very close to their goal.

Another woman behind Jimmy fell, but this time she hadn't died. Just passed out.

"I know what that's like," Truitt said, shaking his head.

Long and Zach simply lifted the woman up and draped her over Zach's horse in front of a small child. If she ended up dying, they would find out at the river and not before.

The last half-mile had to be the longest half-mile Jimmy had ever walked.

The cottonwood trees bordering the river were looming high in front of them now, and the blue of water reflected the sun like a mirror. But they were still a half-mile away under baking sun.

Every footstep felt like sheer agony, and Jimmy seemed to use every ounce of his energy with every step, yet the sight ahead kept him moving, taking another step forward and then another step.

Caroline was walking beside the horse and her sister, and it was clear that at times she was using his saddle to hold herself up from falling.

A few times during that last half mile, Jimmy turned to see how the others were doing.

They were all stumbling like he was, but they were all looking ahead at the water.

Long kept them going at the same speed all the way to within three hundred paces from the river, then he turned and shouted back, "Get the children off the horses without trying to stop the horses, then give the horses their heads."

Jimmy had no idea what Long was worried about with the children. All he wanted to do was stagger at the water and drink. But he didn't have enough energy to ask Long why. He just acted.

They all did.

Somehow, he and Caroline got her sister untied and off the horse without stopping. The little girl was completely limp in Jimmy' arms. Then Caroline tossed the reins back up over the horse's head so that it could go as it wanted.

Just as Jimmy had thought about doing, his horse made a dash at the river, splashing into it right behind Long's horse.

Caroline and Jimmy almost got ran over by Truitt's horse as it went past, also headed for the water.

"Everyone drink slowly at first, just small sips." Long shouted, then turned for the river himself.

Jimmy somehow carried Caroline's small sister the last few hundred paces to the water's edge, then laid her gently on the wet rocks beside the water.

As Caroline was giving her sister a handful of water, washing the young girl's face, and taking a handful herself, Jimmy walked into the water and fell face first into the wonderfully cold, clear river.

Never, in all his life, had anything felt so wonderful.

Beside him, one after another, everyone did the same.

Continued next month...

USA *Today* Bestselling Writer

DEAN WESLEY SMITH

A Story of Conforming...

BRYANT STREET

I fear Bryant Street more than anything on the planet. Honestly, when in a standard subdivision, I always get lost, turned around, and slightly panicked. Not kidding.

In a writer's workshop someone challenged me to write a story with the first line "The Wolves Were Howling on Bryant Street." I knew instantly what the wolves represented. As a fiction writer, doing battle with the wolves never ends.

When starting this magazine, the wolves howled and nipped at my heals more than once. Now at issue ten, they have calmed some.

BRYANT STREET

One

THE WOLVES were howling on Bryant Street.

Duncan nudged the orange slice closer to the edge of his plate of ham and eggs and tried not to listen. He forced himself to concentrate on the loud clanking of pans in the kitchen of the Denny's Restaurant, then the loud, constant chatter of the large-thighed waitress.

It did no good.

He could still hear the wolves.

The waitress had started it all. She'd asked him why he never ate the orange slice that came with his late-night breakfast. She'd said most of her regular customers ate it, why didn't he?

Simple. He hated fruit with ham and eggs. Just the thought made the grease curl up into a ball in his stomach. But for some reason, every restaurant had an orange slice with ham and eggs. Stupid custom.

He had been about to tell the waitress, in so many plain words, that it was his business what he did with his orange slice when the wolves started to howl.

The wolves of Bryant Street.

Bryant Street was after Duncan.

He flipped the orange slice over and thought back to the first and only time he had been on Bryant Street. It had been a warm Friday afternoon two months ago, shortly after he graduated from college with his degree in electrical engineering. Road construction blocked the main street past the mall and he had been forced to turn his VW Bug onto Bryant Street.

Right away he had known he was in trouble.

The perfect houses all looked the same.

Each had lots of shrubs outside, two bedrooms inside, and an attached room for two cars.

The further down the street he got, the more uncomfortable he felt, like he was listening to the music in Jaws before seeing the shark.

He glanced first left, then right.

Perfectly spaced trees planted exactly correct distances apart fought to hypnotize him with their monotone swaying.

The green shutters on all the houses closed in around him and the evenly cut lawns beckoned to him like a soft bed to a man without sleep. He gasped for each breath.

On both sides front doors opened, ready and willing to swallow him.

The smooth driveways sucked at his little car.

Sweat dripped into his eyes as he fought to keep the Bug in the middle of the road.

He glanced back.

He'd only gone a hundred trees.

Five more trees and he couldn't take it any more.

He gunned his Bug into a u-turn between two Pintos.

Bryant Street now seemed to stretch for miles down a dark, forbidding tunnel of jagged branches.

He jammed the gas pedal to the floor, his mind racing with the fear of a flat.

Or engine trouble.

The trees slashed at him.

The street rolled, pitched the car from side to side.

He fought his way down the road tree by tree, the entire time keeping his gaze locked on the faint light ahead.

Finally, after what seemed to be all afternoon, he reached the detour, ducked between a Caddy and a Datsun, and headed back downtown.

He had never gone near Bryant Street again.

Now, it was coming for him, sending the wolves to round him up like so much mutton.

Damn it all, anyway. It wouldn't get him without a fight.

"Mister? You all right?" the waitress asked, popping her gum.

Duncan shook himself and looked up at her. He must have looked a little funny, sitting there, leaning away from the window. The wolves were still howling.

"Can you hear them?" Duncan asked.

"Yeah. They're awful, aren't they?" The whine in her voice reminded Duncan of a smoke detector going off. "Someday they're going to get a good band in that bar and fill the place. I keep telling Craig—he's the boss—that if he would just—"

"No," Duncan said. "Not the band. The wolves. The wolves from Bryant Street. Listen. Don't you hear them?"

She popped her gum once more. "Can't say as I do." She flipped his ticket upside down near his plate and walked away.

He should have known she wouldn't hear them. The street wanted him. He'd have to fight his own battle.

He picked up the orange slice and ate it quickly. He'd give them this first battle, but nothing more.

The wolves quit howling.

He finished his eggs, but left the ham. His stomach was upset enough without putting ham on top of an orange slice.

Two

FROM THAT NIGHT on, the fight with the wolves from Bryant Street became intense.

Every time Duncan got one step out of line, Wham-o, howl-time. And each time the wolves got louder and louder. It drove him crazy. It got to the point he felt they could hear his every thought.

For example, one month after the wolves started howling, on a Wednesday night, he had a date with Constance, a tall blonde with a high laugh and large features.

Constance was the lady who cut his hair while rubbing her large features against his back and arms. He loved the way her fingers massaged his scalp and had dreams of her massaging other places, including her large features.

By eight in the evening they had stormed and occupied a dark, lower booth in a plush hotel bar. One of those places where the backs of the booths were planters and the seats a form of fake leather.

They were getting down to the point of being real cozy, when suddenly, an old woman in the booth behind them looked through the plants and then whispered to her toothless old man, "Is that Constance's husband?"

Duncan turned around slowly, pushed one large bunch of plant leaves aside so he could see the shocked look on the old woman's face, and then looked the old bag right in her gray eyes. "Of course I'm not. What fun would that be?"

The wolves started howling their thing.

Duncan could hear them right over the music and the gasps of shock and indignation from the old woman.

The wolves' howls were long and drawn out and sounded plain vicious. He imagined saliva dripping from their teeth as they threw back their heads and ruined his evening.

And, for the first time, they sounded close.

Almost right outside.

By this point he knew better than to ask anyone if they heard them. "Look," he said to Constance. "I just remembered that I have this appointment. You understand. Maybe another time, huh?"

With one last longing look at those large features, he stood.

Damn it all. He loved those fingers.

He'd fix those wolves for this.

He patted her hand like a father consoling a child, moved his scotch with reverence to the center of the table, and headed for the door of the bar. He had packed his father's deer rifle in the trunk of his car. He was going to bag himself a wolf tonight.

The wolves weren't in the parking lot or anywhere else around the side of the hotel. But the level of their howls never diminished. It was as if he were surrounded.

They didn't stop howling until the police arrested him for scaring hotel guests by stomping through the flowerbeds outside their rooms with a rifle.

Three

WITH THE WOLVES hounding him, life became one big bore.

Time after time they stopped him from one activity or another. He always looked for them without luck. Each time they sounded close, but somehow he knew they were still over on Bryant Street. And no way was he going back there.

No sir.

No way.

After a while he tried to convince himself he was making them up. Didn't work.

Their howls froze him, made him stop whatever he was doing. They were too real sounding.

But there were a few things in Duncan's life the wolves didn't seem to mind. One was his work with a small company downtown. They also didn't seem to mind baseball or Debbie.

Debbie was short and cute in a plain sort of way. She had shoulder length brown hair, perfect teeth, and tiny feet. She was also a complete take-her-home-to-meet-mother prude.

He had met Debbie the week before the wolves started their terrorist action. She worked in a downtown department store in the small-appliance section. He had gone in for a new toaster. The night before, while drunk, he had used his old one for a football. He had thought he

was Joe Willy and threw a perfect pass through the window while fading back behind the blocking of his couch.

For the first month, Duncan wasn't sure why he kept asking Debbie out. Possibly for the challenge. He figured she finally agreed for the same reason.

That and the fact the he had what she called "big potential."

After the war started with the wolves, dates with Debbie were the only peaceful ones he had. For a while he suspected it was something she or her rich father was doing. But after searching a hundred places for speakers, he gave up trying to figure out how.

Dates with Debbie were boring, plain and simple. The same kind he'd had back in high school: movies, hamburgers or dinner, and a lot of talk about everything but the real subject on his mind. Every night, after he dropped her off, he went downtown and got drunk. The wolves didn't seem to mind that much either, as long as he kept his hands to himself.

One night, after six months of dating Debbie and fighting the wolves by alternately running from them or searching for them, the battle shifted.

For some unremembered reason, Duncan had promised Debbie to take her dancing. Debbie was having so much fun, she even had a few drinks. It must have been the drinks, because they started dancing all the slow dances and Debbie kept getting closer and closer.

By halfway through the night she was rubbing up and down and up and down real slow like she was carefully sanding a fine antique. It drove him crazy.

He kept waiting for the wolves to start their howl, but they didn't.

Later, after he was rubbed raw, they ended up at his apartment. That was the first time he had talked her into going up there.

She'd had four strawberry daiquiris and looked dazed. She didn't say a word about the three flights of stairs, but her face looked pale by the time she got inside.

"Bathroom's there," he pointed.

"Nice place," she lied, and headed for the door he had indicated.

He went into the kitchen and poured them both another drink of scotch. He didn't even know if she liked scotch or not, but it didn't matter. He used his best Goodwill glasses and only put one ice cube in hers so it wouldn't be too watered down when he drank it later.

He'd only taken a sip when the toilet flushed and she came out. She staggered straight up to him, pulled his head down, and kissed him with strawberry breath.

He set his scotch down quickly as she started hoeing his mouth with her tongue, planting strawberry seeds with drunken skill.

Fifteen minutes later they had worked their way to the bedroom and removed all their clothes.

"Careful," she said when they started.

He said, "Yeah," and she rubbed and he rubbed and the pace picked quickly up.

Then the wolves started howling.

Major battle time.

Tonight they sounded loud, closer, and extra mean, but there was no way he was going to stop. It was about time he learned to ignore them.

"I love it," Debbie said softly as she twisted her head from side to side. She started rubbing faster and faster. "I love it... I love it... I love you..."

He noticed the word change, but didn't stop.

Nothing was going to make him stop.

No word, no howl, nothing.

Debbie kept saying she loved him and the wolves kept howling and Duncan did his best just to keep up.

Finally, the situation was to that critical time which marked the boundary between thinking, "Why not?" and wondering "Why?" when the wolves stopped howling.

This time the silence made him pause.

"Oh, don't stop," Debbie said. "You feel so good."

A low growl came from near the door.

He tried to ignore it and go on with Debbie's request when a second mean-sounding growl stopped him in mid-rub.

He glanced around.

The wolves were no longer howling from Bryant Street. The battle had moved into his own bedroom where they now circled his bed.

On the left, two were crouched, ready to spring.

Another stood, hair on its back on end, growling. Saliva dripped from its yellow teeth and formed a wet spot on the rug.

He turned to the right. Two more were there.

He was dead for sure. He closed his eyes and waited for the first rip of his flesh. He was going to die in the missionary position without a fight.

What a way to go.

"Duncan, dear. Are you all right?"

"I don't know," he said and opened his eyes. There couldn't really be wolves in his bedroom. Why didn't Debbie see them?

How could they harm him and not her?

Made no sense.

He must be imagining things. That was it. If he ignored them, they would go away.

"Don't stop," Debbie said, her voice almost pleading. She started to move again and without thinking, he did too.

Out of the corner of his eye he saw the largest wolf take a step toward the bed and crouch to spring.

Duncan stopped again, bare essentials cruelly exposed to the pack.

The wolf stopped.

Standoff. Duncan looked both ways. They had all moved closer.

What the hell did they want? He'd been nice to Debbie. This had been mostly her idea. He didn't know what they wanted him to do.

He looked into the pale blue eyes of the largest wolf. It growled real low and angry-like.

Suddenly, what it wanted was clear to Duncan.

He glanced down at Debbie. She was watching him with a look of concern. The wolves wanted him to tell her that he loved her. He might be able to do that.

Maybe.

She was a nice girl. He sort of liked her. Telling her he loved her was the right thing to do and the wolves always left him alone when he did the right thing.

"Debbie," he said, "I... I..."

He turned back to the largest wolf hoping for one last chance. The wolf bared its teeth and growled.

"Debbie, I love you," he quickly said. That should do it.

It damn well better.

Debbie pulled him down into a hard hug that pressed his ear into her right breast. "Really, Duncan? Do you mean it?"

She kissed him with her mouth open and her orthodontist teeth showing. Then, without hesitation, she started to move again. He didn't know if he should join her.

The wolves were still there.

But his body won. He couldn't help himself and he slowly joined her rhythm.

Two of the wolves snarled again and the largest wolf stuck its cold nose against the side of his leg.

He jerked and rolled away from the wolf, pulling Debbie over on top of him.

"Oh, Duncan. You're so much fun."

She pulled her legs up under her and started practicing her belly dancing moves on his stomach. She was a fine belly dancer, he quickly discovered.

He lay there and looked from side to side at the wolves. He hadn't imagined that cold nose. The wolves might be invisible to everyone else, but they were real enough to his touch.

And they still weren't happy with him.

They were in close all the way around the bed. He could smell their stale breath. He had to do something and do it quick.

The biggest wolf again touched him with its cold nose.

Duncan jumped and Debbie gave a little squeal of joy.

"Debbie! Stop!"

Debbie pulled her hair away from her face and looked down at him. Her cheeks were flushed and she had this hungry look in her eyes.

The same look the wolves had.

"I need to ask you something." He checked the wolves on his right and then on his left. He could imagine his blood-stains on their yellowed teeth. They weren't giving him a chance.

They had him surrounded.

They had won this battle and the war.

"Debbie," he said as softly as he could, his mind racing for any other way. Anything. But this was what the wolves wanted. They had him naked, flat on his back, unarmed.

"Debbie, would you marry me?"

"What?"

The wolves all took a few steps backwards. It worked. He couldn't believe it.

"What did you say?" Debbie asked.

"Oh, nothing," Duncan said. The wolves started toward the bed again, all growling.

"Would you marry me?"

"Do you really mean it?" Debbie asked. "You know I've loved you since the first day we met."

"Would I have asked if I didn't?"

Damn the wolves anyway.

She kissed him hard and again started to rub, already trying to polish his rough edges.

He glanced around. Only the largest wolf remained. It curled up and went promptly to sleep in the corner.

After a short time, Duncan started rubbing back.

They were married seven months later in a big church wedding. He was the perfect groom.

Everyone said so.

They moved into a house her daddy bought for them on Bryant Street and he went to work for her daddy's corporation.

People only thought it just a little odd that he built a dog run in their back yard, even though it matched all the other dog runs on Bryant Street.

They don't have a dog.

No one on Bryant Street has a dog.

USA Today *bestselling writer Dean Wesley Smith returns with a second novel to the world of* Dust and Kisses *from the first issue of* Smith's Monthly.

Together, Callie and Fisher work to discover the secrets of a galaxy that have been hidden in plain sight, even from the powerful humans who had rescued millions. And in the process, they just might change everything.

Now Available
from all your favorite booksellers in trade paper and electronic editions.

DEAN WESLEY SMITH

THE ADVENTURES OF HAWK

Chapters 28-30

What came before…

Nineteen-year-old Danny Hawk, his uncle, and his best friend Craig, were in Cairo to look for his missing father. Danny had witnessed the death of his only contact in Cairo, Professor Davis, because the professor had Danny's father's journals.

Danny knows that the men who had killed the professor were now after him and the journals. Danny finds the journals and gets his uncle and friend to safety in an airport hotel where he tells them what happened. They decide to keep searching for Danny's father and try to rescue him.

Along the way, Danny and Craig find some help from a street kid named Bud and twins from South Africa who had worked with Danny's father. They managed to escape the men chasing them twice so far, Danny wasn't sure their luck would hold a third time.

And it barely did. They finally decided to head out of Cairo. Beyond the headwaters of the Amazon, in the Republic of Congo, after a few more close calls, they hire a guide to take them into the jungle in search of a lost ancient city.

Even into the jungle on the Trail of Elephants, they are followed. Then Danny barely escapes death when he falls through a floor in an old temple. The rest rescue him, but when they reach the bottom the men following them throw down the rope and trap them under the ancient city. But what they find next is amazing. An ancient council chamber.

THE ADVENTURES OF HAWK

CHAPTER TWENTY-EIGHT

September 17, 1970
Under the Lost City of Ishango, deep in the jungle of the Republic of Congo.

AS DR. HASSATT, Ernie, and Ed studied the rest of the main platform of the ancient council chamber for any other clues to anything, Danny decided that he and Bud and Craig would look for the way out.

Danny watched as Craig held his torch up. The faint smoke from it drifted to his right and toward the tunnel they had come through.

The three of them climbed down off the large stone platform. "Craig," Danny said, "go toward the left wall. Bud, you go up the right staircase, I'll go up the left. Using the smoke from our torches, we should be able to get some sort of reading on where the draft is coming from."

Danny quickly climbed the stone staircase that went upward between the stone benches. Even fifty rows up in the stands, he could clearly hear everything Dr. Hassatt and the twins were saying. Amazing acoustics in this cave, that was for sure.

He stood about half way up the staircase and let the air around him calm, watching the smoke. It drifted still toward the tunnel, so the entrance was above him still.

"Nothing down here," Craig said from down by the left wall. "Smoke just sort of swirls."

"Mine shows the entrance is up top," Bud said.

"Go slow," Danny said, turning and starting up. "We may have someone waiting for us up there."

Bud nodded and moved at the same pace as Danny up the staircase.

At the top, there was a wide area inside yet another cavern. The entire floor of this cavern had also been paved with stones. The breeze felt clearly more noticeable, and the air was warmer as well.

Craig joined Bud and Danny in the center of the room. They let the air settle, then headed to where the wind was coming from.

At the back of the room were over a dozen tunnels, some made of stone blocks, others cut out of the natural stone. All of them led off the back of the room like spokes on a wheel. Clearly, at one point there had been a lot of entrances to this great chamber, so that a lot of people could come in at once. But now the breeze was only coming from one.

Bud led the way, moving so silently that after a moment, he motioned for Danny and Craig to just stop and he would scout it out. Danny watched Bud's torch disappear around a corner in the stone tunnel.

The waiting seemed to stretch as Danny worked to not hold his breath as he tried to listen for any problems Bud might have.

Then, after what must have been the longest two or three minutes on record, Bud came back, smiling.

"The tunnel was blocked at the entrance a long time ago," Bud said. "Clearly on purpose, so no one would find this place."

"That doesn't sound good," Craig said.

"There was a cave-in just short of the blocked entrance," Bud said, smiling. "We can climb up the rocks and get out just fine."

"Okay, so we can get out," Craig said, clearly feeling as relieved as Danny felt. "Now what do we do next?"

"We look for treasure," Bud said, smiling.

"Besides that," Craig said, laughing.

"I think that's a discussion for everyone," Danny said. "But I'm voting for South America."

"Yeah," Craig said. "Why did I know that?"

Two hours later, sitting on the benches of an ancient civilization's Great Council Chamber, they worked out their plan.

CHAPTER TWENTY-NINE

September 22, 1970
Bunia, Republic of the Congo, on the shores of Lake Albert.

FOUR DAYS AFTER leaving the Great Council Chamber, they made it back down the Trail of Elephants to the shores of Lake Albert.

Dr. Hassatt left them almost at once, headed back down the Nile. He didn't dare stay since he was easily recognized in the area. He planned on holing up in an apartment in London and writing up his notes and publishing a few papers on the great lost city. He had enough pictures, enough evidence, that he hoped to get some decent publications, even though his name had been discredited.

Danny wasn't happy with him leaving them, but they really didn't have any choice if they didn't want to draw attention to themselves. With luck, they would meet him in London after they had found the next Hydra Journal entry in Machu Picchu.

The problem they faced was how to get out of Africa.

At first it had been suggested by Bud that they try to make it across the Congo and to the west coast, but that was ruled out by everyone. Even Danny knew enough about that jungle and the tribes and governments of the Congo to not go that way.

And none of the boys wanted to try going back down the Nile to Cairo, following Dr. Hassatt. Going that way felt to Danny like walking into a huge trap.

Right now, he was convinced that if they stayed hidden, they would have a head start on the Hydra League men still guarding their old camp up in the ruins. It would still be days, maybe weeks yet, before those men discovered that they hadn't died in the cave, but had escaped.

After leaving the cave, Bud had worked his way back down into their old camp in the ruins. The two Hydra League men had been sleeping close by, so Bud had managed to get all their money and a few personal things in packs that the two men wouldn't know were missing. So at least they had money for whatever they needed to do.

"We go east," Ed said after they had all stared at the maps for a time.

"Aren't we trying to go west?" Craig asked. "Seems that South America is west of here, if I remember my world map correctly."

Danny agreed. "Going east across the Indian Ocean and then the Pacific is a long ways out of the way."

Ed nodded. "But we need to go east to get out of Africa. Then we go south and west."

"I agree," Ernie said. He pointed at the huge body of water on the map. "We need to cross Lake Victoria and get into Kenya."

Ed traced the path they were proposing with his finger on the map. "We land in Kisumu in Kenya, take overland transportation of some sort to Nairobi, then a train down to Mombasa on the coast. From there we can get a ship to take us down the coast to South Africa. In Cape Town, we know people who will help us get to Brazil."

Danny looked at the two twins shocked that they would even think of the idea. "You can't go back to South Africa."

"Yeah," Bud said. "They were shooting at you in Cairo, remember?"

Both Ed and Ernie nodded. "We don't have a choice. It is our best chance from here."

Danny didn't like it, but after a few hours of studying the maps, he knew they were right. The twins had to go right back into what might be a death trap if they were all to get out of Central Africa and get on with the search for the Hydra Journals.

CHAPTER THIRTY

October 2, 1970
Cape Town, South Africa.

THE FREIGHTER DOCKED at just after twelve noon in what was clearly a huge, industrial port to one side of Cape Town. From the deck of the freighter as they moved into the harbor, Danny could see at least a hundred ships of all sizes, if not more. It was a very busy international port.

The city itself looked beautiful, tucked in under a long mountain with a flat top the twins said was aptly named Table Mountain. Ernie pointed out Devil's Peak and Signal Hill to the right of Table Mountain. The place would have been interesting to explore if it wasn't so deadly to the twins. They had to get in and out of this port fast.

The sun was high overhead and the air was hot and thick with the smell of oil and sewage. Hundreds of workers swarmed over the docks, loading and unloading the ships.

Danny and Craig were standing on the deck as the crew finished the tying up of the ship. Ed and Ernie had insisted that as a group, they couldn't be seen together. Only Danny and Craig dared do anything, so the twins, with Bud, had stayed hidden below decks, with Bud standing guard for them.

With the apartheid form of government, and the high levels of segregation, two white boys and two black boys were not allowed together. Just doing that would be enough to get Ed and Ernie tossed in jail, and then once the police discovered who they were, they would be killed without trial.

So it was up to Danny and Craig to find a British ship of some kind and book them all passage to Brazil. Danny had no doubt, looking at the busy docks, that wasn't going to be an easy task.

An hour later, they finally found the headquarters of a British ship company, tucked just off the docks on a side street.

The man inside, behind the desk, was dressed in a blue uniform of some sort, with a tie and hat. A fan was working hard in the window to keep the air in the room moving, but it still felt like a sauna bath in the small office.

Danny introduced himself and Craig and told the man that they and three other friends were looking for a way to get to Brazil.

"Americans?" the man said in a fairly proper British accent.

Danny nodded. "Washington State."

The man nodded and chuckled to himself. "We get a lot of American boys these days, traveling the world, trying to stay out of your infernal war in Southeast Asia. Do you have money or do you need to work your way there?"

"We have some money," Danny said. "But we don't need anything fancy. In fact, we would rather not be on a fancy ship."

"Hiding are we?" the man asked, looking at them.

"In a manner of speaking," Danny said, letting the man go ahead and think they were running away from the draft. It was easier than telling him the truth.

The man nodded. "I have a freighter leaving in two days for Brazil. It will be running mostly empty to pick up coffee. I have two spare crew cabins you could have."

"That would be perfect," Danny said.

"All five of you need to be on dock 86-B before seven in the morning, October 4th, with your passports."

"Not a problem," Danny said.

"See to it that it isn't," the man said.

The five tickets cost Danny almost half of the money he had left, but it was worth it. And once in Brazil or Peru, he could wire Uncle Bill and get more.

"That went surprisingly easy," Craig said as he and Danny headed back toward the freighter.

"Yeah, now we just have to hide for the next two days. And try to keep the twins from being spotted."

"From the sounds of it," Craig said, shaking his head, "just being seen with us could be just as bad."

"Yeah," Danny said.

In America, he had watched night after night of civil rights demonstrations on television. He had watched the replay of the assassination of Martin Luther King. Being part Indian, he understood some of what the blacks were going through, but not much. He had been lucky to be raised where he had been raised.

And until Ed and Ernie had mentioned that they couldn't be seen together, Danny hadn't even thought of them as anything but two others his age. Sometimes the world was just a stupid place.

As Danny and Craig moved between two large crates and were just about to step into the open in front of the freighter, Bud appeared beside them.

"Stop! Hide!"

He motioned for them to duck back in behind the crates.

Just as they did, two white men in brown dock police uniforms escorted Ed and Ernie past the crates.

Both men were carrying guns, and had them pointed at the twins.

Danny could feel his stomach twist. They couldn't lose the twins now. They had to do something.

"What happened?" Danny whispered.

"Captain turned them in as being suspicious," Bud whispered back, spitting on the ground in disgust. "I barely got away."

"As soon as they find out who they really are, they're dead," Craig said.

"I know," Danny said, doing his best to keep his heart from beating right out of his chest. He was sweating harder than he should be in the heat. "We follow them."

Bud nodded and led out, motioning to them when it was clear or not.

They didn't have far to follow the two policemen. The twins were taken into a large warehouse two ships down from where their freighter had docked. On the small side door of the warehouse, a sign said simply, "Port Police."

Danny had no doubt that the twins were as good as dead unless he and Craig and Bud could do something, and do it fast.

But what? Danny had no idea.

Continued in the next issue…

USA Today Bestselling Writer

DEAN WESLEY SMITH

CAPTAIN BOB

In His Most Recent Story

THE END OF THE WORLD AS WE KNOW IT

Challenged by another writer to do a story about piranha poodles,
Captain Joe-Jim Bob appeared from the depths of my fevered mind, to fight for what
seems right against all odds.

Or something like that.

And no, I am not writing the novel.

CAPTAIN BOB
In His Most Recent Story
The End of the World as We Know It

March Issue
THE PINK-COLLARED MENACE

IN LAST MONTH'S thrilling episode, Captain Joe-Jim Bob, with the help of his son, Carl, defended the Shady Hills Nursing Home from the rabid looters and pillagers after the simultaneous collapse of the US monetary system and the public water works.

In this months spine-tingling story, Captain Bob faces a far greater threat to Shady Hills. Pouring out of the suburbs is the Pink-Collared Menace: Six hundred piranha poodles, led by Mrs. Dorthey Gillman Dickenson, III.

Captain Bob's only hope is to capture the famed, but very flammable, K-Mart Zeppelin before his son and Shady Hills residents become only so much dog food.

...story to be continued next month.

April Issue
THE GREAT WHITE

REMEMBER IN LAST month's cliff-hanging episode, we left Captain Joe-Jim Bob surrounded by meat-crazed piranha poodles, his right arm missing after having been savagely ripped off and devoured by the Great White Piranha Poodle.

The loss of blood was making him faint.

He only had two bullets left in his gun.

His only hope of rescue, his son at the helm of the very destructible K-Mart Zeppelin.

Captain Bob fans, this month, follow the one-armed Captain Bob as he and his son, Carl, with the help of Grandma and Grandpa Jones as tail gunners, set out in the rather shaky K-Mart Zeppelin to track the 541 remaining piranha poodles, their leader, the Great White Piranha Poodle, and its owner, Mrs. Dorthey Gillman Dickenson, III.

An action packed story for the entire family.

...story to be continued next month.

May Issue
PRISONER IN THE BEDROOM

AS YOU WILL all remember, in last month's heart-stopping episode, we left Captain Joe-Jim Bob desperately trying to escape from the piranha poodles grooming parlor where the beautiful hairdresser, Constance Conraddy, was being held prisoner.

Captain Bob was clutching at a ground rope from the K-Mart Zeppelin as his son, Carl, at the helm of the Zeppelin, desperately tried to pull Captain Bob away from two pink piranha poodles ripping at his right leg.

In this issue's action-filled adventure, follow the one armed, peg-legged Captain Joe-Jim Bob as he sets out with his son, Carl, in the slowly leaking K-Mart Zeppelin to rescue the beautiful hairdresser, Constance Conraddy, from the evil clutches of the 461 remaining piranha poodles, the Great White Piranha Poodle, and Mrs. Dorthey Gillman Dickenson, III.

Will this be the end of Captain Bob?

...story to be continued next month.

June Issue
TORTURE

WOW! IN LAST month's hair-raising adventure, we left the peg-legged, one-armed, Captain Joe-Jim Bob tied to the basement wall of Mrs. Dorthey Gillman Dickenson, III's house and piranha poodle headquarters.

Tied beside Captain Bob was the scantily clad, beautiful hairdresser, Constance Conraddy.

Mrs. Dorthey Gillman Dickenson, III was about to ram a hot fireplace poker into Captain Bob's eyes because she didn't like how he kept looking over at the mostly exposed and very-well-endowed body of her favorite captured hairdresser.

This month follow the daring escape of the one-armed, peg-legged, one-eyed Captain Bob and the beautiful and scantily-clad Constance Conraddy from the 237 remaining piranha poodles, the Great White Piranha Poodle, and Mrs. Dorthey Gillman Dickenson, III.

Will Carl and Grandma and Grandpa Jones in the I-can't-believe-it-is-still-in-the-air K-Mart Zeppelin get there in time to pull Constance and Captain Bob from the teeth of the Great White?

...story to be continued next month.

July Issue
BACK IN THE JAWS OF DEATH

IN LAST MONTH'S spine-tingling story, we left the one-armed, peg-legged, one-eyed Captain Joe-Jim Bob carrying the scantily-clad, buxom hairdresser, Constance Conraddy, through the garden of the Piranha Poodles Beauty Salon.

Up ahead, Grandma and Grandpa Jones and Captain Bob's son, Carl, mow down piranha poodles with machine guns from the barely-in-the-air K-Mart Zeppelin.

The Great White Piranha Poodle is closing fast on Captain Bob and the unconscious beauty, Constance Conraddy.

In this month's chilling conclusion to our story, follow the one-armed, peg-legged, one-eyed Captain Bob, his son, Carl, Grandpa and Grandma Jones, and the hairdresser, Constance Conraddy, as they use the broken-down K-Mart Zeppelin to launch one final attack on the remaining 94 piranha poodles.

Follow Captain Bob and Constance as, side by side, they square off for one final battle, face to face, against the Great White Piranha Poodle and Mrs. Dorthey Gillman Dickenson, III.

Who will win this epic struggle?

Will Captain Bob survive with enough body parts left to show Constance he loves her?

Will Constance fall for Captain Bob's son, Carl?

This is it! The thrilling conclusion to a five-part serial:

CAPTAIN BOB: THE END OF THE WORLD AS WE KNOW IT

The End.

CAPTAIN BOB FANS!!!

Starting next issue an entire new serial starring the never-say-die hero, Captain Joe-Jim Bob and his sidekicks, Grandma and Grandpa Jones, Captain Bob's son, Carl, and Carl's new wife, Constance.

Follow Captain Bob and his crew as they take the mighty K-Mart Zeppelin and go in search of the piranha poodle puppies in:

CAPTAIN BOB: THE RETURN OF THE PINK-COLLARED MENACE

A seven-part serial you won't want to miss.

USA *Today* Bestselling Writer

DEAN WESLEY SMITH

A JUKEBOX
STORY

THE SONGS OF MEMORY

I put this story in here because it is the start of the link between my jukebox stories and my Thunder Mountain series of books and stories with Bonnie and Duster Kendal. I haven't written the story yet with Bonnie and Duster and Stout, but I will.

In this story, as the owner of the Garden Lounge and the time-traveling jukebox, Stout faces a critical decision when the love of his life comes to visit him and the regulars of the Garden.

Many lives hang in the balance, including his and the future of the Garden Lounge. And only a trip through the jukebox might save everything.

THE SONGS OF MEMORY
A Jukebox Story

One

I LOCKED THE front door of the Garden Lounge with a loud click and turned up the lights slightly so that it didn't feel like nighttime. Then I turned back to the six friends sitting on the bar stools, drinking and laughing, with their backs to me.

This was going to be very, very hard to tell them.

Outside, the July sun was beating down on the afternoon streets, sending the temperatures to almost a hundred. But inside the Garden, I kept the temperature at a cool seventy-two. But even with that, I was sweating and worried about what I was going to say.

The old jukebox that had changed so many things for all of us sat in the corner, dark as always, sort of tucked away behind a planter full of natural-looking fake plants. I seldom plugged the jukebox in and turned it on for anything but the special Christmas Eve gathering. The background music in the bar came from an old stereo system tucked under one end of the bar.

That old jukebox could take a person back through time to the memory associated with a song, and the last thing I wanted was to have customers playing songs that took them to memories that they changed and then not come back to be customers. I didn't have enough customers as it was.

But today I needed to turn it on one more time, just for me.

So as I walked toward the bar, I moved around the planter and plugged in the jukebox.

All six regulars turned as one, all stunned.

"Stout?" Big Carl said, frowning. "What are you doing?"

Carl was a giant of a man and as gentle as they come. He worked as a contractor and had skin as tanned and leathery as shoe leather. Of all my friends, he also worried the most about me.

Dave, my best friend, sat next to Carl on Carl's left. He was still in his airline pilot's uniform and he looked suddenly very worried. He had managed to get here by changing flight assignments this afternoon. It was the only time I had ever asked him to do something like that, so he already had a hint about how serious this was.

Sandy, his daughter, sat to the left of him. She was a private eye, one of the best in the city. Beside her, Fred stared at me as well, watching me like I was about to rip off the hotel for older men he ran down on the south side.

Next to Fred on that end was Billy, a rough-looking man with even a rougher past. Billy had moved into Fred's hotel about six months ago, and the two had become like a couple, always seen together and bickering half the time.

Closest to me and the jukebox on Big Carl's right was Richard Cone, a manager of a local factory and the only one of the group besides me who didn't drink. Richard also ran the bar when I couldn't make it or was out of town for some reason. He was the only help I had, and he only worked when I wasn't around.

My six closest friends.

All very different people.

And all but Richard had experienced the effects of the jukebox. Richard just kept declining to go back to a memory, stating his life had turned out just fine and he was happy with where he was. But he loved to watch others disappear back into their memories from a song and then come back with stories.

"So what's happening, Stout?" Richard asked, as I moved around behind the bar.

"Just a little announcement is all," I said. "But before I do it, I need to take a little ride back in time."

"Not to change anything I hope," Sandy said, clearly almost panicked.

I laughed. Sandy existed because Dave had gone back through the jukebox and saved his wife. Without the jukebox, Sandy would have never been born, and no way was I going to take a chance on changing that.

"Nope," I said. "Not changing a thing. I just need to go have a look at someone one more time. Then I'll tell you all what this is all about."

"Jenny?" Dave asked.

I nodded, took a quarter from the cash register, then passed out earplugs as I moved over to the very special Wurlitzer jukebox and dropped in the quarter.

"Stay focused on the bar while I'm gone," I said. "I don't want any of you jumping by accident."

They all nodded. They all knew the drill.

I didn't dare let myself hesitate. It had been ten years since I had taken this ride, ten years since I discovered the jukebox, and I didn't dare hesitate now or I would never do it. But I had to know for sure if my feelings for Jenny were still there before I made my final decision. And the only way to discover that was go be with her for a few minutes.

The length of the song.

I punched A-1, the place on the jukebox where the special song had sat since I found the jukebox.

"Have a good visit," Richard said.

All my friends looked very worried. The next two minutes were going to be a very long time for them, of that I had no doubt. I had done my share of waiting the length of a song while someone was gone, wondering if they would return.

Those two or two-plus minutes could be an eternity.

Behind me the jukebox clicked the 45 record into place. The first note of The Mindbenders song "A Groovy Kind of Love" started and the worried faces of my friends and the Garden Lounge vanished and I was facing Jenny across the hard, polished-Formica top of the table at the university student union.

Two

JENNY HAD BEEN the one true love of my life. She had long, brown hair, very straight, as was the normal fashion of the late 1960s. She wore jeans and a white blouse tucked in with a cloth belt.

We were sitting at our favorite table in the old university student union. She had just told me she was transferring to a university in Southern California and would have to leave in three weeks to get to a promised job and get settled before the semester started. It was the best school for her music degree, and was a great opportunity for her.

Now for the "us" that existed, the couple we had become and been for the last few years, not so good, and we both knew that.

The Mindbenders' song played softly over the student union sound system, which was why the jukebox brought me to this moment.

She had just looked at me and asked me what I wanted to do. And what I wanted her to do.

I had just stared at her and not said a word, and eventually in a day or so we decided she should go and take the job and get the degree and I would visit as often as I could from Eugene, Oregon. I just didn't want to leave the job I had at the moment. She had married someone else six months later.

Now I sat there in that student union once again, staring at her, my stomach twisting just as it had all those years before. My young-self and my old-self memories were all locked into the same brain.

When I was young, I hadn't been willing to give up a job to go with her, and I had lost her. Would I be able to give up the Garden Lounge and all my friends in Portland this time around?

That was the reason I had taken the trip through the jukebox, to try to get an answer for that question.

My young self loved Jenny more than anything. And it seemed my older self did as well. But not just the young girl sitting there, but the woman Jenny had become over all the years.

As I had done when I was young, I just sat there silently and stared at her. Then the short song ended and I was back, standing in front of the jukebox and the worried looks of my friends.

"You all right, Stout?" Dave asked.

I nodded, then unplugged the jukebox and went around behind the bar.

"Not really, huh?" big Carl said.

"Not really," I said as I refreshed everyone's drinks, then leaned back against the back bar with the orange juice on the rocks that I sipped during the summer.

The Garden was as silent as a tomb, so I moved over and turned the stereo back on for background noise. Music was so much of a person's life, it didn't feel right to not have some music playing while I talked with my friends.

I couldn't think of how to start into this, so as I moved back to my position leaning against the back bar facing my friends, I just decided to start from the beginning.

"You know computers can be dangerous things."

"I'll drink to that," Dave said. As an airline pilot, he had told us more horror stories about computers than I wanted to remember. Especially the next time I had to fly.

"About six months ago, I decided to see how Jenny was doing," I said. "So I looked her up on that Google-thing that Sandy showed me how to use when she installed that computer in my office."

Sandy laughed. "That computer was for bookkeeping, not surfing the web."

Billy just shook his head. "Stout surfing. Now I've seen it all."

"Hey," I said, laughing. "I used to surf when I was down in Florida for those jobs."

Billy snorted. "Yeah, thirty years and fifty pounds ago."

"Twenty-seven years and forty-three pounds," I said, laughing even harder. Amazing how good friends could make you feel better even when you were trying to tell them bad news.

Billy raised his glass in defeat.

"So you found Jenny," Sandy said, getting me back on my story. "What was she doing?"

"I actually didn't find her at first," I said, my stomach twisting. "I actually found an obituary for her husband. He died of cancer two years ago. She was mentioned as surviving him."

"Oh," was all Sandy said.

"I searched some more, and discovered she had an account on something called Facebook, so I joined up."

"The world has ended," Billy said.

"My hero is lost," Big Carl said.

Fred just shook his head, saying nothing, while Sandy looked proudly at me and Richard and Dave looked worried.

"So I contacted her and we've been in touch for six months now."

"No wonder you've been in such a good mood," Richard said.

I let them chatter about my mood for a second until Dave said, "Let him finish his story."

"Jenny has two grown kids and a couple of young grandkids. She's living just south of San Francisco and doing fine. Retired from teaching at the university there."

"Is she going to come up and visit?" Fred asked. "I could clean a room in the Golden Dream if she needs a place to stay."

Billy just smacked him on the side of the arm and everyone laughed.

"Thanks," I said. "She actually will be in tonight, and I've got her a room at the Comfort Suites down the street from here."

Now smiles lit up on everyone, and they all started talking at once about how they were looking forward to meeting her.

Finally, after the conversation eased, Dave looked at me and asked, "So, Stout, how come the trip through the jukebox?"

"I wanted to see if the feelings were still there just from the old memories, or if these new memories were building new feelings."

"Getting serious it seems," Richard said.

"Skype will do that for you," I said, smiling.

"The world really has ended," Fred said, shaking his head. "Our Stout is doing the nasty with a woman on the computer."

I just laughed. "Only talking. Honest."

Everyone but Richard laughed. "So what's the upshot of this, Stout?"

I took a deep breath and looked at Richard. "Remember when I had you run the bar for a week two months ago? I was down seeing Jenny and getting to know her family. And that went well, which is why she's coming up here this time. To see my life and meet all of you."

"And if this goes well?" Richard asked.

I smiled. Richard really, really knew me. He was one of the sharpest people I knew. And since he never took a drink, he often caught stuff others missed.

"We might get married," I said, smiling. "We've talked about it, but nothing firm yet. Waiting to see how this trip goes."

Everyone cheered and I quickly hushed them. "Jenny is looking forward to meeting you all, but not a word of that marriage stuff, all right? Promise?"

Six hands went up as one, promising.

"And if you decide to get hitched," Richard said, "you'll need to move down there with her. Right? She's the one with the grandkids and family."

Suddenly even the background music didn't help the dead feeling of the Garden. I made a note to hear the Beatles

song playing on the radio to anchor this moment.

"Actually, we're planning on living both places," I said. "And doing some traveling. But it will be tough to own a bar and not be here six months of the year."

I glanced at all six of the sad faces on my friends. The Garden was as much of a home to them as it was to me. Just like I couldn't imagine shutting this bar down, they couldn't imagine being without it and all the friendships. And that's what they were all thinking at that moment.

No one said a word, so I went on with my plan.

I moved down in front of Richard. "Mr. Richard Cone, sir," I said, acting very formal. "I know you have a great job managing that plant, but I also know you have always wanted to own your own bar."

Richard's head snapped up and he looked me square in the eyes.

A Beach Boys song called "Good Vibrations" was now playing.

"If this works out between me and Jenny, which I have a hunch it's going to, would you be interested in buying the Garden Lounge and running it in any manner you see fit?"

I watched him swallow hard, his eyes slightly misty.

Except for the background song, the bar was dead silent.

Dave leaned over and touched Richard on the shoulder. "I'll back you if you need the help."

"Yeah, me too," Sandy said.

"Count me in," Carl said. "I got some extra if you need it."

"Me too," Fred said.

"Not me," Billy said. "I barely got enough to drink and eat and pay my rent to Fred here. But I'll buy drinks if you'll serve me."

Everyone laughed then, including Richard. Then Richard turned to them. "Thanks. But with my job and low expenses, I've been saving for something like this for a very, very long time."

He turned back to me and extended his hand. "Mr. Radley Stout, if things work out with your new girl, you've got a buyer — as long as that damned jukebox stays with the bar. We can't be changing traditions now, can we?"

We shook hands as everyone cheered, and it felt as if a huge weight had just lifted off my shoulders.

Three

JENNY FIT IN perfectly with the regulars at the Garden. She and Dave and Richard hit it off perfectly, and after just a few evenings, she told me she felt like she had always been sitting at the bar joking with everyone.

And at one point or another every one of my friends told me in private that if I lost this woman, I was dumber than a post.

I had to agree with them, even though Jenny sure didn't look much like the thin, long-haired girl I had fallen in love with all those decades ago. Just as I had done, she had filled out, and now her once-brown hair was short and silver. And she tended to wear dresses more than jeans. And she wore glasses, those thin kind that professors wore.

She actually had been a professor for over twenty-five years, teaching music theory and history before she retired to care for her husband in his last year.

Her husband had been a building contractor, so she and Big Carl seemed to sometimes talk another language that most of us just didn't understand.

After four days, it was clear she and I were going to be together for a lot longer if I could just get past one more hurdle.

Dave reminded me that I needed to tell her about the jukebox.

I had to agree with him. It was important that a future partner would know that I owned — and was about to sell — a time machine.

So once again I passed the word to my closest friends to come in early in the afternoon to help me out in case I needed it. And I asked Jenny to come with me to open the bar. I said I had something I needed to show her.

"This sounds serious," she said, looking at me with those wonderful brown eyes of hers. Those eyes hadn't changed at all, and her ability to really see me hadn't changed either.

"It is," I said. "And I hope nothing serious. Just something you need to know about."

The night before we had talked about me selling the bar to Richard and how happy I was about that.

And sad at the same time.

She double- and triple-checked that I was telling her the truth. After the last few days, she could see just how special the Garden Lounge was to me, and how hard it was going to be for me to let it go.

I told her I didn't plan on leaving the Garden forever. We would be regulars when we were in town. And I told her that every Christmas Eve we had to be there, no matter what. We could fly back to her kids for Christmas Day, since Oregon and California were only a few-hour flight apart.

I told her she would understand why after I showed her what I had to show her at the bar.

Christmas Eve at the Garden Lounge was a special time for all the regulars. It was the only time I ever turned on the jukebox and let customers go back to their memories. Richard had told me that even though he had never gone through the jukebox, he planned on honoring that tradition, and hoped I would be back every year to run the party.

So as I finished getting the bar opened, everyone sort of showed up at once, laughing with Jenny. All of them knew what this was all about, and they were all determined to help if they could.

So with Jenny sitting between Dave and Richard at the bar, I stood against the back of the bar and had no idea where to start. I just sort of stood there as everyone looked at me. I hadn't bothered to turn on the stereo yet, so the weight of the silence made starting even harder.

"Tell her about the glasses first," Dave said, pointing at the case over the bar.

I looked into the eyes of the woman I loved and then said simply. "You are not going to believe most of what I'm about to say, but for now just trust me. Okay?"

She frowned, clearly suddenly worried.

"Trust him," Dave said. "He's not totally nuts, only slightly."

Everyone laughed and I took the key for the cabinet out of the register drawer and went to get the four glasses.

I took three down and left the other in the case.

Then I walked the fine drinking glasses down the bar, putting the one etched with the name Dave in front of Dave, another in front of Carl, and another in front of Fred.

"I made these glasses for these men ten years ago this last Christmas. I served them drinks in these glasses, and none of them remembers that night. Except Dave, who came back after I closed the bar. Long story, but what this is all about."

"If you are trying to explain something," Jenny said, "remind me to never let you in a classroom."

"Now that's a deal, Professor," I said.

I pointed at the old jukebox, dark and sitting in the corner. "You understand the power of music. Music can take a person back to a memory, to an emotion, to an experience."

Jenny nodded. "There have been many studies on the power of songs to trigger memories to try to help some patients with different forms of brain injury and diseases."

Everyone was deadly silent, which wasn't a normal state for the Garden Lounge, so I just blurted it out. "That jukebox actually takes a person *physically* to a memory associated with a song."

Jenny looked at me frowning. Then she smiled. "Okay, what's the joke?"

"Toss me a quarter, Stout," Dave said, climbing off his stool. "She's not going to believe you; no one does, until they see it. I'll go visit Sandy being born again."

I tossed him a quarter and moved around the end of the bar and plugged in the jukebox.

"Give us a minute to get earplugs in," I said.

I quickly dug out the earplugs and handed each person a pair. When I handed the pair to Jenny, I smiled. "You said you trusted me. Just hold on for one more moment and you'll understand what I'm talking about."

She was really frowning now, but she did as everyone did and put in the earplugs.

"Ready," Dave asked, smiling.

I nodded, and he dropped the quarter into the machine and after a moment hit the number to the song that would take him back to the moment when Sandy was born.

I looked into the eyes of the woman I loved. "Cover your ears," I shouted so she would hear. "And think of this moment right here and right now. Think of this bar. Okay?"

She nodded, and then the music started and Dave was gone and we were all still here.

"How?" Jenny said, but I could barely hear her through my earplugs.

I just held up my finger for her to wait and pointed toward the jukebox. Then I put my hand on hers, holding her solidly in the Garden Lounge.

The two minutes of the song stretched into an eternity.

Then, faintly, I could hear the song ending and Dave shimmered back into being, smiling.

We all pulled out our earplugs and Dave rejoined us at the bar. "You know," he said to his daughter, Sandy, "you sure were a damn pretty baby."

"You all right?" Sandy asked, just before I did.

Seeing his wife again had to hurt some. She had died a couple years back from cancer and we all missed her.

"I'm fine," he said, taking a drink.

"So what the hell just happened here?" Jenny said. "What kind of magic trick was that?"

"No trick I'm afraid," I said, pointing at the jukebox. "That thing really takes people back to their memories. You end up inside the body of the person you were, only with old memories. When the song ends, you come back — unless you have changed something."

Dave held up his glass. "One Christmas, ten years ago, Stout gave four of his best friends a very special Christmas gift. He let us go back and change something in our pasts we wanted to change. I went back and saved my wife from being killed in a car wreck; as a result, Sandy, here, and her sister were born."

"That's why we only turn that thing on for Christmas Eve," I said. "And why we're very careful. It's very dangerous and can change a person's life."

I stared at Jenny for a moment, then said, "You still don't believe us, do you?"

She looked me square in the eye and I could tell she was angry. A deep-down angry.

I wanted to throw up. This couldn't be happening.

"You have to admit this is hard to swallow," Jenny said. "And I don't see why you would play this sort of trick on me, Stout."

The silence in the bar could be cut with a knife, I swear. I could hardly breathe. Was I going to lose the only woman I had

ever loved for the second time because of the jukebox?

"No trick," I said, softly. "That really is a time machine."

Again the silence became thick and smothering. I had to do something and do it quickly.

"Do you remember the song that was playing right after you told me about your job while we sat in the student union in Eugene?"

She nodded. "Longest song ever," she said. "I was waiting for you to say something and you didn't say anything."

"Do you remember the name of the song?"

"It was a Mindbenders song about love. Why?"

I took a quarter out of the cash register and went around the bar to her side. I took her hand to indicate she should get down off the barstool. "Let's go for a ride."

She walked hesitantly to the jukebox. "Earplugs everyone," I said.

Then I turned to the woman I love. "You can't change anything while we

are there. Nothing. Our older selves will be in control of our younger bodies, and our younger selves won't remember our little visit. But change *nothing*, all right? Please. A lot of lives depend on it, including your wonderful children and grandchildren."

She glanced around at the people at the bar, then nodded, suddenly very afraid.

I dropped the quarter into the jukebox and once again punched A-1.

A moment later I was sitting again across from the young Jenny.

Only this time Jenny's eyes didn't stay focused on the table in front of her as they had done the first time. They looked up at me, panicked.

The older Judy was in there this time.

Then she looked around, listening to the song over the sound system of the old student union, smelling the greasy fries and smell from the two jocks sitting far too close to us.

Finally she looked back at me. "Is this real?"

I nodded. "Can you remember your life with Stephen? Your kids being born? Your grandkids?"

She nodded, still looking around. "How is this possible?"

"There's some kind of very advanced equipment in the jukebox I've never had the courage to touch. Somehow it lets the power of a memory from a song take the person listening to the memory."

"And our young selves won't remember this?"

"Do you?"

She thought for a second, then shook her head.

"This was our turning point the first time, wasn't it?" she asked

"It was," I said.

"If you had said you wanted to marry me, I would have stayed."

"But sometimes things work out the way they are supposed to," I said. "We weren't ready that first time around."

She nodded. "I would have been angry at you for making me stay."

"I know," I said. "And I would have been angry for you making me leave."

"You've sat here before from the future, watching me, haven't you?"

I nodded. "A number of times. It's how I discovered the power of the jukebox."

"And you never said anything? Never changed our future? Why not?"

"I loved you too much," I said. "And then, after a while, I knew if I changed my future, a number of people wouldn't be alive right now. And that was before I knew about your wonderful family."

The song was slowly nearing its end.

"You are a very special man," she said, smiling.

"Then will you stay with me this time? In the future, of course."

"I want to more than anything. In the future, of course."

I smiled. "Would you marry me the second time around?"

She looked around at the old student union and laughed as the song finished and we appeared back in the Garden.

She put her arms around me and said, "Yes, you stupid fool. Of course I'll marry you."

Then she kissed me in a way I knew I would never forget, song or no song.

And our friends in the Garden Lounge cheered.

This time, it was *my* life the jukebox saved.

~

Now Available
from all your favorite booksellers in trade paper and electronic editions.

USA Today Bestselling Author

DEAN WESLEY SMITH

HEAVEN PAINTED
as a poker chip

A GHOST OF A CHANCE NOVEL

Starting into a brand new series, USA Today *bestselling writer Dean Wesley Smith asks a simple question: What happens if ghosts can fight crime and bad guys?*

Just fifteen minutes after Dr. Jewel Kelly meets Deputy Sheriff Tommy Ralston, they both die. They simply become ghosts, hanging around their own death scene in the mountains of Montana, waiting for something to happen. But even as ghosts they find each other still really attractive.

In life, they both worked to help people. It seems that in the afterlife, their job continues.

The strangest crime-fighting ghost duo ever. And the most sexy.

HEAVEN PAINTED AS A POKER CHIP
A Ghost of a Chance Novel

For Kris
Long live popcorn for the brain.

Section One
That's Got to Hurt

One

TWENTY-SEVEN MINUTES before she died, Dr. Jewel Kelly stepped out of the front door of her small office in Buffalo Jump, Montana, and set her medical bag on the sidewalk beside her. She then made sure the office door was locked tight. With a control on her key chain, she triggered the alarm. She doubted anyone around this town would take anything, but better safe than sorry.

She picked up her bag, pulled her ski parka in close around her, and stepped over under the eve of Bernie's General Store. Her little office was like an outbuilding off of Bernie's store. Three rooms and a bathroom.

Enough for her to get the job done, but not by much.

She again set her medical bag down on a dry spot near the building and turned to face the small town and wait for her ride.

She was a tall woman at five-ten, with long brown hair she loved to keep pulled back, and green eyes people said could stare right through you. At twenty-five, she liked more than anything else to run to stay fit. And she loved reading a great romance novel. In med school in Seattle, she had had time to run, but not read.

Now she had more than enough time for both. She usually put in a five-mile run up near the high school every afternoon, staying off the main highway as much as possible.

The run every day at least made her feel alive.

A cold mist of a late April spring day covered the main street of Buffalo Jump, Montana, which was also a major two-lane north-south highway. The air had a bite to it, and she had no doubt that later tonight the mist would turn to snow and the road would freeze over.

She had planned to spend the night in her log cabin a half mile to the south of town, in front of a nice fire, sipping on a glass of white wine and reading the new Nora Roberts novel. Then maybe later, after a nice bath, she would have a date with her best friend, Mr. Buzzy. She had a hunch that in Buffalo Jump, Montana, she was going to wear out good old Buzzy before she found a real man she wanted to date.

To her right and south was Jay's Gas and Minimart, across from that was Carol's Restaurant, a diner that actually had some pretty good food and was pretty clean. Beyond that, the two-lane highway disappeared off into the pine forest, now growing dark as the early evening wore on.

That was the road out of these mountains to Missoula.

To her left and north sat the twenty buildings that made up the main part of Buffalo Jump, including an old hardware store and some basic offices, two bars, and two antique stores to catch the occasional tourist who thought to stop.

She had been in the antique stores, but not the bars. She wasn't much of a drinker except for a nice glass of good wine after dinner.

On the other end of town, she could barely see through the light rain the white tower of the only church, a Presbyterian church, whose basement doubled for a meeting room for the big town events. She hadn't been in there yet either. She had never been much of a church-goer back in Boise where she grew up.

A sprawling red-brick school sat off the main street against a pine-covered hillside and serviced all grades for most of the county, with dozens of lumbering, bright-yellow school busses pouring in and out of town every day. There was even had a high school football team.

Her favorite running route was from her office, up past the school, out a dead-end gravel road for two miles, then back.

Right now she could run up the middle of the main street and no one would even notice. There was no traffic at all and just a few cars parked in front of the bars.

A typical late Thursday afternoon in small town Montana.

Silence closed in around her and she shuddered. Not even a slight wind through the pines around the town broke the oppressive stillness.

The Third Seeders Universe Novel
now available from all your favorite
booksellers in trade paper and electronic.

She pulled her dark-blue ski parka in around her, making sure it was zipped, then pulled her ski gloves out of her pocket and put them on. She could never seem to be warm enough here, except when sitting in front of the fire in her cabin.

Under the parka, she had on a nice white blouse and today she had worn jeans for only the second time. It seemed everyone else in town wore jeans, including the mayor, who ran the small grocery store, so she might as well.

Besides, jeans were far more comfortable in the cold weather. Not as drafty as the skirts she wore the first month on the job here. Nothing like a cold Montana wind whipping up a skirt and hitting a cotton-covered crotch to give a girl a real thrill.

And not a fun thrill.

She was the town's only doctor, actually the county's only doctor. And at times like this, she had no idea why she had agreed to the tuition deal to practice medicine here.

Sure, she got all her debts forgiven, not a small chunk at all, if she stayed five years, but she wasn't sure if she could handle five years out in the middle of nowhere like this, even though her dream had been to be a GP.

She had only been here for six weeks and mostly been bored out of her mind. She didn't drink and she didn't go to church. That didn't leave a lot left to do except exercise, read and give Mr. Buzzy a workout regularly.

She had delivered one baby in the small building the county called a hospital up beside the school. And she had fixed a few broken bones and one concussion from a bar fight.

For one night, she had even had a woman in the little four-bed hospital with a gall bladder attack. Jewel had to check in on her every hour to make sure the woman didn't get worse and need to take a Life-Flight out to Missoula.

The woman hadn't gotten worse and the woman's husband the next day had driven her to Missoula, four hours away, for the operation.

Today was Jewel's first call for an injury in Jackson Ridge, another small town about twenty miles away on the highway to the north. The call had come into her cell phone from the county sheriff, and he had told her a deputy would pick her up.

She had told the sheriff she had her car and could drive fine, but the sheriff, a man named Martin, insisted a deputy go along with her.

"Trust me," he had said. "The area this call came from is not a place you go in alone. Especially with that little overseas thing you drive."

Clearly, her red Miata had been noticed, and not in a good way.

"Besides," the sheriff had said, "it's going to be snowing soon and the highway's going to be slick. You don't want to be driving after dark out in these woods until you get to know the roads some."

She had thanked the sheriff and said she would be waiting in front of her office in ten minutes.

"Deputy Ralston will be there as quick as he can," the sheriff had said and hung up.

So now she stood under the eve of the general store, moving from foot to foot, her hands deep in her ski parka pockets, watching the excitement of Buffalo Jump on a late Thursday afternoon.

Except for the misting rain, nothing moved.

Nothing.

Total and complete silence.

What the hell had she been thinking coming here?

Two

NINETEEN MINUTES BEFORE he died, Deputy Sheriff Tommy Ralston got into his patrol cruiser that he had parked in front of his family's summer home on the edge of Slatefish Lake, and tossed his hat into the back seat.

Luckily, he hadn't started the steak he planned to have for dinner after the long day on the highways. His shift had lasted ten hours, starting early, and now the sheriff wanted him to take the new doctor down to Jackson Ridge on Mule Dump Creek for an injury call. More than likely one of the Stevens twins had gotten in a fight with a wife and she had stabbed him or something.

He understood why the sheriff had wanted him to go along. Those Stevens' boys had missed the line for brains when they were getting handed out.

Tommy got his patrol car started and headed back into Buffalo Jump. He was ex-military, Marines for three years, and had two degrees that the military had paid for when he got home from the desert. One degree in math from Cal Tech and one in criminal justice from UC Berkeley.

That's when his money had run out, before he could go on into law school as he planned. And he didn't feel much like going into debt just yet. The one thing the Marines had taught him, and that wasn't to be in a hurry.

His family had had the summerhouse on the lake up here that they used rarely, and he had fond memories of coming up here from Spokane where he was growing up. So he figured why not take a law enforcement job for a few years before really moving on into the next phase of his schooling.

The sheriff had been more than happy to have him on board, and for the first year, Tommy had really liked the job. But he was still young at twenty-eight and figured it was time to move on after the summer season.

He had decided he would help the sheriff get through the tourists and then head back to California for the winter. He had saved most of his two years of salary, which would, with a little help from his father, get Tommy through the first year of law school at Berkeley before he had to borrow any money.

Tommy had on jeans, cowboy boots, and had put back on one of his brown sheriff's uniform shirts over a t-shirt with the UC-Berkeley logo on it. He kept his schooling and California roots pretty quiet up here. Not the kind of thing the people who lived in these Montana mountains would take kindly to.

He had tossed a few breakfast bars on the passenger seat to hold him through the drive to Jackson Ridge and back. And a couple bottles of water, in case the new doctor wanted something to drink.

He hadn't met her yet, or even seen her, but he had heard she was young and drove a red Miata. More than likely in another year here she would be trading that in for a Jeep Grand Cherokee or something.

He turned the corner near the big church and onto the silent main street of Buffalo Jump. The towns in this part of the mountains really just rolled up their sidewalks and shut down, except for the bars, by four or five in the afternoon. Only the mini-mart at the far end of town was open to catch a few stray tourists still on the highway. And it would be shut down by nine.

He could see the doctor standing to one side of her office. She looked to be wearing a big blue ski parka and was moving from foot-to-foot as if cold.

He turned up the heat in the patrol car and moved the bars and water bottles to the center console, tossing his clipboard on the floor in the back with his hat.

As he pulled up and stopped, she bent down and grabbed her medical bag, then came over and climbed into the passenger seat, putting the medical bag on the floor between her feet.

"You want me to put that in back?" he asked.

"No thanks," she said, breathlessly, not yet looking at him. "Thanks for having the heat up."

And with that she turned and looked at him.

And he froze.

Flat froze.

That had never happened to him at any point in his past, not with other women, not in the desert while in the service.

All he could see was her smile and those intense green eyes.

She seemed to freeze as well.

They sat there like that, the patrol car idling, the heater running, staring at each other.

Finally she broke first and extended her hand. "Jewel Kelly," she said, with the most incredible and alluring voice he had ever heard come from a woman.

He nodded. "Sorry, Tommy Ralston."

She smiled. "Your first name is Sorry?"

"Tommy," he said, smiling back at her. "Sorry I was staring."

He shook her hand, not wanting to let go of it, but finally doing so.

She was staring at him just as much.

"Before you start," she said, smiling at him. "Let me take this coat off. It's warm in here."

"I thought that was just me," he said, adjusting the heat down some as she laughed.

She opened the door, letting in the cool night air, stood outside the car, and took off the heavy ski parka. She handed it to him before climbing in and he put it in the back seat.

Then, as she was figuring out the seat belt, he turned back to look at her.

She was stunning, with her long brown hair pulled back.

No other way to put it. And clearly in shape, built like an athlete.

And she was a medical doctor, so she was smart.

Holy crap, what was she doing in Buffalo Jump, Montana?

Then she turned and smiled at him again and he wondered if he could even breathe.

"Well, Deputy," she said. "Let's have an adventure."

He laughed. "Doc, not sure if going to Jackson Ridge could be called an adventure. But I'm game if you are."

"In this town," she said, "I'm game for damn near anything."

He laughed. "Bored already, huh?"

She just shook her head as he did a U-turn and headed north.

"You have no idea," she said.

"Been here myself for going on two years," he said, smiling at her. "I think I do."

Three

THEY WERE JUST at the nine-mile mark out of Buffalo Jump and she was still stunned that Deputy Tommy Ralston was as handsome and as smart as he was.

And that he worked in Buffalo Jump. How was that even possible?

In the fifteen minutes it had taken them to go the nine miles on the winding road, she had already discovered he was an ex-Marine, had two degrees from California schools, and planned on heading back to law school.

She had also discovered that he was funny and handsome beyond any hero in any of the romance novels she had read.

And he was single, never married.

Again, how in the hell was that possible?

His dark brown eyes, when he looked at her, seemed to see more than she wanted anyone to see. She didn't seem to mind. In fact, if she had her way, he would be seeing a lot more of her.

The road to Jackson Ridge was winding along the face of a mountainside covered in huge old pine trees. After the first mile, she had forced herself to keep an eye on the road instead of just turning sideways and staring at him, which was what she really, really wanted to do. The last thing he needed was for her, the doctor, to get carsick and throw up in his patrol car.

That would not be a very good first impression.

So she had been staring ahead when a majestic deer with huge antlers jumped up out of the brush and stood right in the middle of the highway in front of them.

"Deer!" she shouted, bracing herself with both hands on the dashboard.

She could see the deer's big brown eyes spotlighted in the headlights of the car. It seemed to be staring at them, daring them to hit it.

"Shit!" Tommy shouted, expertly moving the patrol car to the right to miss the huge animal.

And much to her surprise, he did miss the big majestic creature, but not by much.

But the road on the other side of the deer had turned sharply left.

Tommy had swerved right because there wasn't enough room around the big deer on the left.

She could see the edge of the road ahead as a very dark line. No guardrail, of course. This was Montana. Guardrails were for sissies and city folk.

Tommy fought hard, but couldn't get the car straightened back out on the slick, almost frozen pavement.

But he made an amazing attempt and almost did.

But almost, in this case, wasn't enough.

The patrol car left the highway and got airborne as the hillside beside the road sloped steeply away.

Flying was something she was fairly certain cars were never supposed to do.

"Brace yourself!" Tommy shouted.

She pushed back into her seat.

This was not going to be good.

While the car was in the air, Tommy reached down to the radio and flipped a switch.

The car hit once on the steep slope and bounced violently, again something she was fairly certain a car was never supposed to do.

Tommy fought the wheel, trying to keep the car straight and headed downhill.

That didn't work out so well either.

Right ahead of them was one of the biggest old-growth pine trees she had ever seen.

Far bigger around at the base than the car.

No chance, even as an expert driver, could Tommy miss that tree.

He didn't.

And that was the last thing she remembered.

Four

TOMMY FOUND HIMSELF outside the car, stunned, as the echo of the crash carried through the trees and on down the hill. He must have been tossed clear of the wreck somehow.

Now he was standing near the car on a steep dirt and pine-needle slope. The smell of gas filled the air, but it was raining enough to keep most chances of fire down.

On the other side of the car, Jewel moaned and stood, trying to get her balance.

In the faint light, she didn't look hurt, but he quickly scrambled around the back of the car and grabbed her just as she was about to topple backwards down the slope.

She felt wonderful in his arms and against him. But this wasn't the way he had hoped would be the first time he would hold her.

"Are you all right?" he asked, moving them slowly away and along the slope from the car and gas smell.

She slowly seemed to come around even more, and finally nodded. Then clearly her doctor gene kicked in and she turned her attention on him, stepping back out of his arms so she could look at him.

"How about you?"

He spread his arms for her to inspect him. "I think I'm fine."

After a moment, she released a breath into the cold, night air and nodded.

"Something feels weird about all this," she said. "We might be in some shock."

"I've got no doubt on that," he said.

"And that was some big damn deer we almost hit."

"That wasn't any deer," he said, glancing back up the steep hill toward the edge of the road far above them. The image of those huge eyes staring at him, daring him, would haunt him for a very long time. "That was Ghost Dancer."

She looked at him, clearly puzzled. "You name your deer around here? I thought everyone around here shot them and had them on the barbeque."

"No one, in as long as I have been alive and coming up here, has been able to take down Ghost Dancer."

"Deer live that long?" she asked.

He shrugged. "No one is sure Ghost Dancer is a real deer. Many believe he is some sort of Native American spirit."

"Yeah, whatever," she said, shaking her head. "That spirit or big ass deer caused us to leave the road. What I want to know is how we escaped without injuries."

"Good question." He turned to look back at the patrol car, but something was wrong with his vision. While the dark woods around him seemed perfectly fine and clear, more so than they should be on a dark night, the car was blurry.

They moved back slowly toward the car, but it still seemed blurry for some reason.

He rubbed his eyes, then tried to look again.

Finally what he was seeing cleared and he said simply, "Oh, shit."

"What?" she said, rubbing her eyes. "I can't seem to focus on the car. I must have hit my head or something."

He sat down on the side of the hill, the feeling of being tired overwhelming him. All he could do was stare at the car. "Just keep trying until you can see it, then come sit next to me."

Finally, she said softly, "That's not possible."

She looked at him, a panic in her eyes, then back at the car.

She needed his help and he wanted to give it.

He pushed himself to his feet, feeling just about as tired as he had felt in a long time, and slid and walked the few steps down the steep hill to the driver's side of the car, ignoring the strong gas smell filling the night air.

The patrol car had compacted down to the size of a Mini-Cooper and pretty much wrapped itself like in a lover's embrace around the big old pine. He figured they hit the tree going at least sixty or seventy by the time they left the road and picked up speed in the air and down the slope.

He looked closer, in what was left of the shattered driver's window, and than turned away.

They had not been thrown out.

In fact, their bodies were wedged in so tight, it was going to take the Jaws of Life to even start to get them out.

"We're dead," she said from a few feet behind him.

He could tell from the sounds of her voice that she was barely holding on. He didn't blame her. He wasn't far from losing it either.

He looked back in the window at what was left of his body and face, then turned back to her.

"You're the doc, but I'd sure say so."

"I don't feel dead," she said, not coming any closer, but instead standing there behind the car on the steep slope. She took a deep breath and blew it out. In the cold air, he could see her breath, which considering they were dead, was damn weird.

He moved back up to her and as he got close, she grabbed his arm hard, her strong hands biting into his flesh. "You don't feel dead."

"And that hurt," he said.

She pinched herself and jerked. "That also hurt. How is that possible if our bodies are in there and we're dead?"

"Never gave much thought at what being dead felt like," he said, trying to gather himself as much as he could.

His energy was slowly coming back, which told him he was getting past the shock stage.

Clearly for Jewel, her doctor training had got her right over that shock part.

"Stay here and let me take a look at all this," he said.

He scrambled around the car for a moment to her side, looking at what he could see inside. None of it was pretty. Most of the entire front compartment of the patrol car had been crushed down and looked like it was full of blood.

There was nothing in there that was recognizably Jewel.

In his two short years being a patrol officer, he'd only seen one wreck this bad. If he hadn't been so hardened by what he had seen in the war, he would have quit that first time.

Finally, he moved back up and stood next to Jewel.

"How bad?"

"As bad as it gets. Worse than anything I've seen," he said. "We're dead. No doubt about it."

"So why are we still here?" she asked.

She looked up through the tall pines into the soft rain at the same time he did, but there was no white light or tunnel coming for them. Just more rain.

"Not a clue," he said, "but let's get back up on the road and wait for help to arrive. One way or another."

"No help is coming," she said. "They'll never see the wreck down here. And if we're ghosts, they won't see us either."

"When we went over the side," he said, "I flicked the emergency beacon. All patrol cars have them in these mountains. They're pretty darned near indestructible. The sheriff will be here in fifteen or twenty minutes."

"You want to call a couple white lights while you're at it," she said.

"Out of my jurisdiction," he said.

He reached out and took her hand, which felt wonderful in his hand, somehow. He was a ghost and he was still attracted to her.

That didn't seem right.

Together, they slowly worked their way back up the steep hill toward the road above them.

It took them almost ten minutes of climbing, sometimes on hands and knees.

And by the time they reached the edge of the road, they were both panting, which also didn't seem very ghost-like.

Five

JEWEL FLAT COULD not believe she was dead. The rain had soaked her white blouse making it almost see-through, and she was cold, as cold as she could remember being.

They had found a place to sit under a tree on the far side of the road on the hill, and she had snuggled in against Tommy. She liked how he felt, and could feel his warmth helping her.

She had no doubt that in the war in the desert, he had seen his share of death. But he seemed to be as confused about all this as she was.

"This feels nice," he said, putting his arm around her and pulling her tight.

"It would be a lot nicer if I wasn't so damned cold and already dead."

He said simply, "Someone will be here soon."

She wasn't sure how that was going to help. She had a ski parka and gloves down in that mangled wreck of a car with her body, but no way was she going back down that hill to try to get them.

Something very strange had happened, she had no doubt about that, but being dead seemed to be not part of the equation. She knew death as a doctor. In her residency, she had seen more death than she had ever wanted to see.

And every time, with every patient, she had fought against it. And now, with her body down there, she was fighting against the idea of it now.

This was like no death she had ever imagined.

Finally, through the silence of the dark forest around them, they heard a car coming from the direction of Buffalo Jump.

The bright lights lit up the night before it came around the corner and Tommy stood and stepped down on the edge of the road, flagging down the car.

The car didn't stop, but it wasn't going very fast.

As it passed she could tell it was the sheriff's car, clearly looking for the signal Tommy had triggered. The sheriff was behind the wheel and he had another man beside him.

Tommy shook his head and came back to sit down, again putting his arm around her and pulling her close, which felt damned nice, even under the circumstances.

"The sheriff has Ben with him," he said.

She had met Ben, a young kid with the brain of a gnat, but Ben did as the sheriff told him and that was good enough it seemed.

The Sheriff's car went on around the corner of the road and vanished, leaving the dark night, the gentle rain, and the silence.

"They'll be back once they realize they have passed the signal," Tommy said.

She nodded and snuggled in closer to him, trying to get some of his ghost heat from his hot body.

Three minutes later Tommy was right. This time the sheriff's car was moving very slowly, and it finally pulled over on the side of the road right about where they had come up the hill.

Neither of them moved, but just watched.

Both the sheriff and Ben climbed out of the car, leaving it running. Both were wearing rain slickers and had on hats with wide brims.

She would give just damn near anything for one of those rain slickers right about now.

When Jewel had met the sheriff the first time, she figured him to be about sixty. He also had a solid round ball for a stomach, which meant he was a candidate for a heart attack at any moment. No way was he going down and back up that hill.

Deputy Ben, on the other hand, was as skinny as they came. And young. She guessed Ben to be around twenty-five, more than likely a local who had never left the area.

She watched as they both went over to the edge and looked down.

Then the sheriff said something she couldn't hear and Ben went back to the car and got a huge flashlight from the trunk.

Ben handed it to the sheriff, who clicked it on and shined it down the hill toward the wreck. The powerful yellow beam was clear through the misty rain.

After a moment the sheriff let out some cusswords that made her guess he wasn't a regular at the church with the big white steeple.

Tommy had been right. Help had arrived.

Now what?

Six

TOMMY LOOKED AT Jewel sitting beside him next to the road under the slight shelter of a tree. Her hair was wet and her soaked white blouse was showing a wonderful body very clearly. She had not put on a bra.

He was cold, but she was shaking she was so cold.

There was no doubt in his mind they were dead, that they were ghosts of some sort. But if that was the case, why were they so cold and why were they still getting wet?

"Let's go see if the sheriff and Ben can hear us," Tommy said, starting across the narrow pavement.

"I'll just stay here under the tree and shiver," she said.

He nodded and headed toward the man he had worked for the past two years. Tommy really respected the sheriff for his knowledge, his clear thinking, and his ability to handle the people of this county.

Ben had gone back to the car for a pair of walkie-talkies and a second flashlight.

Clearly he was going to scramble down the slope to the wreck. When Ben came back over to the sheriff and handed him the walkie-talkie, turned on and set, the sheriff said, "Be careful."

Ben nodded.

"Don't bother," Tommy said. "We're dead down there. Call tow trucks and the morgue van."

Neither man seemed to hear him. Ben turned and scouted along the edge of the road looking for a good way to head down.

Tommy stood beside the sheriff, watching, as if he was actually still alive and investigating the wreck.

Finally Ben eased down over the side and started down, using one hand against the steep slope for balance while hold the light in the other.

"He's not going to like what he finds," Tommy said.

The sheriff just ignored Tommy, or more likely didn't hear him.

So Tommy reached out his hand and tried to touch the sheriff on the shoulder of his rain slicker.

His hand went right through.

As it did, Tommy had a sense of the worry and fear and anger the sheriff was feeling, but nothing else.

The sheriff didn't seem to notice at all.

So Tommy stood there and watched as Ben got closer to the wreck. The poor kid slowly came up on the driver's side of the smashed patrol car, then directed his light into the window.

The kid would live with that image the rest of his life, Tommy was sure, because Tommy knew his neck was twisted around and bones were jutting out and blood was everywhere and his nose was gone.

Poor Ben, it was as if someone had punched him.

He staggered a few steps back into the hillside, swung around, and threw up his dinner.

"Told you he wasn't going to like what he found," Tommy said.

"Damn it all to hell," the sheriff muttered and swung around and headed for the patrol car, walking right through Tommy before Tommy had a chance to move.

Tommy shuddered, and again he got a sense of the sheriff's thoughts.

Once again the sheriff didn't seem to notice.

"Was that as weird feeling as it looked?" Jewel asked from across the road.

Tommy stood there shivering, and he wasn't sure if it was from the cold and rain, or the contact with the sheriff. He really didn't want to try that again anytime soon.

But it gave him an idea of what he and Jewel might do to warm up.

He motioned for her to join him and she reluctantly moved toward him, her arms clasped so hard around herself, he thought she might hurt herself, if that was possible for a ghost to do.

Tommy went over to the patrol car, which was still running. The sheriff had just put in a call for a couple of tow trucks, a lot more help, and the morgue van.

Then the sheriff shut the front door of his car and went back over to the edge of the road to check in on Ben.

"What are you thinking?"

Tommy tried to grab the handle on the back door, but his hand passed right through it. Then he stuck his entire hand through the door and could feel the warmth of the inside of the car on it.

He pulled it out and nodded.

Then he took a deep breath, shut his eyes, and just pretended the back door was open and sat down in the back seat.

The wonderful warmth of the car felt great.

And he actually seemed to be seated on the back seat. He wasn't falling through it, and the back seat floor felt solid under his feet.

He had no idea how that worked. Or why it worked that way. But he was just happy it did.

Jewel was standing outside, shaking her head, her mouth open staring at him.

He reached his arm back through the glass of the window as if it wasn't there, indicating that she should take his hand.

It took her a moment, but then she took his hand.

Her skin felt cold and wet against his wet hand, so he made sure he had a good grip, and before she had time to fight, he yanked her into the car with him.

She sprawled across his lap on the seat and it took them a moment, a wonderful moment he had to admit, to get untangled and her sitting beside him on the passenger side of the back seat.

She was breathing hard and her eyes were huge.

"Was that as much fun for you as it was for me?" he asked, smiling at her.

She brushed her wet hair back off her face, took a deep breath while looking around, and then said, "Kinky. You take all your dates to such a high-class place?"

She patted the seat, clearly wondering the same thing he had wondered about how they could be sitting and not falling through, yet able to come in through the door.

He laughed as she once again started shivering from the cold.

"Thank you," she said between shivers.

"My pleasure," he said. "And it was."

Seven

JEWEL WAS SO cold, she could hardly think. Even the warm air in the sheriff's car wasn't helping cut that. She took a deep breath and noticed that Tommy was also shivering. He was even more soaked than she was, if that was possible.

She made herself stop and think for a moment, then realize that if she were facing someone in this condition, this wet and this cold, she would get them into a warm place and out of their wet clothes.

They were in a warm place.

So they were going to need to do that second part as well.

"How long are we going to be here?" she asked.

Tommy shrugged, pretending he wasn't shivering either. "It's going to take an hour for everyone to arrive, then a couple more hours at least to get that car up the bank and our bodies, or what's left of them, out of it. Four or five hours, at least, before the sheriff leaves and takes us back into town."

She was afraid of that.

"We need to get out of these wet clothes," she said, "wring them out, let them dry, and let our bodies get warm."

"You think ghosts can die of hypothermia?" he asked, looking at her, puzzled.

"I don't know about that," she said, "but I'm damn tired of being so cold I can hardly think."

She started working with her numb fingers on the button on her jeans and zipper.

He watched her for a moment, then nodded and slipped off his wet sheriff's shirt, wringing it out onto the floor and then opening it and draping it over the back of the sheriff's driver's seat. Then he pulled off the Berkley t-shirt and wrung it out as well.

She had watched him do that, marveling at how toned and in-shape he was. He must run and lift weights as well to stay in that shape.

"That already feels better," he said.

"When was the last time you undressed in the back seat of a car?" she asked.

She was now working on getting her boots off and failing because of the tight back seat and her cold fingers.

"First year of college," he said. "Her husband was home and my roommate was home."

"Oh, that had to be fun."

"Actually it was. Let me help," he said, indicating her boots.

She swung her legs up and around on his lap and he quickly got them both off.

"So how about you?" he asked as she pulled off the socks and wrung them out and draped them over the back of her seat close to the window beside her head. Her feet were so cold, she couldn't even feel them anymore.

"High school senior prom," she said, remembering that disaster of a night. "I didn't take my dress off, just my underwear. Nothing happened. I touched him, he touched me, and it was all over. But he did have to clean the back seat of his parent's car."

Tommy actually laughed. "Poor guy. That had to be embarrassing."

"I always figured that was something better to learn early about a guy rather than later."

Then she turned back, raised up her hips, and worked her pants down over her hips. She had worn white standard underwear, not some of her fancy stuff. They were so wet, they looked transparent, but at this point, she didn't care.

He managed to kick off his cowboy boots and pull off his socks.

Then as she was working out of her jeans, he pushed his down as well.

His underwear was soaked wet as well and clung to every shape. The cold clearly wasn't affecting that part of him at all, and she liked that view a lot.

Wow. Could ghosts be sexy?

The exercise was warming her right up, or something was.

She wrung out her jeans as best she could, then draped them over the back of Ben's seat. Tommy did the same to his jeans, spreading them out over the two front seats.

Then she unbuttoned and slipped off her white blouse and got the water out of it, hanging it off a door handle. Then at the same time, they both slipped off their underwear and wrung them out as well.

"I think I might actually warm up now," she said, letting out a sigh.

"I know I'm warming up," he said, laughing.

She glanced down at his penis, which was clearly larger. "I can see that. I didn't know you were into necrophilia. I'm dead, remember?"

He just shook his head and laughed again, something she was really enjoying. She loved how easily he laughed, even in this situation. She had only hoped as a doctor after years of practice to be that calm in the face of death and crisis.

"Put your feet up there between the passenger chair and the door," he said. "Should be hot air flowing from the heater there."

She put her feet up toward the passenger door and he turned slightly so his feet were toward the driver's door in the same position. Then she leaned against him and he put his arm around her.

This is nice," she said, taking a deep breath, enjoying the feel of his chest against her back and his strong arm around her.

She was dead, she knew that. They both were dead in a tragic accident.

And now they were ghosts for some reason.

Still, sitting here naked together in the back of this patrol car just felt right.

And she had no idea why.

Eight

TOMMY WAS ENJOYING sitting naked with Jewel in the back seat of the sheriff's car more than he wanted to admit. How they were sitting, he could see everything about her body, from her small, firm breasts with tight brown nipples to her flat stomach and brown pubic hair.

Somehow, he managed to keep his arm on her arm, but a number of times he wondered if she wanted him to just ease his arm over and touch her breast.

Damn, he felt like he was back in high school again. How was that possible? He had just died.

"Shouldn't we be upset that we were killed?" he asked her.

"I would think so," she said. "But I don't feel that way for some reason. In fact, I feel like I'm still very much alive, which is more than likely why being dead hasn't sunk in yet."

She was right. He was feeling alive as well. Very much so, and very much attracted to the woman in his arms.

"Me too," he said. "Maybe more alive than I was before the wreck."

She turned her head and looked at his penis, which was not in full erection, but very much alive as well.

"Yup, I can see that," she said, laughing softly.

"Trust me," he said, "if your fantastic body didn't do that to that part of my body, I really would be dead."

She reached across and squeezed his arm that was holding her. "Thank you."

"My pleasure," he said.

She laughed. "Are you going to have to clean up the sheriff's car before we leave?"

"Not without some pretty significant help from you," he said.

At that moment, the sheriff and Ben got back into the car.

Both Tommy and Jewel sat up quickly, but neither of them had a chance to move their clothing.

The two live men didn't seem to notice them at all, or the fact that two naked ghosts were sitting in the back seat.

"You going to be okay?" the sheriff asked poor Ben.

Tommy really felt sorry for the kid. No one should be forced to look at what that kid saw in that car.

The first time Tommy had seen something like that was after a firefight in Afghanistan. Three Taliban had tried to make an escape in a small car and when Tommy's unit was finished, the small car looked more like sponge.

That had been in Tommy's first month of deployment. No young person should ever be forced to look inside a car like that, or inside the patrol car that Ben had looked into tonight.

Ben nodded in response to the sheriff's question. Then asked, "So what happens next?"

"Help arrives from Bonnie County in the next twenty minutes," the sheriff said. "We're going to need to set up flares to warn traffic."

Tommy knew that, but that wouldn't be needed until more people started to arrive.

The sheriff went on "Two tow trucks from the forest service are headed here now and it'll take both of them working together to pull the car up. Then the medical examiner from down in Bonnie will take the bodies once we get them out."

"We're not going to get them out down there?" Ben asked. Tommy had wanted to ask the same question, but didn't because neither of the men would hear him.

"They're more than dead," the sheriff said. "No point in risking injury and lives of men to go down there and pry them out when they could do it right here on the road. Won't make a damn bit of difference."

Ben nodded.

"But," the sheriff said, "I'm going to need you to go back down there, Ben, and take pictures of everything, including

the best you can of Tommy and the Doc. Think you can do that?"

"I can," he said, swallowing and then nodding. "I'll do it with both the crime scene camera and my phone to make sure we got it all."

"Good," the sheriff said, nodding. "Let's get that going before company starts arriving."

With that both men climbed out of the car and closed the doors, again leaving the car running and the heater going. Tommy knew that was standard on cold nights to leave the car running and the heater going for a place to warm up.

Tommy glanced over at Jewel who sat back, an arm across her chest, her other hand covering her crotch area.

"A bashful ghost?" he asked, smiling at her.

She shook her head, clearly realizing how she was sitting. Then leaned forward and got her pants and again wrung them out where Ben had gotten them wet again with the water off his slicker.

Tommy did the same for his shirt and his pants, wringing both out again. But this time they were feeling dryer.

"I feel bad for Ben," she said.

"So do I," Tommy said. "The kid is young and this will bother him the rest of his life. But the sheriff has no choice. Ben has to do it because the sheriff knows that climbing down that hill might kill him."

"That hill killed us," Jewel said, putting her feet back up and leaning back into him again.

"That it did," Tommy said, enjoying the view once again of her wonderful body stretched out in the back of the patrol car. "But I sure don't feel dead."

"Neither do I," she said. "And that's bothering me a lot. I'm not angry, not sad, not feeling like all my education was a waste. Nothing. I feel like I'm just moving on to the next part of my life and all that training is going to come in handy somehow."

"I feel exactly the same way," he said.

"So what do we do next?"

"We sit here warm until our car is up and on the road and our bodies are taken."

"You think we might end up being pulled with our bodies?"

"I hope not," Tommy said, suddenly very worried about that. "And I hope like hell we're not stuck out here haunting this corner for all eternity."

"Oh, no," she said, sitting up and turning to face him directly. "You don't think that might happen?"

"Never been a ghost before," Tommy said, shrugging. "No clue. We're just going to have to wait and see if we can catch a ride with the sheriff back into town."

She sat there, a horrified look on her face. "That would be hell."

"I honestly don't think that's going to happen," Tommy said. "I feel we're to do something more. Don't you?"

She nodded slowly. "That's what it feel like to me as well."

"Then we relax and wait," he said. "Unless you want to get dressed and head out walking back toward town. It's about nine dark and wet miles. We could make it in a couple of hours."

She turned around and stretched out again, putting her beautiful legs up so her feet would get warm from the heater.

"Let's wait."

"Good," he said. "Because I'm still enjoying this."

"Really?" she asked, glancing at his penis again and then nodding. "Guess so."

"This is heaven," he said.

"So just staring is heaven to you?" she asked.

"A first level of heaven," he said, laughing.

Some Classic Dean Wesley Smith Stories
Available at your favorite booksellers.

Nine

TOMMY MANAGED TO not make a pass at her and she managed to not make a pass at him over the next few hours, although a couple of times she had been tempted. She just didn't feel it was right so soon after being killed.

Something seemed wrong about that. She wasn't sure just what.

They just sat naked, talking about their lives, their years in college, their old boyfriends and girlfriends. The more she heard about Deputy Tommy Ralston, the man, the ghost, the more she liked.

And she really liked his sense of humor and his ability to stay calm in this situation. She tried to get him to talk a little about his three years in the Marines, but he had simply said, "We can talk about that later. Just say it taught me a lot about life and paid for my education so far."

Just as being an intern in a major Seattle hospital had taught her more than she ever wanted to know about life and death.

"So why come to Buffalo Jump?" he asked.

"Pay off debts and get away from the insanity of big city hospitals," she said.

He had nodded and let it go at that. She didn't add in that she had been engaged a year before she left and didn't really want to be married to another doctor. She had broke it off and part of the reason going so far away was to not have to be around him any more either.

She wondered if he had something similar. People moving into the middle of nowhere often did.

After three hours, their clothes were dry enough that she suggested that they get dressed. The clothes were still damp and cold, but would warm quick enough.

She was kind of disappointed he wasn't going to be naked. She had enjoyed him looking at her body and she sure liked looking at his.

Outside, on the highway, it now looked pretty crazy. Two tow trucks with large winches were backed up to the edge of the road and blocked into place so there was no chance they would go over.

The medical coroner's van from Walsa had arrived. It was the only small hospital that had staff and an emergency room between Buffalo Jump and Missoula. And it had the only working coroner in five counties. That van got a lot of mileage she had heard.

After they were dressed, she and Tommy both just sat side-by-side, hips touching, and watched through the rain-covered front window as the two trucks pulled the smashed patrol car with their bodies up the slope and onto the road.

Two of the men who first looked in, turned and lost their lunches onto the side of the road.

"We are not a pretty sight," Tommy said.

"Extreme death never is," she said.

It took the sheriff and three others about an hour to get their bodies out of the car.

Jewel thought it weird to watch her body being laid out on a stretcher on the road and covered.

"I'm still wearing the white blouse and jeans there," she said, pointing to her body. "So what are these?" She pulled on the slightly damp fabric of her white blouse.

Tommy glanced at her and just shook his head. "There's a whole mess of things about this I'm not understanding."

"Me too," she said. And she hated that feeling. She had a hunch Tommy did as well. He seemed like the same kind of person she was, a person who needed answers and reasons why things worked.

The clock on the dashboard said it was a little after two a.m. when the coroner's van pulled away with their bodies in it.

They stayed seated in the warm back seat of the sheriff's car.

She was relieved. And didn't feel a thing as the van disappeared around a corner.

"Looks like we don't have a connection to those hunks of flesh anymore," Tommy said, clearly sounding relieved.

"Yeah, thankfully," she said. "I didn't feel a thing as they were twisting my body to get it out of there."

"I didn't either," Tommy said. "So that answers that question."

They sat in silence as the smashed patrol car was loaded onto one of the two tow trucks and it headed off down the road, followed by the other one.

"Where are they taking it?" she asked.

"A state police impound yard about two hours away toward Missoula."

Sheriff and Ben talked with a few others for a few minutes, then the sheriff nodded and he and Ben came back toward the car.

"Here we go," Tommy said, sitting back.

She pushed closer to Tommy and reached out and held his hand. He squeezed her hand gently, and didn't let go.

The sheriff and Ben got in at the same time. Ben took his hat off and tossed it onto the floor in the back seat. Some water splashed on her, but it didn't matter.

Ben didn't see them.

The sheriff just left his hat on.

The sheriff did a quick U-turn and headed back for Buffalo Jump.

After about a half mile, she let out a breath and squeezed Tommy's hand. "Looks like we're not stuck back there at least."

Tommy let out a huge breath as well and nodded. "That would have not been fun."

In the front seat, neither man said a word to each other. Clearly they were in shock and tired.

Finally, as they got close to Buffalo Jump, Ben turned to the sheriff. "Anything I can do to help?"

The sheriff just shook his head. "Just try to get some sleep and get those pictures into the office when you can."

"I will," Ben said.

"And kid, thanks for the good work tonight. I know it wasn't easy."

Ben only nodded and said nothing.

Suddenly, she had a thought that made her jump. "Sheriff, remember I was going on a medical emergency?"

The sheriff didn't seem to hear her.

She reached forward and tried to touch his shoulder, but her hand went through. She could feel the sadness and extreme exhaustion he was feeling. And the anger at the entire situation.

She pulled back and looked at her hand.

"Weird, huh?" Tommy asked.

"Very," she said. She leaned forward again, tried to just lightly touch his shoulder and then said loudly, "Original medical emergency."

Then she sat back, frustrated.

A moment later, the sheriff turned to Ben as they pulled up in front of Ben's small trailer. "There is one thing you can do for me."

"Anything, sheriff," the young kid said.

"Call down to the state police and have them send a doctor on the original medical call Tommy and the Doc were headed on. I forgot all about that until just now."

"Will do, sheriff," Ben said.

Tommy looked at her, surprise on his face. "That worked. Wow!"

"As you said," Jewel said, smiling, "a bunch of stuff we don't know about this new ghost status just yet."

Ben reached back and grabbed his hat from the floor, his hand brushing Jewel's leg.

And as it did, she got a clear image of the young college girl from Missoula tied up in the shed behind his trailer.

And she knew exactly what he planned to do to her tonight, and it wasn't pretty.

Jewel jerked back and damn near climbed on Tommy's lap.

"What?" Tommy asked.

She stared at Ben, then turned to Tommy. "We got to get out here. Now! I'll explain," she said. "Hurry."

As Ben climbed out one side, Tommy pretended to open the door and just climb out the other.

She scooted over and did the same, finding herself standing on the road beside the car next to Tommy.

The cold was biting and harsh, but at least the rain had stopped. The gravel under her feet felt frozen solid.

Tommy stood to one side of the street, watching as the sheriff pulled away. Then he turned to go into his blue singlewide trailer. There was no doubt, from the rust and the old wooden steps, and broken screens, that this old trailer had seen much, much better days.

She turned to explain to Tommy what she had felt and seen when Ben brushed her leg. It disgusted her to have to even say it.

All Tommy had to say was "Damn it."

And the way he said it was real cold and low and mean.

Ten

TOMMY HAD BEEN shocked when Jewel had wanted to get out at Ben's place. And had so recoiled from Ben's touch.

But then when she explained what she had sensed, he understood completely. He didn't want to tell her but over the last year three college girls had gone missing from Missoula. They had gotten the notices on all three.

One just two days before.

So even though he didn't want to believe that Ben could be the one, he had to believe Jewel at this point.

He took Jewel's hand and they worked their way around behind Ben's old trailer. Ben had always lived in the trailer with his mother and she had left about three years ago, leaving Ben everything.

If Ben was really doing what Jewel sensed, it made sense that Ben had also killed his mother.

Behind the trailer was a big old shed made of large unpainted wooden planks. It had a big lock on the door.

Tommy could see a power cord running to the top of the big shed from the trailer, so at least there were lights and maybe heat in there.

"What are we going to do?" Jewel asked as they got close.

Tommy had no idea what they were going to do, but first off, they needed to see the situation.

He went to the locked door of the shed and tried to grab the lock. His hand went right through it.

So without stopping to think, he let go of Jewel's hand, closed his eyes and stepped toward the door.

And through the door.

He felt nothing at all.

Jewel, with her eyes closed, stepped through behind him and bumped right into him. For each other, they were solid. But doors were not.

Inside the shed the smell hit Tommy first. Things had died in here, of that there was no doubt. Most of the shed held old rusted tools and moving equipment. None of it usable at all.

An electric heater kept some of the chill off, but not much.

The floor was dirt and wet, which accounted for some of the mold smell, but not the death smell.

In the back of the shed, to one side, was a ratty, stained mattress on wood planks and sprawled on it was a young woman, tied up and partially covered by a light blanket.

Jewel got to her before he did and tried to pull the blanket back, but failed.

She gently touched the girls shoulder and then recoiled.

She looked at Tommy with her eyes huge and wide. "She's freezing, but other than Ben looking at her breasts, she hasn't been touched or harmed yet. But she's terrified."

"She should be," Tommy said. "Ben's clearly a monster."

"What are we going to do?" she asked.

"I honestly don't know," he said. "Touch her, try to get her calmed down and ready to run if we figure something out. Just repeat that over and over to her."

Jewel nodded and touched the girl's shoulder.

Tommy tried touching anything in the shed, trying somehow to find a weapon.

His hand went through everything.

Everything.

He was dead.

He had to stop thinking like a live person and looking for weapons a live person would use.

He had to learn how to think like a dead person.

There had to be something he and Jewel could do. They couldn't just stand by and watch Ben rape and kill this poor girl. He couldn't allow that to happen.

But he was dead.

What could he do?

Then he remembered how Jewel had touched the sheriff and got him to remember why she and Tommy had been on the road.

And when he had the sheriff step through him, he knew what the sheriff was thinking, even though the contact had only been for a moment.

So maybe, just maybe, he could control Ben.

"She's calming down," Jewel said. "She's going to look for any chance to run."

"Good," Tommy said, nodding to Jewel. "I'm going to try to take over Ben's body and get him to turn himself in."

"You're going to what?"

"Only thing I can think of," Tommy said. "I hate the idea, but no regular weapon works."

Jewel looked very worried, but then nodded.

"Stay close to me," he said. "I may need your strength. We're still new at this ghost stuff."

"With you all the way," she said, standing and stepping toward him and taking his hand.

He felt her strength and resolve pour into him and he felt so much better.

"Let's go get the little bastard," Tommy said.

With that, the two of them went through the locked shed door and into the cold. Thirty steps later, they were through the back door and into Tommy's trailer.

He was just finishing with a call to the State Police and was hanging up the phone.

"I'm going to get him to call the sheriff and confess," Tommy said.

Jewel nodded and squeezed his hand, then let go.

Tommy forced himself to take a deep breath. This was just like any combat mission.

He could do it.

He was stronger than anyone.

He stepped forward and right through the back of Ben, making sure he stayed covering Ben as much as possible.

The kid was sick.

Really, really twisted sick.

And he had long ago lost the ability to tell right from wrong.

Tommy felt dirty just seeing Ben's thoughts and his life. But this was a mission to save a life.

First, Tommy forced Ben's feet to not move.

He needed Ben to stay still so that he could maintain his connection to him completely.

His entire will just forced its way into Ben, freezing his feet to the floor next to the phone.

Then Tommy had an idea on how to get Ben to confess.

Tommy remembered back to that first mission in Afghanistan and the huge amount of guilt he had felt for killing those men in that car.

Ben had no guilt, so Tommy started to give him some.

And then he flooded it at the sick kid, making him feel the pain, the loss, everything.

Ben bent over and supported himself on the table, scared for the first time, and wondering what was happening.

Tommy kept inside him completely, even bent over.

Tommy kept repeating over and over, "I saw too much death tonight."

Finally Ben said that. "I saw too much death tonight."

"Tell the sheriff what I have done."

Tommy started repeating again and again, pounding at Ben, never letting up on his guilt feelings from those missions.

Finally, Tommy willed Ben to pick up the phone and dial the sheriff's number.

Tommy heard through Ben the sheriff come on the phone with a gruff "Yeah."

"Girl in my shed." Tommy willed Ben to say. Tommy poured on even more guilt. And kept repeating "I've seen enough death. Girl in my shed. I don't want to kill her. Stop me."

Finally Ben said those exact words to the sheriff.

"What?" the sheriff said.

Tommy really, really pushed, hard, pouring on every bit of guilt he had, forcing Ben to say those words again.

"Girl in my shed," Ben said. "I don't want to kill her. Please stop me. Too much death."

On the other end of the line the sheriff laid down the phone softly.

Tommy really understood now how smart the sheriff was.

Tommy wanted to get out of this sick kid's mind and body, but he didn't. He kept Ben's feet pinned to the floor and repeating over and over what he had said into the phone.

Two of the longest minutes Tommy had ever spent, he heard Jewel say softly, "Sheriff's here."

Thirty seconds later she said, "Looks like Carl from the gas station is also here. He's armed with a rifle as well."

Tommy kept focused on Ben, keeping his feet firmly planted to the floor, keeping him repeating over and over into the phone his confession.

"Sheriff just looked in the window," Jewel said. "They are coming in, guns drawn."

Tommy heard a smash as Carl kicked in the door, but didn't let Ben react. Tommy just kept Ben repeating over and over that there was a girl in his shed and he didn't want to kill her.

"Ben!" the sheriff said, pointing his gun at the young kid.

Tommy decided it was best to get it all out now, everything he knew about this sick kid.

"I killed my mother," Tommy had Ben say. "I killed the other two. They are buried in the back woods behind the shed. I've seen too much death tonight. I don't want to kill the girl in the shed."

Tommy could feel the sheriff come around behind Ben, take the phone out of his hand, and quickly slip handcuffs on him.

So Tommy stepped away and back into only his own thoughts, out of the sick perversions of a very evil person.

To Tommy, it felt like he had just climbed out of a dark cesspool and into sunlight and fresh air.

Tommy could feel that most of his energy was gone. He staggered and Jewel caught him.

"You did it," she said, hugging him, beaming. "You did it. Are you all right?"

Tommy nodded, feeling the energy from Jewel flowing into him. "I will be."

She hugged him again.

Tommy looked over at Carl, a tall man with a good heart, who fixed cars for a living. He was about Tommy's height and had gained a beer gut. He was clutching his 30-30 deer rifle in his hands and looked like he might be sick. He had tossed on his overalls and boots, but didn't have a shirt under the overalls.

"Sheriff?" Ben said, suddenly coming back to his senses. "What are you doing here? Carl? What did you do to my front door?"

Tommy glanced over at the door that was now smashed and hanging barely by one hinge.

Ben looked at the phone on the table, then felt the handcuffs. "What's happening?"

"We're going to go have a look at that shed of yours," the sheriff said, yanking Ben by the arm and out the back door of the trailer.

Jewel looked at him. "Seems anything we have someone do or say, they can't remember," she said. "Learning a lot this first night of death."

"Too much," Tommy said.

He kept leaning on Jewel and enjoying the feel of her beside him. His strength was coming back and at the same time he was pushing the thoughts of being inside Ben's head away.

He felt a little like he was just scrubbing out his mind.

"Do you have a warrant, sheriff?" Ben asked as they started across the backyard.

The sheriff damn near knocked Ben to the ground with that statement. Tommy wished he had.

"You told me, flat out to my face, there's a woman in there and you don't want to kill her," the sheriff said, his voice so angry he could hardly contain himself. "Like you did your mom and two others. I think that's enough reason to go in there, don't you?"

Ben went silent.

Big Carl took an old rusted ax from beside the shed and knocked open the lock.

A few minutes later, Ben was sitting handcuffed hands and feet in the back of the sheriff's car where an hour before he and Jewel had sat naked.

Jewel had gone to the girl again and worked to keep her calm, telling her that Carl and the sheriff, even though scary-looking, were her friends.

Tommy watched her, nodding. They really had saved that girl's life and they were dead.

He had no idea how that worked. But he wanted to find out. Being dead was one thing.

Being dead and still useful was another.

Eleven

BY THE TIME they had walked the mile, hand-in-hand, down to Tommy's home on the lake, Jewel was again frozen and her teeth were chattering. The sun was starting to paint the tops of the mountains with a slight orange color.

It was really, really beautiful but she couldn't enjoy it because her clothes were again wet.

But even shivering and knowing she was dead, she somehow felt great. They had managed to save that poor girl. The images of the girl's terror were slowly fading from Jewel's mind as she shoved them back.

Tommy had said that it felt like his brain was scrubbing out Ben's thoughts. That was exactly the way it felt with the poor girl's thoughts. Jewel didn't want to remember them and they were fading quickly.

Tommy's home turned out to be a beautiful lakefront house with a dock and everything. The lake was a black, flat surface and the mountains were white and showing orange from the sunrise.

And as they walked through the closed front door, the heat hit her.

"Thankfully, I left so fast, I didn't turn down the heat," Tommy said.

"Tough to turn up a thermostat when your hand goes through it," Jewel said.

She had no doubt that if it was possible for ghosts to touch something, they were going to need to learn how to do that.

"This way," he said as she marveled at his fantastic kitchen and the view out the back.

He led her into what was clearly his bedroom. The room was comfortable and lived in. The quilts on the bed had been pushed up, but the bed wasn't made. The furniture was a solid-looking wooden chair sitting beside a wooden chest of drawers. A couple of pairs of boots and a pair of tennis shoes sat beside the chair.

One side of his wall closet was open and she watched as almost without thinking or remembering he was a ghost, he reached up and grabbed a flannel shirt from a hanger.

The shirt stayed on the hanger, but a ghost shirt came off in his hands.

He stood there staring at the shirt on the hanger and then at the one in his hands.

She moved over and touched the ghost shirt. It felt as real as anything.

"Who knew clothes had ghost shadows," she said, laughing.

"You know," he said, "I always thought death was just going to be blackness and nothingness. I never expected to have to learn a brand new world."

She had thought a lot about death when in Seattle. She had seen so much of it, she honestly never came to any conclusions about what death would be. But if she had, it wouldn't be the death state she found herself in now.

"Get out of those wet clothes and put that on," he said, handing her the soft flannel shirt.

Then he grabbed another one for himself, again looking at the shirt still on the hanger and the one in his hands.

"I wonder if this is just because it's your clothes," she said.

She reached up and pulled down another shirt. It was soft in her hand, but the original stayed in place.

"That's just too weird," she said.

Then she started to undress again, for the second time, in front of a hot man she had only known for about fourteen hours.

She hoped he was watching her.

Twelve

TOMMY FLAT ENJOYED watching Jewel once again strip out of her wet clothes and then put on his soft, flannel shirt. She buttoned up the shirt, pulled her wet hair back and then stood there, smiling at him.

"You look stunning," he said. "But wish that shirt wasn't so long."

She laughed. "Got some running shorts around here somewhere?"

"In the third drawer," he said, pointing to his wooden chest of drawers in his bedroom.

He watched as she went over and tried to pull it open and failed. Then she just stuck her hand through the wood and pulled out a fistful of his shorts. She tossed them on the bed, took one pair, and slipped it on much to his disappointment.

"Slippers?"

He pointed to the bottom of the closed part of the closet.

Seeming like she had been doing it forever, she stuck her head and shoulders through the wooden closet sliding door, letting her butt stick out, sadly covered by his running shorts.

After a moment she pulled out two pair of his slippers.

"I'll wear the dark brown ones," Tommy said, also pulling on a pair of running shorts. "The lighter ones are too small for me."

"Perfect," she said, slipping her feet into them.

Her feet looked like a child's feet in his big slippers, but she nodded.

"I won't be running in these," she said, "but they feel warm and soft."

They hung their clothes around in the bathroom to dry, then headed back to the kitchen.

"Now what do we do?" she asked, sitting down on a stool pulled up to the island area in the big kitchen.

Tommy looked around a little. The entire kitchen was all wood cabinets with state-of-the art appliances his dad had put in last year. Then he heard what he had thought.

"Dad."

"Oh, shit," she said, her eyes wide, understanding exactly what he meant. "Family and friends."

He nodded, trying to push away what his death was going to do to his father. "I feel so much alive, I forgot we were really dead."

"Me to," she said, clearly lost in her own thoughts.

They remained in silence for a minute. He couldn't imagine how his dad would feel. He had two sisters, but he wasn't that close to them. But his father was, and his father would need them now.

He knew his father had come to terms with the chance that Tommy might be killed in Afghanistan, but this sudden accidental death would knock him down. Mother had died slowly, from cancer, and that damn near killed his father. This would be as bad, if not worse.

"Are your parents still alive?" she asked.

"Father," he said. "He and I were pretty close. This is his house, actually. Two sisters, some buddies from the Marines. How about you?"

"Both parents died in a boating accident when I was a senior in high school," she said. "No brothers or sisters. Just friends from college and med school and my residency."

Again they dropped into silence before Tommy looked out at the sun coming up over the lake. "Dad is in Spokane, along with one of my sisters. They will be up here later today. So we need to get out of here."

"Don't want to be here when they arrive?" she asked.

"No," he said, shaking his head. "That's the last thing I want to do."

He wasn't sure if he could handle seeing how much he had hurt his father by

dying. He needed to leave them to grieve on their own.

"Let's go to my place," she said. "Since the city is leasing it to me, no one will bother with it or my stuff for a few days I bet. We can decide what we are doing next there."

He nodded. "We have a few hours here to let things dry out again first."

She nodded. "And if you can find a ghost pack, you can take some clothes as well."

He had to switch the topic from thinking about his father and family. "Are you hungry?"

She looked puzzled. "I just might be."

Then, as she said that, she said, "Damn it, now I have to pee as well."

He laughed. "Now I do as well."

"Guess things turn on slowly in this ghost world," she said as she started down the hall.

"Second door on the left," he said. "Closed one. Hope I left the lid up."

"I can go in the sink just fine if I have to," she said, smiling at him as she headed down the hall.

He headed for the bathroom off his bedroom. He knew for certain he had left the lid up there.

Strange things ghosts had to worry about. He could go through doors, get people to confess to crimes, but couldn't lift a toilet seat lid.

This ghost world was going to be interesting, he had no doubt.

Thirteen

HE HAD HIS head in the fridge, through the fridge door, actually, when she came back to the kitchen. He couldn't see a thing because the light was off in there, but it frosted his face quickly.

"That looks really strange," she said.

He managed in the dark, from memory, to grab a couple of apples and pull them out. At least ghost apples. He was fairly certain their original real-world partners were still in the fridge.

He held one up for her and she nodded and took it. She bit into hers first, then smiled. "Wow, that's good."

"How is this possible?" he asked, staring at the apple and then biting into it as well, getting juice on his chin. Jewel was right, it tasted wonderful. Better than any apple he had remembered.

"Seems that most everything has a ghost component," she said.

"Including us, it seems," he said.

"Yeah, does seem that way."

"Bottle of water?" he asked as she took another bite of the apple.

She nodded, so he stuck his arm back through the fridge door and grabbed a couple of bottles of water. Ghost water again. He handed one to her, then opened and drank out of the other.

Tasted just like water.

She looked at him and frowned. "How long do you want to stay here?"

The image of his father flashed into his mind. Knowing his father, he would have gotten the news in the middle of the night. He would have called Carol, Tommy's youngest sister, and the two of them would have headed this way within an hour.

More than likely they got the call last night while Tommy and Jewel were still on the mountain road. Tommy knew well that the drive from his father's place to here was five hours, so they might be getting here in a couple of hours.

"We need to be getting out of here," he said.

Jewel nodded and took one more bite from her apple.

He set his bottle of water and half-eaten apple down on the counter.

"Let's get dressed, see if we can find you a coat and hat and gloves for the walk to your place."

"Mind if I just keep this shirt on?" she asked, smiling at him. "It's toasty."

"I'm disappointed I won't get to see you nude again," he said, "but sure."

She laughed. "I'll flash you for good measure."

"Promises, promises.

As they packed clothes for him, and found her a coat, she did as promised, which made him smile.

Twenty minutes, with a very light bag of ghost clothes over his shoulder, they headed out.

Jewel had put on her still-damp pants and shoes, borrowing dry socks from him as well. She had on his blue ski parka that draped on her, a matching ski hat, and gloves that made her hands look huge. But at least she would be warmer in the two-mile walk they had to do right through town.

He had on dry jeans, with two more pair packed in the bag. And a bunch of socks and underwear and shirts, plus an extra pair of shoes. He had no idea where they were headed, but better to take what he needed at the moment.

The rain had stopped and the clouds were now high, with occasional sun breaks. It was still cold, but it looked like the day might turn out decent weather.

On the way into town, as they walked along the road, not really talking, he looked up and saw his father's white Jeep headed toward them. His father loved that older Jeep Cherokee and drove it more than he drove his Lexus.

Tommy could feel his stomach twist up into a knot.

He took a deep breath of the fresh morning air and that calmed him a little.

"My father and sister," he said to Jewel.

They both stood to one side of the gravel road as the Jeep drove past.

Tommy saw that his father had the look of grim determination, as was normal for his father in tough situations. His sister looked like she had been crying.

As the Jeep passed them and went on toward the lake home, Tommy said out loud, "Good-bye Dad. Sis."

Jewel reached over and took his hand and squeezed it gently.

They stared at the departing Jeep until it vanished around a corner on the gravel road.

Together, they then turned and kept walking.

He had no idea where they were ultimately going, but he knew now that part of his life that was his family and friends and job was done.

They walked on, not talking, their footsteps silent on the gravel.

Fourteen

JEWEL DIDN'T KNOW what to say to Tommy after they passed his father. So she just walked with him, hand-in-hand toward town, letting him stay in his own thoughts.

He needed to know she was there if he wanted to talk, even though they really didn't know each other very well. She did understand family. And right now, even though he was the one that was dead, it felt like he was losing them instead.

This all was flipping strange, of that there was no doubt.

She knew one thing for sure. She loved being with him and was growing to care for him more and more with every second.

When they finally reached the big church on the edge of the small town, she looked at it and felt nothing.

"You'd think we'd want to go in there," she said, breaking their silence and indicating the church.

"Not much of a believer," he said, shrugging.

"Yeah, me either," she said. "And all this that is happening to us is making me wonder even more."

"Yeah, this kind of stuff would do that to anyone," he said, shaking his head.

They walked up past the now closed bars and toward her office, their steps almost matching, which was unusual for her. Her longer legs and height usually meant she walked faster than anyone around her.

She liked that he matched her step-for-step and it felt comfortable.

Nothing seemed out of place or different in the small town, which sort of surprised her, for some reason. There were a few people out and about, but not many, even though it was after ten in the morning now.

Shouldn't they all be in the streets upset at her and Tommy's death?

She knew that was silly, but dying seemed important to her.

"Going to miss that little place?" he asked, indicating her office ahead.

"Wasn't here long enough to grow fond of it," she said. She honestly didn't feel even the slightest need to go inside. There was nothing in there for her or that she needed.

Ahead of them, a man sat against the wall of Bernie's General Store on a part of the pavement that had stayed dry in the night's rain. The guy had put a newspaper under him.

Jewel didn't recognize him, but that didn't surprise her from her little time in town. The guy had on a dark suit and light shirt, with a fashionable tie of some sort. He had matching patent leather shoes. She hadn't seen shoes like that since she watched part of an old golf tournament from 1970.

The guy sitting on the sidewalk was way, way underdressed for being in Buffalo Jump, Montana, in this cold.

He was looking down at the sidewalk, his blonde hair perfectly styled and in place. Jewel had no idea what he was doing sitting out here. The day would warm up to maybe fifty eventually, but it was far from that at the moment.

As they approached, staying to the outside of the sidewalk to go around him, he glanced up and then smiled, clearly happy to see them.

"Hey, Doc, Deputy. I was hoping you two would be show up before I froze my tush off."

The guy pushed himself to his feet, smiling as Jewel and Tommy just stopped in their tracks, stunned. She couldn't believe he had talked to them.

The guy brushed off his suit, making sure it was in perfect condition. Who wore dark suits and patent leather shoes in Montana?

"You can see us?" Tommy asked a half second before Jewel could get the same words out of her mouth.

The guy laughed. "Of course I can. I'm a ghost like you two. He extended his hand. "I'm K. J. Moore, originally of Los Angeles, now of San Francisco."

Tommy shook his hand, looking stunned and Jewel did next, noting the guy had a weak, but firm grip, as if she was shaking another woman's hand.

K.J. looked to be about their age, not more than thirty, that was for sure, and was fairly short, maybe five-three, if that. His eyes were dark brown and his smile seemed genuine.

"So are you from here?" she asked as she let go of his hand. "You die around here?"

He glanced at the small town of Buffalo Jump and then shook his head. "Not a chance," he said. "This is really the back-end of nowhere here. I died in Los Angeles in 1951. Too ugly to talk about, but since you asked, I was caught by the wrong people kissing another man." He waved away the idea and said, "Ancient history."

She opened her mouth, then shut it because she honestly had nothing to say. This ghost had said he died sixty-five years before.

"Tell me," K.J. said, looking around, "where do the buffalo jump around here? Never seen anything like that."

"That's just a name from history," Jewel said. "At least I think it is?" She turned to Tommy. "Do buffalo jump around here."

Tommy just shook his head and focused on K.J. "So what are you doing here?"

"Looking for you two, of course," K.J. said, again smiling as he pulled back on his glove. "My job to brief you and get you started."

"Brief us on what?" Tommy asked.

"Oh, why you are ghosts and not headed on to the next world," he said. "But can we go someplace warmer? I'm not used to this kind of cold. Not like this in San Francisco, let me tell you. This is just brutal."

"We're headed to my rental place," she said, pointing ahead down the highway past the mini-mart. "That's about a half mile walk."

K.J. frowned. "Too far for me in this cold and that gravel road might just ruin my ankles. How about your office, Doc? It's warm? Right?"

"It should be," she said, nodding, feeling stunned that she was talking with this man. She wasn't sure why she was stunned, but she felt stunned.

She glanced at Tommy and he was looking just puzzled and a little amused.

"Great," K.J. said, turning and heading toward her office. He walked through the closed front door without seeming to give it a second thought.

Jewel looked at Tommy and laughed.

"Maybe we can get some answers, now," he said, shaking his head.

"Wouldn't that be nice," she said, still laughing.

With that, she moved toward her office door, closed her eyes, and went through the door.

Tommy was right behind her.

Fifteen

K.J. WAS STANDING inside and as they came through the door he smiled at them. "Going to need to learn how to walk through doors with your eyes open. Never really know what's on the other side."

"We will," Tommy said, looking around at Jewel's small office. "We haven't been dead that long, remember?"

"Ah, that's true," K.J. said.

They were in a waiting room with five wooden chairs, a coat tree, and some old magazines on scarred wooden end tables. Tommy was surprised that the room was smaller than a normal bedroom, smaller than he remembered, but at least it was warm.

He had been in here only once before to bring a sick woman, but that was a year before Jewel had arrived and two doctors before her. The place didn't look any different from the previous doctors, so clearly Jewel hadn't settled in enough to put her touches on the office.

"My office is bigger and likely warmer," Jewel said, leading the way through an open side door and into a larger room with a large wooden desk dominating one side. There was an old metal gooseneck lamp on the desk, a clipboard, and a penholder. Nothing else but a calendar blotter on the big desktop.

"You really hadn't moved in, had you?" Tommy asked.

"Didn't seem much point in changing anything during the winter," Jewel said, shrugging off her coat and hanging it on a coat tree, even though it was a ghost coat.

Three chairs faced the desk, so she went around and sat behind her desk, rolling up the sleeves of the big red and brown flannel shirt of Tommy's that she was wearing. She looked great in that shirt as far as he was concerned. She looked better without any clothes, but he hoped that would come later.

Tommy sat in one chair facing her.

K.J. sat in the other chair, looking very official in his business suit.

"How long had you been out there waiting for us?" Jewel asked before Tommy could think of a first question out of the hundreds he had.

"An hour, but a long cold hour," K.J. said. "Not sure I could get used to this kind of cold ever."

"It gets worse," Tommy said. "This is spring."

K.J. just shook his head and made a production out of shivering.

"So start from the beginning and tell us what all this is about," Tommy said, turning slightly in the chair so he could see K.J.'s face better.

The guy clearly was from a different climate and world. His skin was smooth and his nails polished red, which Tommy hadn't seen on a man in this part of the world. He was short and frail and sat in the wooden chair across from Jewel like a kid in a principal's office, his posture perfect, his smile bright.

"You died in that horrid wreck," K.J. said.

"We know that," Jewel said.

"Did you cause the wreck?" Tommy asked and saw Jewel sort of jerk back at the idea.

K.J. just shook his head and covered his mouth in fake horror as if appalled at the idea. "Oh, my, no. Everyone has a time and you both had run smack into your time, no big tree pun intended."

Jewel didn't smile at the bad attempt at humor. Tommy nodded that K.J. should just continue.

"But since your time had come, and you were together, my bosses decided you both, as a team, would be good candidates to join our ranks."

Tommy felt stunned.

"What ranks? What team? What bosses?" Jewel asked.

K.J. held up his hand, smiling. "You wanted me to start from the beginning, so let me start."

She nodded, and Tommy made himself take a deep breath.

"For longer than any of us can imagine," K.J. said, "there has been an organization called A Ghost of a Chance. Ghost for short."

Jewel started to say something, but K.J. held up his hand for her to stop and she did.

"Ghost is an offshoot of a much larger universe you will come to understand in

Former PGA Golf Professional and USA Today *bestselling writer Dean Wesley Smith walks you step-by-step, club-by-club from your car to the first tee and beyond in a laugh-out-loud style that not only teaches, but entertains.*

Now Available
from all your favorite booksellers in trade paper and electronic editions.

time," K.J. said. "But our official mandate is to help set things right that are going to go wrong. We fight for a future that is peaceful. I understand that before I got here this morning, you already stopped a serial killer from killing again."

"We did," Tommy said, stunned that he knew.

"That's the kind of thing we do, and much more."

Tommy liked the sound of that, but asked his first question instead of making a comment. "So does everyone that dies become part of your organization?"

K.J. laughed really hard at that and his laugh sounded more like a young girl's laugh than a man's laugh. Tommy and Jewel watched him laugh for a moment until he finally gathered himself enough to answer.

"Oh, my, no," he said, trying to catch his breath because to him something seemed very funny. "My bosses only recruit who they think are the best candidates. The rest catch the white tunnel express and move on, thankfully. We wouldn't want them all hanging around, now would we?"

"You know what's on the other side of that white tunnel?" Jewel asked.

Tommy was about to ask that same question exactly.

K.J. shook his head. "Not a clue. It's a pretty closely guarded secret by everyone who does know. The standard answer everyone gets when they ask is that you'll know when you take the white tunnel yourself."

"So how long are we going to be in this ghost state?" Tommy asked.

"As long as you want to keep working for Ghost," he said. "There are agents I know who have been here since the time of Atlantis and before. It's a pretty

darned good job, to be honest. Rewarding when you get to help someone. No real expenses, no costs, great sex. So, not a lot of us want to move on."

Tommy rocked back, not even knowing what to ask next. And the entire Atlantis reference just had him confused.

"Agent of Ghost?" Jewel asked.

"Yes," K.J. said, "that's what you are now."

He looked at Tommy and smiled. "You went from deputy to agent in one fell tree."

Tommy did not laugh and after a moment K.J. stopped laughing at his own attempt at humor.

Sixteen

JEWEL MADE HERSELF take a deep breath and focus on the man, or ghost in a suit, in front of her. Her office was warm, and it was her office, so even though she hadn't used it much, and now never would again, she at least felt in charge in here.

"So we have been recruited as ghosts, or agents, for an organization called Ghost," she said, staring into the blue eyes of the short, petite man next to Tommy. "Is that correct?"

K.J. nodded, still half giggling at his stupid attempt to be funny with their deaths.

"How many Ghost Agents are there?"

K.J. shrugged. "Not that many. A couple hundred or so, if that, in the United States and Canada. Sweetie, I honestly don't know. A lot more around the world, but you don't run into other Ghost members very often unless you are living together, or having a party, or on a similar mission."

Jewel tried to ignore the hundred questions that sentence brought up and forced herself to just ask more important questions. "Do we have extra powers or skills besides being invisible and being able to walk through doors?"

"You will, given time," K.J. said. "But at the start you both need to figure out what you can and can't do in this ghost state. Sort of a stumbling trial and error."

"I controlled that killer this morning by being in his body," Tommy said. "You mean things like that?"

"Exactly," K.J. said, nodding. "And so much more. Just enjoy yourself. Try everything. This is a lot more fun than being alive ever was."

Tommy shook his head and Jewel again ignored questions around that, figuring she would come back to it.

"You said you had bosses," Jewel asked. "Are there ranks in this organization?"

"Well, dear, it's an organization," K.J. said, smiling at her. "What do you think? And you'll learn the ranks given time, don't worry."

"So you're our boss?" Tommy asked.

K.J. thought that really funny again. Then after laughing his strange and high and slightly forced laugh, he shook his head and said, "Oh, heaven's, no, Deputy honey. I'm just your coach and someone to help at times if you need me. I'm still new at all this myself on the scheme of things."

"Will we meet our direct boss?" Tommy asked.

K.J. shrugged. "At some point, I suppose. I sure don't see her very often and she's my boss too."

"And this isn't heaven or hell or purgatory?" Jewel asked, finally getting to the point she had been aiming at.

K.J. just shook his head. "This is still very much the real world and your job is to help real people into a more peaceful future. It's what both of you did before that accident, wasn't it? So now you just keep doing that."

Jewel looked at Tommy who seemed to be deep in thought. She still had so many questions, she didn't know where to go next.

"Look," K.J. said, checking a bright pink watch that looked like it was made

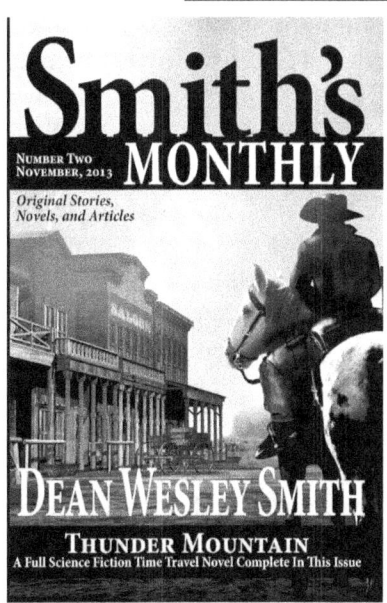

for a teenage girl that had been hidden under his suit sleeve, "I have to be getting ready for a smashing birthday party in San Francisco in about an hour. It's going to have all kinds of really fun games like bobbing for your partner's junk. So let me get right to it. Your first mission is pretty clear. In five days, in Las Vegas, someone is going to try to cause a powerful US senator to have a stroke and die in a bad circumstance. Your job is to stop that from happening."

"A senator?" Jewel asked, shocked.

"Yup, one of the big one hundred," K.J. said, nodding. "Can't tell you any more than that right now because, to be honest, I don't know anymore. Just get to Vegas and get settled, have some fun, explore a little, and I'll contact you."

Jewel didn't even know what to ask.

Tommy looked to be in the same state.

"Great!" K.J. said, standing. "Got to party! I've been so looking forward to this all week. See you in Las Vegas."

And with that he vanished.

No sound, no pop, no whoosh.

He just vanished.

Seventeen

TOMMY STARED AT where K.J. had been a moment before, then laughed. "Think that transporting or vanishing or whatever he did will be one of our future powers?"

"Might be," Jewel said, still staring at the empty chair on the other side of her big desk. "But I like how our reason for being like this is to just keep on helping people."

"Yeah, me too," Tommy said. "I liked helping save that girl's life this morning. And I like that this is still the real world."

"Real, but not really what we are used to, it seems, when it comes to our connection to it."

He agreed and stood as she did. Once again, he was struck at how good she looked in that big shirt of his with her long brown hair pulled back. And her green eyes seemed to be getting brighter as the day went along, as if she was coming alive.

She grabbed his big coat and wrapped it around herself and dug the gloves out of the pocket. "Time to go get you some clothes and head for Las Vegas," she said. "Ever been there?"

"A couple times when I was younger and on leave," he said, trying to remember anything about the two trips. "I wasn't actually present for parts of the trips due to extreme alcohol poisoning."

"Never been to Vegas," she said, smiling as she pulled on his big gloves. "Never had the time."

"We got the time now," Tommy said, "if we can figure out a way to get there."

"How about we figure that out on the walk to my place," she said.

"After we stop at Carol's Diner and grab a couple of those fantastic cinnamon rolls of hers," Tommy said. "That apple isn't holding me." He had slowly been becoming aware he was getting hungry.

When he said that, she smiled. "I've been feeling hungry as well. And getting a little tired as well."

"It seemed ghosts have to eat and sleep and pee after all," he said, following her out into her office waiting room.

"Not something the movies ever got right," she said.

They went through the front door and out onto the sidewalk, then stopped.

He looked both ways up and down the quiet little town. He had enjoyed his time here, but he wouldn't miss it. He turned to Jewel and her large green eyes.

She gave him a mock salute. "Lead on, Agent Ralston."

He laughed and took her hand. "To the cinnamon rolls, Agent Kelly."

As they turned and headed across the street toward Carol's Diner, she asked him one question. "Did buffalo actually jump around here somewhere?"

"Damned if I know," he said. "But I think it's too late for either of us to ask anyone."

"One big damned tree too late," she said.

And at that, he laughed.

Eighteen

CAROL'S DINER was a small place with a glass front door. They both went through the door quickly. Jewel actually managed to keep her eyes mostly open. It was strange, like a slight blurring of her vision.

What was amazing is that the diner smelled wonderful, a mixture of coffee and cinnamon rolls baking. Jewel was surprised that as a ghost, she still could smell things.

The diner was not much more than a long counter with brown stools bolted to the floor along it and vinyl booths along the front window looking out over the highway. There were only five people in two booths. Two men in one and a man and two women in the other. Jewel didn't recognize any of them.

Carol, a solid, middle-aged woman had a coffee pot in her hand, her brown hair up in a bun, and an apron that had seen a better day about two decades ago. Carol always seemed to have a smile, but not today. Now she looked sad.

"Sense of smell is still with us," Tommy said.

He reached over the counter near the old cash register and grabbed a cinnamon roll from a huge plate of them sitting near the register, right where Carol always set them to tempt customers. And Jewel had been tempted many times over her short time here. Every time she ate one of the incredible cinnamon rolls, she had run an extra mile. Since she loved to run, it wasn't much of a price to pay for such a wonderful taste.

The ghost part of the cinnamon roll came away in Tommy's hand. He grabbed a napkin and then took a bite.

"Better than they ever tasted in real life," he said. "And that's going some."

She reached over and grabbed one of the soft rolls, feeling the sticky sugar frosting against her fingers.

And it actually felt warm.

The real-life roll she had grabbed was still sitting there on the big plate, but at the same time she had the ghost image of it in her hand.

With her other hand, she reached for the same roll again. And came away with a second ghost roll.

Tommy just shook his head and smiled, white frosting on both corners of his mouth. "Seems we have unlimited food."

"It does, doesn't it," she said. She set one roll down on the counter and grabbed a napkin. Then decided to try something.

"Watch this," she said.

She took another ghost napkin from the pile, then put her hand through the entire large stack of napkins with no resistance.

"How in the world does that work?" Tommy asked.

"I'm betting we control what we want with our minds," she said, pulling her hand back out of the pile of napkins and then picking up one as if it was a regular napkin.

Then she looked back at the glass door. "I wonder if everything has a ghost element to it if we want it to have one?"

"Not following you," he said, chewing on another bite of cinnamon roll.

She went back over to the front door of the diner, then reached out and pulled open the glass door.

A ghost glass door opened, but the real door stayed in place.

She let the ghost door go closed and came back toward him near the front counter.

"This is going to take some figuring out," he said.

"A whole bunch," she said. Then she took a bite of one of the cinnamon rolls and let the fantastic, sweet flavor fill her mouth.

"You're right, the rolls are better. I didn't think that was possible."

At that moment, the conversation between Carol and two men in one booth got heated and fairly loud.

"You need to have some respect for the dead," Carol said loudly before turning away.

"Both jerks," Tommy said. "Reedman brothers. They live on a ranch about twenty miles from here and spend more time in the bars around the county than on their ranch. Glad I won't be dealing with those two anymore."

One of the brothers said loudly to Carol. "I just said that more than likely the doc was giving the deputy a blow job when they left the road. How is that not respectful? I wouldn't mind going that way."

"Yeah, me too," the other brother said.

"They only wish," Jewel said, laughing.

But Carol didn't seem to be taking the joke too well. With a full, steaming coffee pot, she walked back over toward their table and before either of them could move, she poured the scalding coffee in their laps.

"Oh, oh," Tommy said, shaking his head.

"That's going to scar where they might not enjoy scars," Jewel said, laughing

Carol turned and headed for the counter as the two jumped up swearing and trying to dab at their crotches and brush away the burning liquid, as if that was going to help.

Jewel knew that the only thing that was going to help those kinds of burns was to get their pants off and pack the parts in ice quickly. But she doubted either of them would do that here, so they were going to be really burned by the time they got done moving around.

Tommy set down the rest of his roll and stepped toward the two men.

Jewel had no idea what he was thinking, but she followed.

After the two brothers got done swearing, and dancing and smashing around, they both turned toward Carol. "You're going to pay for this," one of the brothers said.

"Wow, movie cliché and everything," Jewel said.

"Not a lot of brain cells in those two heads," Tommy said.

They both started toward Carol who had the empty coffee pot in her hands and was starting to look slightly scared.

Tommy got in front of one of the brothers, and she got in front of the other brother. He didn't smell that good and his eyes looked mean and angry. She had no idea what she was doing, but she had seen Tommy do it earlier, so she knew she could as well.

As Jewel merged inside him, she ignored the desire to just run and take a shower and used all her thought and energy to force him to stop.

He did, but she had to take one step back to stay inside before he actually stopped.

Tommy had been right, not a lot of thinking in this one. More like animal behavior of rutting and drinking and eating and not much more. It made her feel like her skin was crawling and she hoped his thoughts would not be part of her. If it worked like before, that feeling would pass quickly after she left.

She hoped.

Beside her, Tommy forced the other brother to sit on the floor, his back against a stool with a big metal base that was bolted to the floor.

She used all her focus and forced the brother she was in control of to the floor as well.

Tommy then had the brother he was controlling say, "Someone please call the sheriff. Carol, please tie our hands securely to these stools so we can't move. We do not want to hurt you, but we will if we get loose."

Jewel could tell from the brother's mind she controlled that the two brothers had beaten up a man in Missoula three days ago. And they had raped a few women.

Jewel could tell, from the guy's thoughts, he was in intense pain from the burns in his crotch and legs. Served the bastard right.

"We need to confess what we have done," the other brother said as Tommy controlled him.

The two women in the other booth had their cell phones out and were recording everything. The guy was busy calling the sheriff on a third phone.

Beside the man Jewel held, she saw Carol come around with strong wrapping twine and cinch it around the guy's hands. Then wrap it around the post of the stool a few times and then back around the guy and back around the post and then around the guy's neck and back around the post.

The guy was not moving. The twine hurt.

Jewel focused on ways of helping the guy feel the extreme burn pain even more, unlocking pain blockers that had been working in his mind. He slowly started whimpering and then peed himself, the hot liquid making the burns feel even worse.

She dropped what pain blockers his mind had up and shut them down permanently.

Carol went around and quickly tied up the other brother as Tommy had him recite the crimes they had done, who the victims were, and why they did what they had done.

Carol finally finished tying up the second man.

Jewel climbed out of the guy she had been in and stepped back. He was nothing more than a whimpering pile of humanity sitting in his own pee.

Tommy forced the last guy to finish his list of crimes.

As Jewel moved back, outside the sheriff pulled up. Gun drawn, he slammed his car door and came running in.

"Might want to have him recite what they did one more time," Jewel said to Tommy. "Sheriff has arrived."

The sheriff stopped near the cash register, stunned at the sight he saw in front of him. The brother Tommy controlled again recited what he and his brother had done, right down to the rapes and how they had enjoyed it and planned it.

Jewel was disgusted, and Carol had her hand over her mouth in shock.

The two women in the booth were recording everything.

Finally Tommy stood and left the guy.

Jewel moved over and hugged him. "Nice job, agent.

"You two, agent," he said, smiling at her.

"What's happening?" the one brother said, struggling and discovering he couldn't get loose.

"Damned if I know," the sheriff said, shaking his head.

"What did you do to that guy?" Tommy asked Jewel as the other brother just whimpered at the pain.

"Took down the pain blockers in his mind," Jewel said, "made him feel everything intensely, especially the pain from the burns on his crotch."

"Wow, that's really great," Tommy said. "Explain to me exactly what I look for when I'm in there."

She tried to tell him, as best she could, not using medical terms.

Finally Tommy nodded and went over and sat down inside the body of the guy he had been in before.

After a moment the guy stiffened, then slowly started squirming and whimpering and begging for someone to stop the pain. The transformation of the tough guy to a whimpering sick monster was pretty amazing to Jewel watching it.

Carol, the sheriff, and the other three in the booth just watched, mouths open.

A moment later Tommy came back out of the guy and shuddered.

"That should do it," Tommy said. "I made sure he would always feel any pain far, far worse than it actually is.

"I think you did it just fine," she said, as the wet spot on the guy's crotch from the steaming hot coffee got larger as the guy peed himself and squirmed even more.

"Agent, I think out job is done here," he said.

She nodded, and they headed for the front door, each grabbing another cinnamon roll as they went by from the big plate of them.

Suddenly, the sheriff turned around and said into the air up toward the light fixtures. "Thanks, Tommy. I got it from here."

That froze her and Tommy both in place.

Jewel looked at Tommy. "Could he see us?"

"No," Tommy said. "But the sheriff is a very smart man and can put two and two together with the best of them."

Tommy stopped, went back over beside the sheriff who was still watching the two tied-up criminals whimper and squirm against their ropes.

Jewel watched as Tommy gently touched the sheriff's shoulder and said, "You are welcome, sheriff. It was an honor to work with you. I've got to go now."

The sheriff nodded, then said softly. "I'll miss you. Good luck wherever you are going."

Tommy took his hand away and went back to Jewel.

"Who were you talking to?" Carol asked the sheriff, puzzled.

The sheriff looked at her, then back around before saying, "Deputy Ralston. He's been helping me out one last day."

Carol touched the sheriff's arm sadly and nodded, saying nothing.

Jewel took Tommy's free hand and with their cinnamon rolls in their other hands, they went out into the chill of the day.

"That was nice," she said.

Tommy nodded. "It was. I kind of like this new job." Then he took a large bite out of the cinnamon roll.

"Yeah, me too," Jewel said. "But can't help but wonder what the sheriff would have thought if he knew we were headed to Las Vegas instead of the next world."

She had to pat Tommy's back because his laughter made him choke on the roll.

Nineteen

TOMMY FELT WONDERFUL walking along the edge of the highway toward Jewel's cabin. The images from the brother's mind back in the diner had almost faded, cleaned out very quickly.

He really liked that it worked that way. Last thing he wanted to do was walk around with other people's horrors in his mind.

He was already enjoying this Ghost Agent job, and he hadn't even been dead for a full day yet.

He couldn't believe he was enjoying being dead. That was just flat weird, but true.

And he was really growing closer and more attracted to Jewel. She was smart, stunningly attractive, and fun to be with. He was very glad she was with him on this adventure.

So he was enjoying being dead and falling for a dead woman. Yeah, this is what he expected to have happen exactly after he died.

Maybe in a wet dream.

They talked most of the walk, trying to decide the best way out of these mountains and to Las Vegas. They both had decided that just catching a plane in Missoula would be the best, but neither of them had many ideas on how to get out to Missoula.

Hitchhiking was sure out of the question, since no one could see them.

Finally, they decided that in the morning they would walk back to the mini-mart and gas station and just wait until someone on the way toward Missoula stopped for gas. Then play it by ear from there.

When Jewel pointed down a small gravel side road off the highway, Tommy nodded.

"You been down here before?" Jewel asked.

"Dropped Doc Craigston off here about a year ago," Tommy said. "He was far too drunk to drive and the bartender at the Oasis called me."

"Ben Horseman owns both the little office and this place," Jewel said. "He's got quite a rental gig going with the county."

"As long as the doctors stop dying on him," Tommy said.

"Did Doc Craigston die as well?"

Tommy nodded. "Heart attack coming out of the Oasis one night."

"Didn't know that," Jewel said, shaking her head. "I thought he just retired."

"In a way he did," Tommy said.

Ahead of them the small log cabin with cedar shakes sort of set alone in a clearing in the tall pine trees. It had no view, and sometime in the past someone had tried to plant a garden and fence it off from the deer. That area was all weeds now. Jewel had seen that and just shook her head. Not in a million years would she have planted a garden. Not her thing in the slightest.

Otherwise, the cabin looked kept up and lived in. The blinds on the windows were drawn and since Jewel wasn't home, there wasn't any smoke coming out of the top of the stone fireplace.

"Was it comfortable to live in?" Tommy asked as they stepped up on the porch.

"Actually," Jewel said, "it was. Great bathtub with shower, great reading lights, great fireplace. I liked it."

Jewel went through the closed front door first and Tommy followed, closing his eyes.

Inside the house did feel comfortable. The large brown logs of the walls and the beams overhead gave it a soft feel. And it was warm.

Also, luckily, one lamp was still on.

"Nice," Tommy said, dropping his pack of clothes beside the door.

"Living room up front here," Jewel said. Kitchen and dining is the back half of this big room. Bathroom off the kitchen, bedroom through there. Simple and small, but nice."

"First at the bathroom," Tommy said. "Hope you left the lid up."

"If I didn't, try lifting it and see what happens," Jewel said.

"Good idea."

He didn't need to lift the lid, and by the time he was finished, Jewel was in the bedroom and pulling down some ghost clothes and packing them in a small satchel similar to the one Tommy had left in the front room.

"Figured I might as well get this done in case someone shows up."

Tommy nodded. "Good thinking."

Then, as if he wasn't standing there watching, she started to unbutton her shirt. When she had it off and was nude from the belt up, she tossed him the shirt. "Might want to pack that."

"Can I do that in a minute," he said. "I'm enjoying the show."

"Not much to look at," she said, spreading her arms and giving him a full view of her breasts. Both were wonderful. Pert, and firm, with hard brown nipples.

"Fantastic to look at," he said.

She then worked at getting out of the pants she had had on all day and yesterday. "I'm going to take these," she said, wadding them into a ball and putting them into her bag. "I figure at some point we'll either figure out a way to wash clothes, or just get new ones all the time."

Tommy only nodded because now she was standing there only in her white underwear. She worked for a few more minutes like that, stuffing ghost clothes into her bag, then finally slipped off her underwear, tossed them into the back of the open closet with other dirty clothes, and picked up the bag.

She went to hand it to him.

"You want to put this in the living room with yours?"

"I'd much rather watch you do it," he said, moving to one side so she could go past him and out in to the living room.

She smiled, clearly knowing damn well what kind of impact she was having on him, as she went past him out into the living room and dropped her bag, then headed for the bathroom.

"What are the odds we can get some ghost hot water running?" she asked.

"I honestly have no idea," he said.

He followed her into the bathroom and she went to the tub with a shower over it and turned the handle.

He wanted more than anything to just reach forward and touch her, and he was pretty sure she wanted him to do that as well, since how she was acting. But he honestly felt almost paralyzed like a young high school boy.

So he just watched the fantastic show of the most beautiful woman he had ever known get ready to take a shower.

The handle actually didn't turn in Jewel's hand, but water started flowing, so she must have turned a ghost handle.

She waited a moment and then made the motion to turn the other handle and smiled. "We have perfect shower water. "Get out of those clothes and come and scrub my back."

He didn't remember shedding his clothes. But somehow he did, never taking his gaze off of the vision of nakedness under the water.

And in record time he was stepping under the warm shower and washing the back of a dream come true.

"I'm starting to think old K.J. was wrong," Tommy said as Jewel sighed and leaned forward, clearly enjoying his touch.

"Why is that?" Jewel asked.

"Because I know I'm dead and I'm pretty sure this is heaven."

She laughed. "Keep that gentle touch up much longer and I'll show you the pearly gates."

"Promises, promises," he said.

She pushed back against his hard penis with her butt. "That's a promise," she said.

There was not a thing he could say to that, so he just kept washing.

Twenty

SHE AWOKE the next morning to the wonderful smell of eggs and pancakes. Tommy was gone from the big bed and the morning light filtered around the edges of her bedroom curtains.

She stretched, pushing away the blankets, feeling more relaxed and at ease with the world than she had felt in a very long time. Having a real man make love to her was so much better than Mr. Buzzy. She had almost forgotten.

After the shower, they had managed to get dried off and to her bed. He had been gentle and passionate both, just as she always hoped a man would be.

And the sex had been even more intense than anything she had ever remembered. K.J. had made a comment that the sex was good, and wow had he been right.

Tommy appeared in the bedroom door. He was dressed in jeans and a blue t-shirt that had a Berkeley logo on it. He smiled when he saw her awake and naked, stretched out on top of the bed.

"Breakfast in five minutes, Doc, so hurry up and get dressed."

She laughed and sat up. "I'd suggest another round in the sack, but I just realized I'm famished. How did you manage to cook something."

"Seems everything has a ghost element to it," he said, smiling. "Pans, gas burners, eggs, milk, you name it. Now hurry up. I have a hunch ghost eggs can burn just as easily as anything else."

He vanished and she rolled out of bed and slipped on the clean clothes she had left out of her bag for this morning. Then she slipped on her running shoes and headed for the bathroom.

Five minutes later exactly she had her hair combed and pulled back and her face washed and was being served a plate of eggs and pancakes at her little dining room table.

"This really is a nice place you had here," Tommy said as he took another plate, dished up his breakfast, turned off the gas burner, and came over to sit across from her.

"Thanks," she said. "I liked it the best of anything here. Every day I looked forward to coming here and just reading and being alone."

"You going to miss it?"

"Honestly, no," she said, digging into the fantastic-tasting eggs, salted just perfectly. "I'm ready to do some real work and I think this new job is just what I needed."

"Too bad we had to die to get it," Tommy said.

"Regretting that part of it?" she asked, digging into the pancakes after smothering them in butter and maple syrup.

"I keep thinking I should, but I sure don't," he said, shaking his head and continuing to eat. "I think that's because for us this feels just like real life, only we have super powers."

"Super powers?" she asked. She couldn't completely grasp what he was saying.

"Never read comic books?" he asked.

"Never did," she said. "I was one of the serious types and just never got started on them."

"Well," he said, "we are invisible, that's a super power. And we can walk through walls, which is a super power."

"We can read minds and control people," she said.

"Another super power," he said, nodding. "And from what K.J. said and did, we might have more if we can figure them out."

"So I died and become a comic book heroine," she said. "Not the afterlife I had expected, I can say for certain."

"That happens in comics," Tommy said, laughing. "I could name some characters if you want."

"Thanks," she said, finishing up her pancakes. "Maybe later."

"As foreplay?" he asked, grinning.

"Agent," she said, standing and moving over to kiss him. "You make me hot all by yourself."

She kissed him long and hard, then moved over and put her plate in the sink and ran some ghost water over it.

He put his plate on top of hers.

"I wonder if these ghost plates will be here forever now?" she asked, staring at them in the sink. "Or do they merge back with their real plates at some point or just vanish?"

"We've got a lot to learn about this new state we are in," Tommy said.

"We do," Jewel said.

She started to turn away, then turned back and keeping the water running, she spent the next minute washing the plates and frying pan while Tommy used the restroom.

She put them away where they all belonged as Tommy came out and headed for the front door.

"Ready to go on an adventure?" he asked as he slipped on his heavy coat, picked up his bag, and slung it over his shoulder.

She looked around the cabin she had enjoyed for a time, then nodded.

"I am if it's with you," she said, pulling on her ski parka and then pulling on her gloves.

She then picked up her bag.

Tommy stepped through the big wooden door and outside.

With one last look at the cabin where she had actually lived, she stepped through the door and out into the cold, fresh, morning air to really start the journey into a new world.

Section Two
What Happens In Vegas

Twenty-one

AFTER THEY GOT back to Jay's Minimart, a middle-aged couple driving a big brown motor home pulled in for gas and some snacks. They were pulling a big new Jeep. Both vehicles had Texas plates on them.

Tommy was surprised. You didn't see many big motor homes way up here in winding, mountain roads, let alone ones from Texas. They were a very, very long ways from home, that was for sure.

Tommy, with Jewel at his side, was just inside the minimart, trying to stay out of Jay's way, yet stay warm. The day would maybe get up to near fifty and sunny by four in the afternoon, but at nine

in the morning it was still just above freezing. After their experience yesterday at the wreck scene, neither of them had much interest in getting that cold again.

Jay was a skinny little guy, about the size of a small high school kid who hadn't gotten his growth yet. But he was at least forty, with a face covered in wrinkles and only a wisp of gray hair. The sheriff had told Tommy one day that Jay had been born here and inherited the old Chevron station from his father and turned it into the minimart because he hated working on cars.

"Let me see where they are heading when the husband comes in," Tommy said as the woman from the motor home came inside and went into the restroom.

"That does look comfortable," Jewel said, nodding, staring out the window of the minimart at the big motor home. "We could spend the trip on the bed."

"Now wouldn't that be fun," Tommy said.

"Play your cards right," she said, giving him that smile that he was coming to love, "you might get lucky."

Tommy pointed to some playing cards for sale. "Want me to get a pack?"

"Not the kind of cards I'm talking about," she said, laughing.

It took almost fifteen minutes for the big motor home to fill with gas. Then the guy came in, all talking and happy, one of those kind that loved to talk with anyone along the way. He was about three times Jay's size and clearly had money and didn't care if anyone knew. And his accent clearly put him from Texas.

The woman had come out of the restroom a few minutes before and now stood at her husband's side, but said nothing. She was dressed like a tourist in very expensive clothes that included more pink than Tommy thought should be allowed inside the borders of Montana.

"How far do we have to Missoula from here?" the guy asked Jay as he dug into his wallet. Tommy just smiled at Jewel.

"Two hundred miles," the clerk said. "In that rig of yours about four hours."

"Is it a pretty drive?" the guy asked.

"Just about as scenic as it gets."

"Perfect," the guy said.

"Perfect for us as well," Tommy said.

He grabbed his pack and led the way outside to the motor home. Jewel followed closely and he quickly shut his eyes and went up the step and through the door into the motor home.

He took two steps and stopped.

The smoke smell was about as bad as he had ever smelled.

Jewel came in behind him and then coughed.

Tommy pointed to the full ashtrays besides both seats. "I don't think I want to spend four hours in this, do you?"

"Not a chance," she said.

She turned around and went back out and he followed her into the crisp, but fresh mountain air.

"Wow," she said, coughing to clear her lungs. "That was something."

"Never know on what level a couple will bond," Tommy said, between taking a few deep breaths of fresh air.

"Let's just keep bonding on sex, all right?"

Tommy laughed. "No argument from me."

They were just about to go back inside when a big black Cadillac pulled up to the pump on the other side of the motor home. Tommy watched as Moore Williams climbed out and worked at the pump to fill his car.

Moore was an accountant from Missoula. He had a big second home on the lake not far from where Tommy had lived in his father's home. Tommy liked and respected Moore and his wife and kids. His wife was a lawyer in Missoula and the kids went to school there and the entire family spent most of the summer on the lake.

Moore also played at painting landscapes, and he liked to be up here when he had time to paint and be alone.

Luckily for them, today was one of the days he had to head back to the big city.

"That's our ride," Tommy said, pointing at the Cadillac.

"You know him?" Jewel asked, following Tommy.

"Moore Williams, a friend of the family," Tommy said. "Moore is headed for Missoula. This is part of his normal routine."

Jewel laughed. "Amazing what you learn about the locals when you're a deputy sheriff."

"Sometimes too much," Tommy said as he moved around to the passenger side and climbed into the back seat. The car smelled fresh and was fairly warm. The seats were dark leather and Moore had his suit jacket draped over the passenger seat.

Tommy indicated that Jewel should take off her coat before getting in and he worked at doing the same. He could have just stepped back out to do it and should have. The back seat in the Cadillac sedan was big, but not that big.

Ten minutes later, they were both very comfortable in the back seat of a smooth-running Cadillac, headed out of Buffalo Jump for the last time.

She was holding his hand and Tommy liked that a lot.

Even going off into an unknown world on an unknown adventure, he felt right being with her.

Moore Williams expertly took the smooth-riding car down the highway, staying just over the speed limit, taking the curves with ease. He had soft jazz on the fantastic sound system and the temperature control set perfectly.

For Tommy, it didn't get much better than this.

Twenty-two

THEY MANAGED TO get out of Moore's car at a stoplight not more than a mile from the airport. The weather in Missoula was warmer and neither of them needed their coats.

Jewel had really enjoyed her ride with Tommy from Buffalo Jump. A lot of the time they had just sat silently holding hands, the rest they had talked about their history, mostly about old boyfriends for her and old girlfriends for him.

It had felt right to tell him some of those things. It felt like he was more than a lover. It felt like he was her friend as well and that felt right.

After the walk to the airport, they both used the restrooms, then stood off to one side out of the flow of people and studied the flights.

There was one headed to Las Vegas in thirty minutes, so they decided they'd try to catch that one.

The airport was fairly modern and had wide, carpeted aisles, so they spent a lot of time walking along the edges where there were pictures of Missoula and different national parks close by on the walls, trying to not walk through anyone.

But at one spot she failed that, having a guy turn suddenly and walk right into her and through her.

She caught a glimpse of his life as he went through. Deep in debt, deep in the closet, afraid his wife would find out about both the debt and his male lover.

"You all right?" Tommy asked after it had happened.

"I'm fine," she said, shaking her head. "Just stuff about some stranger I didn't want to know."

"Clearing?" Tommy asked.

She nodded. The memories and thoughts she had glimpsed from the guy were clearing, quickly as they had before.

When they finally reached the gate, it looked like the plane was almost finished boarding.

"What happens if this is a full flight?" she asked, staring at the open door.

"We stand," Tommy said. "Or we find a couple sitting together and join them, give them a little nap while we use their bodies."

He smiled at her and made her laugh, the worry vanishing. She loved how he could do that for her.

"Always wanted to see Vegas," she said, heading for the door.

"I want to see it and remember it," Tommy said.

It felt weird to Jewel to just walk past the attendant at the gate. It felt like they needed to pay or something. She had felt the same way when Tommy had gotten them both a couple bottles of water and some candy bars from a newsstand on the way to the gate. Even though the candy bars and water were ghost echoes of their real sides, and he hadn't stolen anything, it still felt weird to her.

They headed down the breezeway and into the airplane just as the flight attendant was about to close the door. She had dark brown hair and looked to be around thirty. Both Jewel and Tommy had to brush through the flight attendant to get in.

Jewel saw instantly that she wanted to have sex with the captain of this flight, had a bad marriage, and wanted to lose ten pounds.

"After the last two heads I've been in," Tommy said, "that was refreshing."

"What? Jewel asked as she turned toward the cabin. "Shallow?"

"No, not evil."

"Yeah, that was nice," Jewel said, nodding and looking for any empty seats. "I have a hunch there will be far more of that than the evil we encountered before."

"I sure hope you are right," he said.

As she feared, there were no empty seats. Not one.

She headed down the aisle, looking for a young and handsome couple sitting together. After a moment she saw some candidates. They both looked to be in college. He had long dark hair and a baby face that was handsome. He had on a button down shirt and jeans. She also had long dark hair and a trim body and wore a thin white blouse, a lace bra under it, and jeans.

They both looked very nervous, as if this was their first flight.

They were sitting beside a middle-aged woman in a business suit who had a laptop out and was already working. The woman was in the window seat.

Tommy looked at them when Jewel pointed the couple out.

"Eloping," Tommy said, smiling. "Any bets?"

She looked back at the young couple and knew he was right. "Shall we see if they are a match for each other?"

"I sure don't see any open seats at all," he said. "So might as well."

She brushed through the guy and sat down on the girl's lap, sinking right into her completely as if the poor young girl wasn't there at all.

"That sure looked creepy from out here," Tommy said and Jewel realized he had never watched that before. She had watched him do that but he had never seen her do it.

He settled into the guy's body and both of them stuffed their packs under the seat in front of them.

The moment she had brushed through the guy, she knew Tommy had been right. They were eloping.

But it was when she sat down with the girl that she got the big surprise. Her name was Spring Stevens and she was still a virgin with boys. She and Bryan, the kid beside her, had never had sex, even though they had been dating for two years and she loved him. They had done a lot of heavy petting, but no sex.

And both of them were freshmen in college, both over eighteen.

But Spring had had lots of sex with other women, mostly her two best friends. And she wasn't sure she was making the right decision at all marrying Bryan, even though she loved him.

Through them holding hands, Jewel could feel Bryan's thoughts as well.

Bryan wasn't sure either and was scared to death. She got lots of images of Bryan masturbating to pictures of Spring in a bathing suit. But actually seeing her nude had him scared to death.

Then she felt Tommy put Bryan to sleep and she did the same thing with Spring.

Both Spring and Bryan closed their eyes and put their heads back, acting like seasoned travelers. The woman pounding her laptop in the window seat beside them didn't even notice and Jewel doubted the woman would even care.

Jewel could now only sense Spring and Bryan's deep thoughts, nothing else, like a light background noise.

"Well, that worked," Tommy said.

"Don't you think this is sad?" Jewel asked, squeezing Tommy's hand.

"Real sad," he said. "The poor kid is going to be a mess the moment he sees her without clothes and compared to her girl-friends, he's going to be a bumbling fool."

"But they seem to be in love," Jewel said. "And they seem to be good kids from good families."

"Yeah, they are in love, that much is clear. Maybe for the use of their bodies for the flight, we can implant some pointers to help them along."

Jewel laughed. "We could let them wake up with his hand in her crotch and her hand in his crotch."

"If I do that now," Tommy said, "whose crotch would I really be touching? Yours or hers?"

Jewel laughed. "Your hand would go right through her crotch. Mine, on the other hand, your hand did some nice things to last night."

"Oh, yeah, good point," Tommy said. "His hand would feel her crotch, my hand would feel yours. We might want to wake them up some and test that."

"Later," she said, laughing. "Watch the safety lecture. We might need to know what to do in case of a water landing."

"Between Missoula and Las Vegas?" Tommy asked, laughing.

Jewel leaned her head out of the sleeping Spring and faced the side of Bryan's head. "You just never know. Now come on out of there and kiss me."

He did.

And the kiss lasted until they were in the air. And she didn't want it to end even then.

Twenty-three

JUST AS THEY had done on the drive from Buffalo Jump into Missoula, Tommy and Jewel talked most of the way to Las Vegas. They kept both kids asleep and when the woman next to Jewel started to say she wanted to go to the restroom and had actually touched Spring's shoulder to wake her, Jewel just put the woman to sleep as well.

Tommy could tell, because he was touching Jewel, that the woman really hadn't needed to go to the restroom, but only wanted to try to make a cell phone call from the bathroom.

"Wow, she's a piece of work," Tommy said. The real sense he had gotten from the woman was cold. Ice cold. She was in a sex-less marriage for looks only and cared only about her job and the status of what people thought of her.

"There is no world but her world," Jewel said, shaking her head. "At least these two kids eloping are worried about what their parents might think and their friends. That woman cares for no one but herself and her job and the things her money will buy her."

"So we live trying to help people," Tommy said. "And then there are people like her."

"I can see why K.J. laughed when we asked if everyone ended up Ghost Agents like us."

"Yeah, now that I think about it," Tommy said, "that would be pretty silly. And make a real mess in the world in very short order."

At that moment the flight attendant indicated they should start getting ready for landing.

"What should we do about these kids?" Jewel asked.

Tommy had been wondering the same thing at times during the flight. "How about we implant some sexual pointers for them to try in their hotel tonight. Give them a running shot at enjoying that."

"I like that idea," Jewel said. "But how about we also plant a few suggestions that they don't need to get married here, that if they love each other, they can go home and get married with their families and friends. They can use this trip as an engagement trip."

Tommy smiled at her. "You're a real romantic, you know that?"

"I am," Jewel said, smiling back at him. "And I love reading romance novels. So now the truth is out."

He laughed. He really liked how amazing Jewel was and the more he found out about her, the more he liked.

"So we give these kids a running chance at a decent life," he said.

"I think we should," she said. "Seems like the least we can do for them after these last four hours."

"Let's start to wake them up and plant the ideas and sexual hints as we taxi toward the terminal," he said. "Then before anyone gets up, let's move up front and try to be the first out."

"Yeah, getting tapped in this crush could be more than I want to know about far too many people."

"My fear exactly," he said.

Ten minutes later, the plane was on the ground safely in Las Vegas. The sun was low over the mountains from what Tommy could tell out the windows. And it looked like a clear day.

Tommy slowly worked to bring Bryan up from his deep sleep. And as he did, he planted some deep suggestions about how to please Spring. And how to help himself last longer to please her as well.

And then as Bryan woke up completely, he gave him the strong idea that they should call this trip their engagement trip and go home and get married if they still loved each other after having a few days alone together.

Tommy was pretty sure that they would.

"Ready," Jewel said.

They both grabbed their packs of clothes and as Jewel stood, she brushed the woman asleep near the window one more time.

"What did you do?" Tommy asked.

"Made sure she would sleep through everyone getting off the plane," Jewel said as they headed up the aisle, doing their best to not touch anyone as they went past. "This flight goes on to Los Angeles. She might wake up there."

"Perfect," Tommy said, laughing. "I'm starting to really love being a Ghost Agent."

"I thought you said this morning that we were superheroes," Jewel said, laughing.

Tommy glanced back at the two kids who were waking up, surprised they were already in Las Vegas. Two kids who might now have a much better start into their future.

"You know," he said. "I think we just might be."

Twenty-four

GETTING OUT OF the Las Vegas airport was a lot harder than getting through the Missoula airport. Jewel couldn't believe how busy the place was, and how narrow some of the hallways were, often cluttered with slot machines.

She ended up walking through or brushing a good ten people before they got to the taxi stand. Most of them were just regular people, but one guy was working some sort of scam she didn't want to think about at all.

Tommy had the same problem.

"There has to be a better way to get around," Jewel said. "Or a way to block people's thoughts when we want to."

"We need to ask K.J. when we see him," Tommy said.

"How will he know we are here?" Jewel asked as they stood off to one side of all the massive rope and chains that directed people in a steady stream toward taxies.

"I have a hunch he'll know," Tommy said. "But let's find a room and get settled and then shout out for him."

"And you have some ideas on how to find a room?" she asked. She sure didn't, but clearly Tommy had been here before and had been thinking about this.

"I do," he said.

Then he pointed to a taxi that was actually a van pulling up at the taxi post labeled 61. "Our ride somewhere. We'll see how many people are riding in the van and where they are going before jumping in."

She nodded and they walked through the ropes to a place out of the way, but close to the taxi van.

Around them, the warm air felt good to Jewel. It wasn't a hot day, but after being so cold at the wreck, this felt wonderful.

Way down the line an airport worker was directing people to taxi stands. As it turned out, only one guy was going to end up riding in the van, and he was headed for the MGM Grand on the strip.

"Perfect," Tommy said.

The guy climbed in the front seat beside the driver and Tommy and Jewel climbed into the second seat.

As the taxi left the airport, Jewel was stunned at the huge buildings of the strip she could see and how close it was. The postcards and photos of Vegas didn't do the place justice.

And the late-evening sun was lighting up some of the tall buildings, making the scene even stranger.

Even though the buildings looked close, it still took almost fifteen minutes to get to the big unloading area in front of the MGM Grand. Jewel was overwhelmed and just gawking at everything, from the tall, ornate building shooting into the air from the desert to the sparkling lights and the size of everything.

They climbed out of the van and stood against a decorative pillar to one side under the massive parking area that looked like it was six or seven cars wide. Jewel just kept looking at the incredible bustle and numbers of people moving here and there. About half of the people wore blaring loud shorts and loud-colored shirts and many had drinks in their hands.

Some men wore expensive suits and the women with them wore slinky, expensive-looking dresses. They were overdressed, clearly trying to impress someone, or headed to some formal event. Jewel just felt out of place completely in her Montana comfort white blouse and jeans, even though no one could see her.

"Looks like we got here at a peak time," Tommy said.

"Top check-in time," Jewel said.

"Afraid so. This is going to be hard to get from here to the front desk without walking through some people," Tommy said.

"Just get us a good room and that will make up for it," Jewel said, smiling.

"Stay close to me," he said.

"I like doing that," she said.

He laughed and headed across the unloading area toward the huge entrance glass doors.

They made it to the doors without touching anyone thanks to Tommy being able to almost outthink where a person was headed.

On the other side of the doors, it was the sounds that hit her first. Fantastically loud noises of slot machines and hundreds and hundreds of people talking and laughing and having a great time.

The lobby area of the MGM Grand was exactly that: Grand. Huge marble columns seemed to hold the ceiling up and bright chandelier lighting filled the entire space with bright, warm light. Most of the flooring was a brown and gold and tan marble and all the colors were gold or muted browns.

A massive curved wooden and gold and marble front desk with a good fifty people behind it stretched along one wall with lines of tourists waiting in places to check in or get other services such as show tickets and such.

Tommy led her over quickly to the wall area on the right of the big room from the front door and toward the front desk. He found an alcove that was out of any traffic pattern and stopped.

"Wait here," he said, handing her his pack. "Got to secure a room for us. Then we can get out of these crowds until we learn to handle it a little better."

She nodded and watched as he went around to the end of the big counter and stood there a moment, seeming to study the people behind the counter. Then he went through the counter and toward one woman standing near a back countertop, watching. Jewel had a hunch she was the front desk manager.

The woman wore what was clearly an MGM manager outfit, with a trim brown skirt, a tan blouse, and a nametag. She had her hair pulled back up and tight on her head and had glasses around her neck on a chain.

As Tommy got close to her, he reached up and touched her shoulder. Then he nodded and disappeared inside her.

Then, less than five seconds later, he came back out and stood, his hand touching her shoulder.

Jewel was going to have to ask him later what it was like being in control of a woman like that. Jewel had a hunch that anything Tommy might say might get him in trouble.

A moment later the woman, with Tommy still touching her shoulder, moved over to a terminal and started typing. It took about five minutes, including the woman printing out two keys and putting them in an envelope and placing them on the back counter in a special file there.

Finally Tommy nodded and then walked the woman back to where she was and took his hand away. The woman stood there as if nothing had happened, watching her clerks help customers.

Tommy stood beside her for a full minute, then nodded and smiled at Jewel and headed her way.

"Got us a suite," he said as she handed him his bag back.

"How did you do that?"

He laughed. "Just had her believe that a large whale, meaning a big spender, was coming in later or tomorrow or maybe the next day and they had to reserve a suite for him just in case."

"So we have a suite for three days?" Jewel asked. "In this place?"

"Only a two thousand dollar a night suite," Tommy said. "But we're dead, so I think we can afford it."

"I don't want to take that kind of money from the hotel," Jewel said, shocked. She didn't feel right doing that. She didn't need a suite, just a nice hotel room would be fine.

Tommy laughed. "They never charge for these rooms," Tommy said. "That's just the rack rate to make the whales feel like they are getting something when they are given the room for free. The rooms are not designed to actually rent out. They are always comp rooms."

"Oh," she said. "How did you know that?"

"Always thought it would be interesting to be a professional poker player," he said. "So I studied all this stuff while I was in a boring semester in college. Back in the big poker craze days."

"Did it lead to one of the drunken trips down here you mentioned?"

He laughed. "Nope. You can't drink and play cards. This is my first time back after doing all that study."

"I'm afraid you can't use the card part this time either," she said. "But if this suite is as good as I think it's going to be, I'll reward you in other ways."

He leaned over and kissed her, then said, "I'll take you up on that."

Twenty-five

TOMMY HAD TO be honest, the suite was so big and spectacular, it even surprised him. Four huge rooms, two of them bedrooms, each with large bathrooms. A giant sunken living room with large leather furniture that looked almost too expensive to sit on, a large dining area that could seat twenty easily around what looked like a pure oak dining table, and a kitchen area. Plus there was a stocked wet bar to one side of the living room.

Back in his college days, this would have been a kid's dream come true. It wasn't bad now.

Everything in every room was done in brown tones, with gold trim that made the place feel comfortable, yet ornate. Huge windows, with the drapes pulled open, looked out over Las Vegas toward the center of town.

"Now this is amazing," Jewel had said when she saw the big tub in one bathroom. "I've died and gone to heaven."

"Died, yes," Tommy said, laughing. "Not sure if a suite at the MGM Grand is heaven. But I have to admit, it's darned close."

So after taking the grand tour and hanging their clothes up in one of the closets, she sat down on the bed and asked what they should do next.

Tommy had all sorts of ideas that included that big bathtub and the huge bed. But he was getting hungry and he knew Jewel was as well.

"I have some ideas about that big bed, but I think we need to do a few other things first to get settled."

"Food?" she asked.

He nodded. "How about we call K.J. and see if he'll come and give us some pointers on how to get around in a crowded city. And get decent food."

Jewel nodded. "A plan."

He took her hand and they went out into the living room. She sat on one of the big couches, he sat in a big overstuffed chair that felt even too big for his frame.

"K.J. we're here!" Tommy shouted up to the ceiling. He had no idea why he shouted at the ceiling, but he did.

Nothing.

So he shouted again.

Nothing.

"Maybe he can't hear us," Jewel said.

"I can hear your bellowing just fine," a voice said from out of nowhere that was clearly K.J. "Give a guy a second to put on some pants and I'll be right there."

Jewel laughed and Tommy just shook his head.

A half-minute later K.J. appeared, his hair wet and his face flushed. He had on a tight pair of jeans that left little to the imagination, a frilly pink shirt, and his nails were painted pink now.

"Sorry, bad timing?" Tommy said.

"Nah," K.J. said, waving his hand limply, "the orgy was just winding down and if I didn't get out of the hot tub soon, I was going to prune up like bad fruit in a hot sun." Then he looked around. "You two learned some quick ropes I see. Nice place."

"The casino likes us," Tommy said, which made K.J. look at him puzzled and Jewel smile.

"So we could really use some pointers," Jewel said. "Especially on how to get around through crowds without having to hear a dozen people's thoughts."

"You can't," K.J. said, moving over and sitting down in another of the big overstuffed chairs. He sat on the edge of it, his back straight, his posture perfect. "You touch someone you get what they are thinking and all their memories and everything icky about them. That is one of your powers and no way to block it. But the thoughts fade quickly when you are not touching them."

"We noticed that," Tommy said. "But besides teleporting as you do, which we haven't learned yet, how would you suggest we walk from one side of a crowded room to the other."

"With style," K.J. said, waving his arm in the air like a dancer. "And flare." He waved the other arm.

Tommy just shook his head as K.J. laughed at his own joke. Then, when he saw Jewel was only smiling and Tommy wasn't even smiling, K.J. said, "You two need to lighten up and have some fun. What's the point of being dead if you can't enjoy life a little?"

"We haven't been dead two days yet," Tommy said. "We will have fun if we can learn some of this stuff."

K.J. sighed and said, "Hitchhike. Both of you pile into the same person and just ride with that person across a busy room."

Tommy nodded. Not sure why he hadn't thought of that, since they had basically done that on the plane. And got a guy on the elevator to push their floor button for them.

"Food?" Jewel asked. "We discovered that all foods have a ghost component. Any suggestions on how to get a great meal in a restaurant?"

"Sure," K.J. said. "Wait near the kitchen door for a meal to come out that looks good and then take the ghost component off the waiter's tray. But it's often easier cooking your own. That works just like in the life side of things."

"Tommy discovered that," Jewel said.

"Food tastes better, doesn't it?" K.J. asked. "I just love that."

"When we take a ghost plate," Tommy asked, "what happens to the plate when we are finished."

K.J. shrugged in an exaggerated way. "After a few hours of you not touching it, it vanishes. No clue where they go. Dish heaven, maybe. A little white dish tunnel to the great dishwasher in the sky."

Again K.J. laughed at his own joke and Tommy actually found himself smiling.

Jewel was just shaking her head and smiling.

"Tough crowd tonight," K.J. said. "I might need a drummer to give me an occasional rim shot, which actually sounds dirty."

Tommy ignored him and asked his next question. "So can we die in this ghost state, get hurt, whatever?"

"You can't die unless you ask to move on," K.J. said. "But trust me, pain is very real and you could wish you were dead. I mean this one time I got shot by one of the Brigade right in the leg, right here."

K.J. pointed to a spot covered by his pants and then waved his hands in exasperation. "Painful, let me tell you. I couldn't dance for almost a month. But at least it didn't leave a scar."

"Shot?" Jewel asked, clearly alarmed. "I thought real stuff just went through us."

"Oh, sure, real bullets do. But ghost bullets can certainly slow you down some until you recover, as I discovered. No dancing, let me tell you, it was pure torture. I love to dance the night away."

Tommy wasn't sure he was liking what he was hearing at all.

"So who is firing these ghost bullets and why?"

K.J. signed heavily. "As in the real world, in this ghost realm, there are two sides to everything. We are in a battle for the future."

"And which side are we on?" Jewel asked.

"You are agents who work for the agency, as I told you in Montana, called "Ghost of a Chance.""

"And the other side is called what?"

"The Brigade," K.J. said. "You know those two brothers you took care of in the diner after I left? That was really nifty by the way, how you got them to feel the pain and pee their pants like that. Had me rolling in laughter and if I hadn't been in a compromising situation, I would have given you both a standing ovation. Well, I sort of did, but with a different part standing, if you get my drift."

Jewel just held up a hand. "More information than we need on that topic."

K.J. just stuck his tongue out at her and then smiled.

"So what about those two," Tommy asked.

"Those are the type recruited by the Brigade when they die."

"Why?" Tommy asked, feeling completely puzzled. "What's the fight?"

"K.J. looked a little flustered. "As I said, we are in a battle for the future. Both our bosses and the Brigade bosses can see possible futures. And both try to direct the present to get to the future they want. Our bosses want peace and democracy and Brigade bosses feed on the energy of anger and destruction and would rather have anarchy than stability for who knows what silly reason."

"How and where has this played out?" Jewel asked.

"Everywhere for centuries and centuries," K.J. said. "Small things and huge things. For example, there were major battles ahead of the Bush/Gore presidential fight that went on for years ahead of the actual election. I was involved in a couple of those fights. We lost a few battles big time, so Bush ended up winning and there ended up being two wars and everyone completely ignoring how the climate is changing. Chaos, death, and anarchy. The Brigade bosses thrive on it."

Tommy just sat there silent. He had no idea what to think. Jewel seemed to be looking at her hands in her lap, clearly thinking as well.

Finally, Tommy had another question. "So how do we know a Brigade agent when we see one?"

"Honestly," K.J. said, "if they weren't as stupid and slow as a high school dropout smoking too much of the funny weed, you wouldn't. Kind of like those two brothers. But when they join the Brigade, they are issued weapons. I've never seen a Brigade member walking around without machine guns full of ghost bullets. They love those guns more than I love a good blow job."

"They have guns?" Jewel asked. "Seriously? Dead people walking around with guns?"

Tommy felt the same way. Just flat stunned.

K.J. nodded. "They are horrid shots and dumb as hell, but you still don't want to find yourself in front of one of those bullets, as I said."

"So how do we fight them?" Tommy asked. "Do we have weapons with ghost bullets or something?"

"Can you see me carrying a gun?" K.J. asked, laughing. "That would do really bad things to my nails and I'm sure I'd scream and drop the gun and run in

the other direction the moment I fired the first shot."

"You didn't answer my question," Tommy said.

K.J. pointed to the side of his head. "We outthink them. Ghost of a Chance recruits brains like you two."

"So let me get this straight," Tommy said. "We can't really die again, but we can get hurt."

"Yes, but you recover faster than in real life."

Tommy nodded to that. Didn't like it, but he nodded to it and then asked his next question. "We have to go against people with machine guns unarmed. And we do assignments that might change the future, but we don't know how. Do I have all that?"

K.J. smiled. "But don't forget the great-tasting food, free time, and wonderful sex. Plus you get to help others along the way."

"Oh, yeah," Tommy said, "How could I forget that?"

"You had better not forget that sex part," Jewel said, smiling at him.

K.J. covered his mouth in fake shock and surprise.

And that made Tommy laugh.

Twenty-six

"SO WHAT'S THIS assignment we are supposed to do?" Jewel asked, feeling a little stunned that she and Tommy had actually been recruited to fight in a war she didn't really understand yet.

K.J. looked serious.

He stood and went over to one of the big windows and indicated they should come with him.

As Tommy got near one window, he noticed a square thing floating high in the air, clearly not flying, just floating in one spot. "What's that?"

Jewel was stunned. She had never seen anything like it before. She had no idea how it stayed up there. It looked to be the size of a large room.

K.J. looked up. "Oh, that's one of the gambling god's or hotel god's offices. Not sure which one. I don't pay any attention to that side of things. I stay on the ghost side."

"Gambling gods?" Jewel asked a moment before Tommy could.

K.J. waved away the question. "Trust me, don't worry about it at the moment. They only deal with the present, not the future, and work with Ghost of a Chance at times against the Brigade. But first you have a great deal of things to learn and a job to do. You can learn all the organizations and structures later. What I need you both to focus on is that tall building in the downtown area."

Jewel looked at where K.J. was pointing. Tommy had said earlier that was the downtown Las Vegas area. Right now they were out on what was called "The Strip."

"That's the Golden Nugget, right?" Tommy asked.

"You got it," K.J. said. "My bosses tell me that a powerful senator, which one doesn't matter, will be there in two days, doing who knows what to whom. My gut sense is that he likes little boys, but that's just me guessing."

"What's going to happen," Jewel asked.

"The Brigade is going to try to cause the senator to have a stroke, more than likely while in a compromising position or two, and thus swing the balance of the Senate. Your job is to not let them cause the senator to have a stroke in a bad position."

"How could they cause the senator to have a stroke?" Tommy asked.

Jewel knew and didn't want to think about it, but K.J. turned to her. "You want to answer that for your boyfriend, Doc?"

"You know how we unblocked the pain dampening agents in those two in the diner?"

"Ahh, that was just wonderful," K.J. said.

Tommy nodded, suddenly clearly starting to understand where she was headed.

"If the senator has a weak blood vessel in his head, a fast increase in blood pressure could cause it to blow out. We could cause it to happen easily."

She never wanted to think about ever doing that to anyone, and if she was asked to, she would decline. Killing was not why she became a doctor.

"Oh," Tommy said. Then he turned to K.J. "What's to stop these same people from following the Senator back to Washington and doing the same thing."

"Nothing," K.J. said, "and if they did, it wouldn't matter to the future, from what I was told when I asked the same question. What's important is they do it here, in two days, in his room at the Golden Nugget around six in the afternoon. More than likely to discredit the senator because of something he's doing at the time. I honestly don't question why. Gives me a headache."

"So we save the senator's life in two days and that's the mission?" Jewel asked.

"That's the mission from what I understand it at the moment," K.J. said, smiling. "Now, go get some food and do all the other things later that you heterosexuals do to each other and then test out some of your ghost skills tomorrow. The senator doesn't arrive in town for two days, so you got some time."

"Any hints," Tommy asked.

"About sex?" K.J. asked. "Trust me big guy, you wouldn't like what I would suggest."

Jewel laughed.

Tommy blushed slightly and then said, "No, I mean about how to fight."

"Remember when you are inside a live human, you can't be seen," K.J. said. "The Brigade carry machine guns, so when they are inside a live person, you can still see their guns. They are not rocket scientists, thankfully, and they do love their guns. I'm betting a lot of them sleep with the things and more than likely use them for sex toys."

Tommy nodded and Jewel couldn't think of another question. She was sure she had them, just couldn't think of a one at the moment.

K.J. said, "Well, better get back and see if there is any water left in my hot tub. And see if anyone is up for a rematch. All these questions have me all fired up again."

He smiled at Tommy, then winked at Jewel and vanished.

"I'm really starting to like him," Jewel said, moving over and putting her arm through Tommy's arm as they stood staring out the window at the downtown area. It felt wonderful to be with him. In all her life she had never felt this comfortable with anyone.

Of course, she had never been dead before, but she didn't think that had much to do with how she was feeling about Tommy at all.

The sun was slowly starting to sink below the hills to the west, painting everything in the city and surrounding desert with shades of red and pink.

The lights of the city were coming up. She was surprised at how really beautiful Las Vegas was. She had seen pictures of the lights, just never expected the beauty of it all.

"I wonder what the view's like up there," Tommy said, pointing to the floating office. "With this sunset, it would be really something."

"Maybe someday we'll find out," Jewel said, "but it's not bad right here."

He looked down at her and smiled. "Not bad at all."

And with that, she just had to kiss him.

Twenty-seven

TOMMY COULDN'T remember an evening he enjoyed as much. They had walked down a few flights of stairs to find someone waiting for the elevator, then rode down with them.

Instead of hitchhiking inside a live person, they stayed along the edge of the hallway after leaving the elevator area and made it into a wonderfully smelling steak restaurant off to one side of the casino. There was nothing like the smell of steaks sizzling on an open grill mixed with the smell of freshly baked bread.

He couldn't believe how hungry he was and when they moved inside the restaurant and the smell hit Jewel, she said she was so hungry, she could eat a chair leg.

"I think the steaks will be better," he said. "Let me get us a table."

He moved over and touched the shoulder of one of the greeters named Tami who was seating people and marking off tables that were occupied on a big chart.

He could see in her mind that she was a young woman working her way through college. She had a test in physics she really needed to study for tomorrow, so she hoped she would get off early tonight, even though she could use the money. And at the moment, she was mad at her boyfriend for not remembering their third month anniversary.

Tommy planted the idea in her mind that a special table needed to be reserved for a few hours in case a special guest decided to show up.

She moved over to the reservation board and crossed off a table Tommy could tell was off in the back, out of sight from the front area.

Tommy nodded and moved back over to where Jewel waited, out of the traffic pattern.

"Around the corner in the back," he said.

Then as a waiter set a bottle of white wine on a table nearby and opened it, Tommy took the ghost version of the bottle and they set off toward their table.

Tommy set the bottle down on the cloth-covered table and they both turned to go back to the exit from the kitchen.

The first waiter coming out had a tray of Caeser salads in large bowls, already mixed.

Tommy pointed and Jewel nodded, so they both grabbed a ghost salad and headed back to the table.

"This feels like a buffet," Tommy said, sitting down and grabbing a fork and digging in.

"It kind of does," Jewel said, laughing, as she also dug in.

About halfway through the fantastic salad, he looked up. "K.J. said the food would taste better, but this is crazy good."

"Better than that," she said.

They just ate, then went back to the exit from the kitchen and waited for

a waiter carrying a tray of plates with steaks on them.

They both grabbed a plate as he went by and went back to the table. Tommy grabbed a basket of fresh soft rolls from a table near his and Jewel scored them two glasses of water.

For Tommy, the steak tasted so good, he didn't want to stop eating long enough to even talk. And clearly Jewel felt the same way. Granted, it had been a long time since that breakfast in her cabin in Montana. But not that long, not long enough to make this medium-rare top sirloin and asparagus spears in butter taste so good.

He cleaned his plate completely just a moment before Jewel did.

"Think ghosts can get fat?" she asked.

"With this incredible-tasting food," he said, "I'd like to try."

"I'm going to have to go out for a run in the morning to work this off. I don't ever remember eating like that."

"I sure don't remember a steak tasting that good before."

They sat and sipped their wine, watching the people around them, and talking. Tommy was amazed at how easy it was for them to just talk about everything. They had only known each other for two days. Two very traumatic days, true, but he felt like he had already known her for years.

After dinner, Tommy grabbed a basket of rolls and another bottle of open wine from a table they passed, then headed back to the elevators, again staying to the edge of the wall to avoid contact.

Jewel got a blonde woman with a short skirt in the elevator to punch their floor, then when Jewel pulled back, she smiled at Tommy. "She's a high-priced escort headed for a date with a regular customer and his wife. She likes them a lot."

Tommy just shook his head. "We're not in Buffalo Jump, Montana, anymore, that's for sure."

"Are you saying that kind of thing wouldn't happen in Montana?" she asked, laughing.

"Oh, I'm sure it does," he said, "but not with someone who looks like that."

"From what I saw," Jewel said, smiling, "the couple she is meeting are very attractive people as well."

He turned to her and held up the wine. "Are you saying we should go watch? Maybe even ride along with one of them in the process?"

He laughed when she blushed and shook her head a little too quickly.

It looked as if he had just found an area just a little beyond Jewel's range of desires. If she asked him, he would have to admit, it was just outside his as well. But now that they were ghosts, it looked like they could sure watch others have sex if they wanted.

And for some reason, sex was sure a lot more open now that he was a ghost and could see people's thoughts. Amazing how many people thought about sex or had different sexual desires than they showed on the outside.

And with Jewel, sex was a lot more fun as well.

And over the next two hours, both in the big tub and in the bed, he had more fun with sex than he could remember ever having.

Wow, what a first night in Las Vegas.

Twenty-eight

THE NEXT MORNING, Jewel let Tommy sleep and showered and got dressed before waking him up with a long kiss. She loved how he felt, how he smelled, and how he kissed.

"That was nice," he said after she pulled back. "What time is it?"

"About nine-thirty," she said.

"Wow, haven't slept this late in a long time."

She laughed. "The life of a ghost isn't bad, is it?"

"Not at all," he said, smiling and motioning for her to come back and join him in bed.

"If I do that," she said, we won't get out of the room for hours."

"And that's bad how?" he asked, smiling.

She wanted to crawl back in bed with him, but she was also hungry and desperately needed to go for a run to clear her thoughts.

"I'm going for a short run around some back streets," she said. "How about I meet you in the buffet in thirty minutes. They will serve breakfast for another hour."

"Deal," he said.

She bent over and kissed him again, then pulled away, even though she didn't want to, and headed for the door. The wine bottle and basket of rolls they had brought with them from the restaurant last night were gone from the coffee table in front of the couch. Clearly K.J. was right, if they didn't touch something in a number of hours, it vanished.

That meant never having to do dishes again. She was really starting to like this ghost living.

She ran down four flights of stairs, going slow to get loosened up, checking at each floor to see if anyone was waiting for the elevator, but no one was until the fifth floor down. Somehow, in the small confines of the elevator, she managed to not touch the elderly couple who got on.

There was an emergency exit near the elevators on the main floor and she went through that and out into the warm morning sun near some restaurant supply doors and dumpsters tucked in behind the building.

The sun and warmth felt heavenly. She had been so cold all winter in Montana. Now this just felt perfect.

And it was stunningly quiet. Inside the noise was a constant drumbeat from the casino and all the talking. But outside, even with the traffic sounds, it seemed almost silent.

She headed down a side street lined with a construction area and palm trees, moving slowly at first, then finally striding at her normal pace. It felt great, perfectly normal.

There weren't many people on the sidewalks of the back streets behind the MGM Grand, so she had no trouble doing a quick mile into a residential area and then back, going in through the emergency door of the MGM near the restaurant.

Inside the sounds of the casino hit her solidly again. She wound her way through the crowds, mostly moving at the same speed as everyone, and managed to get to the ornate buffet while brushing only one person, a young woman who was hung over and wasn't sure she could eat.

The poor woman didn't remember much about last night and had woken up naked and wrapped in a blanket on a couch, not something that usually happened to her.

Jewel was glad to see that the buffet was huge and mostly empty, so she took a table near the back, not one that anyone would likely want to sit at. On the way to the table she took an orange juice from one table that the person hadn't yet touched and a glass of water from another.

There was no sign of Tommy, but that didn't surprise her. More than likely he had fallen back asleep.

As she sat sipping on the orange juice, enjoying watching the few people that were in the restaurant, a man with a hotel security uniform on came in and started toward her.

She was fairly certain she couldn't be seen, but since it had only been a few days, the confidence wasn't high.

The security guard, a guy with a slight gut and a blue uniform walked straight at her. Then he stopped a few feet short and said, "Young lady, you know that taking ghost food robs the human person of necessary ghost nutrients vital to their health in the afterlife?"

She jerked back, stunned that the guard could see her.

The guy was smiling.

Then it dawned on her what was happening. "Tommy, let that poor guy go."

Tommy stepped from the security guard smiling and came over and kissed her.

The poor security guard blinked twice, then looked around, muttered something about needing to get more sleep, and headed back for the entrance.

"Is that poor guy going to be all right?" Jewel asked.

"He needs to lose about thirty pounds," Tommy said, "and stop playing the horses, but otherwise, yes. I thought I'd test the ride-along and it works great."

"I could see that," she said. Then she stood and said simply, "Food."

They both headed for the buffet to start off their second full day of being dead.

Dead in Las Vegas. Beats the hell out of Buffalo Jump, Montana.

Twenty-nine

TOMMY HAD BEEN stunned how easy it was to get inside the security guard and just give him suggestions as to what to do and say and where to walk and he did it. And he knew that the guard would have no way of knowing he had been directed, or even what he did while directed.

The guy just thought he had daydreamed and ended up in a strange place. Tommy had done that a few times himself and now he wondered if some ghost had been directing him.

But K. J. was right. Having that ability to direct someone and not be seen was a very powerful weapon.

After breakfasts, once again some of the best-tasting buffet food he had ever eaten, they went back up to their suite and Jewel changed from her running clothes into something more suited for the warm day ahead. They were both excited about testing some of their new powers and seeing Las Vegas at the same time.

They had decided that their best bet was to get downtown and explore the Golden Nugget first, check out the entire area, then take a look around the rest of the town and some of the hotels on the Strip as well.

And one of the keys was learning how to get around town easily. It seemed everyone in Las Vegas took cabs, so they headed out to stand out of the way near the MGM taxi stand, listening as people talked about where they were going.

But after fifteen minutes of no one going downtown, Tommy knew that they were going to have to take a person into control to just get there.

"Let's see if we can both be in the same person," Jewel said.

"Might as well try that right here," Tommy said. "Let me get in and in control, then you join me."

Jewel nodded.

He looked for the richest-looking guy he could find so that the extra cab fare wouldn't bother him.

There was a guy standing off to one side of the departure area, wearing a silk suit that had clearly been tailored for him. He had dark, perfectly cut hair and seemed bored. He looked like a model or a romance hero standing there with a briefcase and a small carry-on leather bag.

Tommy pointed to him.

Jewel nodded and said, "Yummy."

Tommy just shook his head and went over and merged with the guy. It turned out, the guy wasn't a model or a romance hero. But he was rich, and ran his own corporation that dealt with internet gaming and had his jet waiting for him at the airport to take him back to the San Francisco area after meetings here the last two days. His name was Rocky Manning

Tommy had the guy motion in Jewel's direction that she should join him and Jewel came over and merged with the guy as well.

It felt like he and Jewel were suddenly in a small old phone booth, or a tiny broom closet. Only they both could see out of the guy's eyes, feel what he was feeling, hear everything going on around him, and read his thoughts.

"This is cozy," Jewel said, pressing up against Tommy.

"Now don't start that in here," Tommy said, laughing as she pressed her crotch against him and rubbed. "We'll get this guy arrested."

"Spoilsport. So get us a cab," Jewel said, putting one arm around Tommy and clearly settling in just to let him do the driving. Tommy had no idea how the two of them could fit inside a guy smaller than Tommy, but they clearly did.

The guy had been waiting patiently for a limo to arrive to take him to the airport. Tommy got him to go over to the bellman and slip him twenty dollars. "Changed my mind, I need a cab."

The bellman nodded and within two minutes, they were inside a cab, the guy's briefcase and bag on the seat beside them, and headed toward the Golden Nugget downtown.

"Should we stay in here or spread out?" Jewel asked.

"Let's see if we can do this for a period of time comfortably," Tommy said. "I think we need to test just about everything we can test."

"Fine by me," Jewel said, again rubbing her crotch against Tommy.

"Now see what you have done," Tommy said, indicating to Jewel that their poor ride now had an erection.

"Now isn't that interesting," Jewel said.

Tommy could feel Jewel moving around in the guy's mind.

"What are you doing?"

"Just remembering parts of my medical school and what parts of the brain do what," Jewel said. "Figured it might come in handy like that pain thing we did to those two."

"Very good idea," Tommy said.

The guy they were riding in suddenly moaned softly and then to Tommy's horror, had an orgasm in his pants.

"Found that control just fine," Jewel said, laughing.

"The poor guy," Tommy said. "He's going to be mortified when he realizes what happened."

"Just plant a really good dream about his assistant he was with last night and when we leave, he'll think that caused it."

"It does look like they had a great time in that hot tub," he said, laughing. "And this morning in the shower. No wonder he was so relaxed waiting for his limo."

"Hang on," Jewel said and Tommy could sense her worry and sudden panic. "What happened to the assistant? Where did she go after their shower this morning? Why wasn't she going to be with him on the plane back. Can you access that information in his mind? I don't see it."

"Wow," Tommy said. "I don't either. Her name is Annie Small and she has worked for him for six months."

Tommy had the guy pull out his cell phone and look at the numbers. Annie Small's number was there. But when he dug a little deeper into the guy's thoughts, Tommy also got a sense that a man named Monte was to take care of her.

"What does "take care of mean?" Jewel asked, seeing the same thought.

"This guy honestly doesn't know or seem to worry about it at all," Tommy said. And for Tommy, that worried him a lot.

Tommy had the guy call Annie's number.

A moment later Annie answered, "Yes, Mr. Manning."

"Checking to make sure all was going well," Tommy had the man say.

"Perfectly, sir," she said, clearly all business when outside the hotel room shower. "We are about to take off for Dallas. I'll report back after the first meeting, sir."

"Thank you," Miss Small," Tommy had the guy say. "Safe trip."

And then Tommy had the guy hang up and put his phone back in his pocket.

"So no wonder we couldn't see her," Jewel said. "She left before he got dressed and he wasn't worried about her at all, so he gave her no thought at all. Good lesson there."

"I'll give him a really good dream," Tommy said, "to explain the mess in his pants, and a feeling that he needs to treat her better and think of her more often."

"Perfect," Jewel said as the cab driver pulled into the Golden Nugget arrival area and Tommy had the guy hand the driver a hundred and say, "Keep the change."

Then Tommy climbed them out of the cab, the briefcase and bag in the guy's hand as Jewel rode along comfortably.

"That actually works," Tommy said, turning as the cab drove away.

"It does," Jewel said.

Tommy moved the guy over to a sheltered place out of the traffic and said, "Ready to jump ship?"

"You got him all prepared?"

"He's going to discover he likes Miss Small a lot more than he thought he did," Tommy said.

With that, Jewel moved away from Rocky Manning and a moment later Tommy followed her into the warmth of the early morning.

They both stood there watching as poor old millionaire Rocky shook his head and looked around, clearly surprised at where he was. Then suddenly he looked down at the wet spot on his crotch and instantly put the briefcase in front of it.

Rocky moved over to the bellman and said, "Cab please." He handed the guy a twenty and two minutes later good old Rocky Manning, their first ride together, was headed off toward the airport without them.

"That was fun," Jewel said, taking Tommy's hand.

"And even more importantly," Tommy said. "We can do it. Who knows when that's going to come in handy?"

"Handy? Jewel asked. "Good old Rocky didn't even need any hands."

Tommy laughed and kissed her. "Who knew such a horny and sexy woman lived in Buffalo Jump, Montana."

"As we're discovering," Jewel said, smiling. "You never know what's just below the surface of a person."

"Boy is that the truth," Tommy said. "But I have to tell you, I really like what's just below the surface of your clothes."

She kissed him again for that one.

Thirty

THE GOLDEN NUGGET was nothing at all what Jewel expected. It was beautiful and ornate, in a comfortable way, with the center of the entire hotel being an outdoor pool enclosed with glass from the hotel itself.

And over the center of the pool sat a massive fish tank full of huge sharks and other sea creatures in deep blue water.

Staying inside the hotel, you could walk around the giant pool area on three sides. And there were many very attractive women and men out there sunbathing so that everyone walking inside could see them.

And there were a few others who should have never been allowed out there.

Jewel was really shocked at one woman who had to be in her thirties, at least, who stood no more than five-two and must have weighed over three hundred pounds. She was out there so everyone could see her in a far too tight bright pink bathing suit that left no fat roll to the imagination.

Jewel and Tommy were standing off to one side of one of the main hallways as traffic went past, looking around. Jewel pointed to the pink-suited woman on the other side of the glass. "You want to explain that to me."

"Las Vegas," Tommy said, shaking his head. "She doesn't know anyone here in Las Vegas, so who back home is going to care that anyone here sees her like that?"

"So no shame and enjoying herself," Jewel said, admiring the woman's courage. Jewel never wanted to even wear a swimming suit when she got more than five pounds overweight. She couldn't imagine the confidence and self-image that woman must have to be in front of thousands of people per hour dressed like that. Or not dressed as the case might be.

She and Tommy managed to walk around the pool and into an older wing of the hotel, then back around the pool again to a newer tower without brushing through more than three or four people.

In the new tower area, there was a second front desk with a huge fish tank behind it that filled the middle area of what looked like a fancy dinner restaurant. There was no one at the counter and a woman behind the counter looked bored waiting for someone to come up. She was shifting from side to side slowly.

"Let me see if I can get the senator's room number and when he arrives," Jewel said.

Tommy nodded, so she headed through the big front desk and merged with the woman.

The poor woman had to pee really bad, and the person who was working at the desk with her was late getting back. Since she was the supervisor, she was going to have a thing or two to say to him.

Jewel forced the thinking of having to pee down and got the woman to the hotel reservations screen. A moment later she had pulled up the reservation for the senator and his staff. It was blocked, but she used her supervisor status to get through with the late-arriving employee's identification number.

It seemed the senator and his party was taking over two 23rd floor suites at one end of a short hallway. He was checking in the day after tomorrow at 2 p.m. and would be staying for only one night. Both suites were one bedroom and very nice.

Jewel cleared the board and then made sure the woman didn't leave any trace in the system that she had accessed that information from her board, so if anyone checked, it would look like the guy who was late coming back had done it.

Jewel then left the woman and moved back to Tommy.

"Got it?" he asked.

"Got it," Jewel said, "I'll tell you about it in a minute, but right now I really have to pee."

Tommy glanced over at the woman shifting slowly from foot to foot and then laughed.

She hadn't felt that she needed to pee before taking the woman's mind over, but now it was really strong. Power of suggestion or reality, she didn't know, but she didn't want to test it.

Jewel headed at a quick march back down the hallway to where they had passed restrooms with Tommy following close behind.

Thirty-one

THEY SPENT THE rest of the afternoon exploring along the giant Fremont Street covered mall area, looking into gift shops and playing tourist. Tommy was impressed at how nice the entire area felt. Tourist, yet welcoming and comfortable, at least as much as a casino culture could be welcoming.

They went back into the Golden Nugget and were heading for the buffet when they passed the poker room.

"Shall we test a little something," Tommy asked, pulling Jewel off to one side near some empty slot machines and out of the traffic pattern.

"We got forty-eight hours until the senator arrives to do just that," Jewel said.

"I want to see what it would be like to play some poker," Tommy said pointing to a table with five guys around it. From the looks of the chips and such, it was a no-limit hold'em game.

"This should be interesting to watch," Jewel said.

"Don't play poker?" he asked.

"Strip poker once in high school. Bored and scared at the same time."

Tommy just was never going to be surprised at Jewel. She had so many levels that he wanted to keep learning about.

"You're going to have to tell me all about that later," he said, giving her a smile.

"Have fun," she said as she moved over and stood with her back against a wall close to the table.

Tommy picked a young man with brown hair who had the least amount of chips at the table and sat down with him. The guy was named Richmond and he played every day in one room or another in Vegas. He was good, but he didn't make a lot of money at it. Just barely enough for a small apartment, a car payment on a used Lexus, and food, mostly with coupons at buffets.

The guy wanted to prove to his family and friends back home that he had the ability to play and be a professional, but after six months now in Vegas, he was starting to have his doubts. He had a master's degree in math and really had no desire to teach college.

Tommy stood, staying attached to the guy as the dealer shuffled and started to deal. "This kid's name is Richmond and he is a good guy," Tommy said to Jewel. "I'm going to see if I can give him a boost.

As Richmond looked at his cards, Tommy could see he had a pair of tens. A decent starting hand, but not great. The kid would have to play it right or fold it.

Tommy reached over and picked up the ghost cards for the man across from Tommy. He had a king-seven suited. Horrid.

The next guy over came out with a twenty dollar raise with a pair of sevens. The right play.

The next guy folded before Tommy could see his cards, but the guy next to Richmond hesitated and Tommy picked up his cards to see a pair of nines.

The guy called. Richmond had the best hand, but he had no way of knowing it. Both the raiser and the caller were good players, so chances are they had strong hands. Richmond was about to fold, but Tommy stopped him.

Then in Richmond's mind he put the simple thought, "The reason these guys run over you is that you play scared and they can see it."

Richmond stopped.

Tommy could see that the realization that Richmond had been playing scared made sense to him. He looked down. He had about seventy in front of him.

Tommy smiled when Richmond pushed his chips forward. "Raise all in."

The initial raiser stared at Richmond, then folded his small pair. The guy beside Richmond folded as well, and Richmond took down the forty dollars plus blinds.

Tommy sat with the kid for two more hands as the kid went back to tossing bad cards away.

On the fourth hand, Richmond called the five dollar blind with a ten jack. Three others called and the first three cards on the board came out Ace, queen, six, missing Richmond completely.

"Aggressive," Tommy planted in his mind.

Richmond nodded, as if understanding and bet out thirty. He got one caller.

Next card on the board was a four.

Tommy wasn't even going to look at what the other players' cards were. If he was going to help this kid take the next step to making his dream, he had to help him cleanly.

Tommy nodded and bet out forty bucks.

The guy who had called him the first time looked at the board and then called.

Richmond clearly thought "The guy is waiting for a flush. More than likely has a pair of kings."

The last card was a jack that made Richmond's straight, but did not match the suit on the board.

Richmond didn't even hesitate. He shoved his entire stack of chips forward again.

The guy shook his head and tossed in his cards and Richmond pulled the pot once again.

"Alternate timid and scared with aggressive," Tommy planted in Richmond's mind. "They won't know what hit them."

Again Richmond nodded and Tommy stood and moved over to Jewel.

"Was it fun?" she asked.

"It was because Richmond there is a good kid with a dream. Felt good to help him a little."

Jewel looked at Tommy. "When did you learn how to play top-level poker?"

Tommy laughed, not wanting to tell her right there that he had earned some of his way through college by playing online poker before they banned it. And that one of his drunken trips to Vegas was playing in the World Series of Poker main event. He hadn't started drinking until he got knocked out of the tournament on the third day.

"After you tell me about your strip poker," Tommy said, "I'll tell you about how I learned how to play poker."

"Deal," Jewel said, giving him a sexy smile with those green eyes that promised a wonderful evening ahead.

They stood there watching the table for another ten minutes in which time Richmond took down another big pot.

Suddenly Tommy had an idea. He turned to Jewel. "How about I get inside the senator and plant in his mind that he really, really needs to play poker after he gets done with his meeting here?"

"So he doesn't go back to his room until very late?" Jewel said.

"Poker rooms are open all night," Tommy said, smiling. "How about he never goes back to his room? If I'm inside him, I can keep him alert and playing and winning until he needs to catch a flight."

"You think it might really be that easy to stop this attack?" Jewel asked.

Tommy had no doubt that it wouldn't be that easy to save this senator. "No, I don't. But it might be a start to a plan."

"And a good one," she said, nodding.

Thirty-two

BY THE TIME they got through most of their lunch in the sparsely filled Golden Nugget Buffet, Jewel had more questions about how to fight these other ghosts that neither of them had answers to.

She had thought that she would just have a salad for lunch after the huge dinner last night and breakfast this morning, but after the salad, she had gone back for some wonderful deep-fried shrimp, some freshly cut turkey, and some corn-on-the-cob dipped in butter.

And it all tasted wonderful.

"We need to talk with K.J. again," Jewel said, wiping some of the butter from the corn from her mouth and the side of her face. Ghost food was as messy as real food it seemed. Ghost food just tasted better, as if they were taking the essence of the food out of it.

Tommy nodded. Then he said into the air, "K.J., when you get a chance, we have some questions."

This time K.J. appeared in a tight pink dress, black gloves up to his elbows, and bright red lipstick. He had a black, wide-brimmed felt hat on and he looked to Jewel like he was straight out of the 1940s. He was also wearing bright ruby shoes and carrying a wicker picnic basket with a pink ribbon on it.

The tight dress showed areas of K.J. that Jewel was sure he wanted to show. He clearly wasn't wearing any underwear at all under the tight cloth.

Tommy blinked twice, and Jewel was proud of him for not laughing or saying something.

"Like the outfit?" K.J. said, spinning around once before sitting in an extra chair at the table. "It's my costume for tonight's costume ball."

"What are you going as?" Jewel asked.

K.J. smiled. "A slutty old Queen Dorothy from the Wizard of Oz," he said. He reached into his basket and pulled out a long, pink penis-shaped vibrator.

"Meet Toto," he said, petting the long vibrator like it was a dog.

Jewel loved it and laughed. Tommy laughed, but looked just a little shocked. She liked that about him.

"So much about my coming night's adventures," K.J. said. "Or better put, my night's coming adventures."

He laughed at that play on words and then looked at Tommy. "What's the questions?"

"If the senator is killed playing poker, will that cause the problems?"

Jewel watched as K.J. seemed to be listening off into the distance, then he came back into his dark eyes. "No. What causes the problem is if the senator dies in a compromising position in his room with a teenaged girl."

"Good," Tommy said.

"If one or both of us are inside a person," Jewel asked, "and someone from the Brigade wants to get inside, how do we stop them?"

"Fill the entire body," K.J. said. "Did you try riding in the same person?"

"Yes," Jewel said.

"And it felt like we were both in there, cuddled together," Tommy said.

Jewel nodded.

"If you don't want someone to join you," K.J. said, "just imagine yourself filling every inch of the person's body, matching the person in size and shape. No one can get in then with you. Might need to practice that a few times."

"But that would let the Brigade know there was a Ghost Agent inside the person, right?" Tommy asked.

"Afraid so," K.J. said, nodding, his big felt hat flopping as he did so.

"So if the Brigade agent started firing at the person I was inside," Tommy asked, "would I be hit?"

"Not if you went to the person's toes," K.J. said. "Remember you can move around inside of people as much as you want, be as big or as small as you need to be inside there."

Both Tommy and Jewel nodded. Jewel could see all kinds of possibilities, but she wasn't sure how any of them would work.

"Looks like you two agents have some practicing to do before you start your first mission," K.J. said.

He stood and twirled around in his tight, pink dress and ruby-red slippers. Then he pulled Toto from the basket and waving the big pink vibrator he said, "Me and the big dog here have some baying at the moon to do."

Then he clicked his heals together three times saying three times, "There's no place like an orgy."

Then he vanished, leaving them sitting with their mouths open.

Thirty-three

AFTER LUNCH BUT still in the buffet, in quick practice sessions, Tommy occupied a man completely and Jewel failed in trying to join him, saying that it felt like she was just running into a normal person.

Then they reversed that a few times on different people in the buffet, Jewel in the women, Tommy in the men.

To Tommy, when Jewel fully occupied the woman, it felt as if he could actually touch the woman. Tommy figured that had some interesting possibilities down the road, but not for this first mission.

Then they both climbed into a woman who wanted to go back for another helping, but was afraid of what her husband would say about her weight. He wanted her to stay very, very thin.

They had her stand up anyway and go for a third plate of food, and while she was walking and they were controlling her, they went to her feet, Jewel in the right foot, Tommy in the left. Worked fine.

Tommy felt like he was a tiny person inside a giant. He could still see out of the woman's eyes and control her, but from a distance.

"That was weird," Jewel had said after they got the woman back to the table and her frowning husband. "As a doctor, having that skill would have sure come in handy to explore what was wrong with someone."

"You're still a doctor," Tommy said. "And it's going to come in real handy tomorrow, I hope."

After a bunch of experiments with other customers, they decided to head back out to the MGM Grand.

Tommy took over a cab driver just to make sure he could drive while in control of someone. He wanted to make sure that was possible and thankfully, it was.

After they got back to their hotel and got out of the cab in the huge parking area, Jewel practiced walking a woman into the hotel while in her right foot.

"Don't let me join you," Tommy said as they neared the front desk of the hotel in the huge front lobby and then he just tried to step into the woman. No luck. Jewel had gone from the woman's foot to filling her completely in just a fraction of a second.

"Well done," Tommy said as Jewel appeared out of the woman, smiling. "That seemed almost instantaneous."

"Speed of thought," Jewel said, watching the woman walk away.

"What's wrong?" Tommy asked.

Jewel turned and looked at him and Tommy could see a real depth of seriousness in her eyes, something in their short time together he hadn't seen much of yet. He liked it and it worried him.

"As you said, I'm still a doctor."

Tommy nodded. "You are. So what's wrong?"

Jewel pointed at that woman. "After you said that, I decided just how much I could sort of scan about a person. So as I entered her and went to her foot, I also scanned her body. Amazing I can do that like that. Just amazing."

"But she has something wrong?" Tommy asked, glancing over at what appeared to be a perfectly healthy mid-thirties woman waiting in line at the desk. She wasn't thin, but she wasn't heavy, either. She had short black hair and looked like a businesswoman of some sort by the pantsuit she wore and comfortable shoes.

"She does," Jewel said, also looking at the woman and nodding. "She used to be a smoker and she has the start of lung cancer in her right lung. Still small, but it needs to be caught now."

Tommy kept staring at the woman. It was amazing what they were learning about people by just suddenly being inside them. He knew that three days ago, when he was still alive, the very idea of another person poking around inside his body would have appalled him and made him angry.

Now it was starting to feel natural for him to do as they practiced more.

"Did you give her a suggestion that she have a check-up?" Tommy asked.

"I did," Jewel said. "But she already has one scheduled in eight months and her doctor won't catch it in time, if they even notice it then."

"Would they catch it if they did a chest x-ray of her lungs?" Tommy asked.

"Without a doubt," Jewel said. "The tumor is big enough."

Tommy looked again at the woman still waiting for an open clerk to check in. She looked perfectly healthy. "So let's send her to the hospital."

"How do you suggest we do that?" Jewel asked.

"We have two choices, as I see it," Tommy said, smiling at Jewel. "We either get inside her and trigger some sort of breathing attack that forces her to be taken by an ambulance to the hospital."

"Think we can do that?" Jewel asked, a serious expression on her face and in her green eyes, clearly trying to figure out how medically she could do that.

"I'm sure there's a lot of things that we can do that we don't know about yet," Tommy said, smiling at the woman he was quickly starting to fall deeply for. "But I think my second way is much better."

"What's that?"

"We just jump back inside her and make her take herself to the hospital," Tommy said, "When we get her there, she can complain of intense shortness of breath and maybe we can make her look

like she's passed out there to get some quick action. Then we jump into the doctor and suggest to the doctor that they need to look for a lung tumor."

Jewel just shook her head, smiling. "I'm still not thinking like I can control other people."

"Too many patients not doing as you asked, huh?"

"Far too many," she said, laughing. "So let's go save this woman's life and then come back to our suite."

"And then what?" Tommy asked.

"Then we practice something else that has to do with a shower and a big bed."

"I like that kind of practice," Tommy said, laughing, as they moved toward the woman in line.

Thirty-four

JEWEL STRETCHED, NAKED on the big bed. She must have dozed off a little. Tommy was on his back, a sheet covering him from the waist down. She was pretty sure he was asleep.

And her stomach was rumbling, she was so hungry. It was well after eight in the evening and that lunch in the buffet had been a long time ago.

They had taken the woman to the hospital to save her life, then come back and had some wonderful times in the shower and then back here on the bed.

Jewel turned to lie on her side, facing him, just staring at his handsome face and watching him breath lightly, his strong chest moving up and down.

Sex with Tommy was so much more intense than she had ever experienced before. Some of that might be from being a ghost, but she had a hunch that sex with

Tommy would have been wonderful even if they were alive.

They just fit together, and she was starting to wonder what she had done before the last three days without him in her life. They had already packed a lot of living in their deaths, and she had a hunch it wasn't going to slow down any time soon.

At least she hoped it wouldn't.

"You ready to go again?" he asked without opening his eyes.

She laughed and moved against him, cuddling under his arm and putting her head on his shoulder. Her stomach rumbled again. "Aren't you hungry?"

"Food instead of sex?" he asked.

"Oh, no chance of that," she said. "Just food before sex."

"In that case," he said. "I am hungry."

He hugged her and then kissed her and for a moment she had second thoughts on the order of importance. Then he pulled away and stretched before going for his clothes where he had taken them off near the bathroom. A lot of men didn't look that good without clothes on. He looked more like a Greek god statue. She could stare at that body for a very long time, of that she had no doubt.

As they got dressed, they ran over the plan they had for saving the senator tomorrow. They had worked it out in detail at the hospital and on the way back.

"So we meet the senator at the airport when his plane lands," she said.

Tommy nodded, then pulled on his shirt. "I jump inside the senator, but don't control him in any fashion, just ride along through his day while you follow and watch for Brigade members."

"Exactly," Jewel said, slipping into her running shoes. She was going to dinner in her jeans and WSU sweatshirt.

Tommy was wearing jeans and a dress shirt and tennis shoes as well.

"So when the senator is done and thinking about going back to his room," Tommy said, "I'll get him to sit down in a poker game and help him do some winning and really enjoy himself."

"That's when the Brigade will try to take him over," Jewel said, to get him to go to his room."

"I'll make sure that doesn't happen," Tommy said.

"You know, about a thousand things could go wrong with this plan," she said.

"We wing it if it does," he said, smiling at her.

In medicine, a doctor sometimes had to just make due with what was at hand. She knew that. It was one of the many things that attracted her to being a GP.

But winging on this mission just seemed really, really dangerous. And since she and Tommy had no idea about this Brigade, she felt unprepared and somewhat helpless.

And she hated that feeling.

"We need one more talk with K.J.," she said.

"I was just thinking that," Tommy said.

"But let's get some food first, then call him," she said as her stomach rumbled again.

"And with that I also agree," he said.

They went through the door to the suite and out into the hallway when two men came around the corner from the elevators.

Both looked like they hadn't shaved in months, both wore bib overalls, and both carried what looked like military-style machine guns.

Jewel knew that they hadn't been seen, so she shoved Tommy through the hotel room door they were passing and went after him.

He started to say something, but she put her finger to her lips, then whispered, "Brigade."

He nodded and eased toward the wall, keeping his eyes open and kneeling so that his face was near the bottom of the wall near the door. Then he eased through.

After a moment he pulled back and stood. He whispered, "They got their guns ready and went into our room."

"How did they know we were here?" Jewel asked in a hushed voice.

Tommy shook his head and indicated that she should follow him.

The hotel was a standard room, not one of the big suites like theirs. And no one had checked into the suite yet.

Tommy led her through the wall and into yet another identical room, also unoccupied.

Behind her, she heard gunfire, but it sounded off, like it was muffled in some fashion.

At the sound of the gunfire, Tommy picked up speed, moving through one room after another toward the elevators and the center stairwell, Jewel right with him.

They got to the stairwell and headed down at top speed, not slowing until they were five or six floors down.

Then Tommy stopped them.

Jewel was breathing slightly harder than normal. Luckily she was in such good shape or that would have been painful. Tommy didn't look like he was even bothered.

"K.J., need your help," Tommy said.

A few seconds later K.J. appeared with only a towel around his waist. His make-up was smeared and he looked more like a character out of Rocky Horror Picture Show than The Wizard of OZ.

K.J. looked around, then at them. "What happened?"

"Two men with machine guns went into our room and started firing," Tommy said.

"We were headed to dinner and saw them coming, so they didn't see us escape," Jewel said.

"Damn," K.J. said.

The next moment K.J. jumped them to a booth in the back of the buffet. Jewel found herself sitting across from Tommy and K.J. was standing there by the booth like a naked waiter.

"Get something to eat," K.J. said, "one of you watching, the other getting food. I'll get dressed and be right back."

He vanished without a single word of humor or a single joke.

And that bothered Jewel more than she wanted to admit.

Thirty-five

TOMMY INSISTED THAT he stand guard first and Jewel quickly filled a plate of food, even though she wasn't that hungry anymore. She knew she needed to eat.

Then she sat facing the crowded area outside the buffet while Tommy got some food.

They were both eating when K.J. appeared, now clearly showered and all make-up gone. He was dressed in what must have passed for San Francisco casual. Loafers, dark slacks, a light pink shirt, and a matching dark blazer with a rose in the pocket. His hair was still wet and combed back.

"What did these two look like?" K.J. asked, making Jewel slide over so that he could sit beside her and see the restaurant.

"Dirty coveralls without shirts," Jewel said, remembering them very clearly. "Black hair, dirty faces, work boots, and machine guns."

"Standard low-level Brigade men," K.J. said, shaking his head.

"How did they know we were there?" Tommy asked a fraction of a second before Jewel could.

"I honestly don't know that," K.J. said. "People above all three of us are working on that right now."

That was not the answer Jewel wanted, so she asked the next question that had her scared to death. "If we had still been sleeping and they shot us, what would have happened?"

"You would have woken up a couple days from now," K.J. said, "in pain, and it would have taken about a week to recover fully. Not fun."

"So they wouldn't have killed us," Tommy said.

K.J. frowned at Tommy and stuck his hand through the table and then brought it back up. "You're already dead, remember. You can be stopped with ghost bullets for a time, but you can't be killed. Painful though, so avoid getting shot if you can."

"Always thought that good advice when alive," Tommy said. "Sure can't imagine altering the thinking now."

K.J. nodded, still looking far too serious for Jewel's tastes.

"And you are saying that we can't fight back in any way?" Tommy asked.

"Well, I didn't exactly say that," K.J. said. "I just said we don't use guns."

"So I'm faced with one of those Brigade men in a hallway, what do I do?" Tommy asked.

Jewel really, really wanted to know the answer to that question.

"What you did," K.J. said. "Run, outthink them. I once had one lumbering after me and I got him to run right off an edge of a building. We may all be dead, but none of us can fly."

"You seem to be able to," Jewel said. "At least transport."

"They can't," K.J. said. "None of them can."

"Will we learn how?" Tommy asked. "Sure would help in tight situations."

"Given time, yes," K.J. said, nodding. "It's only been three days since you died, remember?"

Jewel was very glad to hear that eventually they would be able to just flick in and out, but she needed some larger answers.

"So tomorrow we're going to risk a lot of pain to save a senator some embarrassment," Jewel said. "Correct?"

K.J. nodded.

"Why?" Jewel asked. "I know you told us, but fill us in more on all the reasons we are risking a lot of pain for this."

K.J., still not joking at all, nodded. "There are two sides fighting in this realm we find ourselves in, this real world, but not-real world."

"Got that," Tommy said. "And we have been picked and saved from the white tunnel by your side. We got that. But who is our side, really? Who is the big boss?"

K.J. sighed and then looked around. Then he said simply, "Ghost of a Chance agents work ultimately for old man time himself. Father Time, whatever you want to call him."

For some reason, that was not at all what Jewel was expecting.

"The guy with the long beard and a staff?" Tommy asked.

"Actually," K.J. said, shaking his head, "he looks like any rich businessman, with light gray hair always kept perfectly, and expensive silk suits tailored to him. I always wanted to know who his suit maker was, but he won't tell me, just makes me squirm. He now calls himself Charles Aeon actually lives here in a gated community on the edge of town and has corporate offices all over the world."

Jewel just opened her mouth, then shut it. She had no idea what to ask next.

"Is he dead like us?" Tommy asked.

"Oh, heavens no," K.J. said, laughing. "He's one of the thousands of gods that roam all over the place. And that's not saying anything about all the superheroes working for the gods. Never know who's a god and who's a superhero. Being an agent is so much easier. There aren't that many of us. And we all work for Aeon. We got immediate bosses up the ladder, but it all ends at Aeon."

Jewel started to open her mouth and K.J. held his hand up. "More than enough time for questions about all the world of gods, superheroes and agents. You need to focus on tomorrow."

Jewel nodded and took a breath and asked the next logical question. "I understand we need to focus, but we need some reason to fight. If Father Time is the powerful old god, whom is he fighting? Who is trying to alter the future and who but him can even see it?"

"One of his own kids," K.J. said. "The kid holds a grudge because when he was born, Dad ate him."

"He did what?" Tommy asked, stunned.

"He spit him out later from what I understand," K.J. said, shuddering. "Sort of grosses me out, to be honest, and there's not a lot of things that gross me out."

Then Jewel saw a look of slight panic in K.J.'s eyes.

"If you ever meet the old guy," K.J. said, "don't mention it."

Jewel knew whom K.J. was talking about since she had studied mythology in undergraduate. She just never expected to die and find out it was all real, in some form or another.

She looked at Tommy, the man she was falling for more every moment, who looked very puzzled. "We're fighting the forces of Hades," Jewel said to Tommy. "The brother of Zeus, the son of Kronos."

"Yeah, all that," K.J. said, "Zeus runs everything now, the top dog, but they don't go by those names anymore."

Tommy shook his head. "If I wasn't dead and sitting here enjoying ghost food, I wouldn't believe a word of this. And honestly, I'm still having troubles."

Jewel understood Tommy's point exactly. "How long has this fight between father and son been going on?"

K.J. shrugged. "More centuries than I want to think about. Zeus forgave his father after the brothers defeated the old guy and the other Titans, from what I understand. But Hades never really did."

"So Hades wants to have the future be one way, Charles wants it another?" Tommy asked.

K.J. nodded. "Just like it was in your life, Tommy. You had rules and wanted them followed, others, like those two men you did a number on in the diner thought the world should be a darker and nastier place. Same fight. Just slightly different rules."

Now that was something Jewel understood. And from the way Tommy was nodding, he did too.

"So it's against the rules that we hurt the Brigade members?" Jewel asked.

K.J. laughed. "Heaven's no. We just don't carry guns. But you can sneak up behind one of them and hit them with a pan or bat if you want. I've done that a few times. Pans make such a wonderful sound."

Jewel glanced up and saw two members of the Brigade walking by. "We have company," she said.

"Let's follow them and see where they are going," K.J. said, standing.

"We're going to follow them?" Jewel asked, shocked.

"Sure," K.J. said. "Do they look like ghosts?"

"No," Jewel said, watching the two men as they headed for the lobby. They just looked like dirty construction workers carrying guns.

"To them, we don't look like ghosts either," K.J. said. "So just take his arm and walk like a couple enjoying the night in Las Vegas. I'll be close."

With that K.J. vanished.

Quickly she and Tommy headed out of the restaurant and got into a pace about forty steps behind the two men that had tried to shoot them with the machine guns they now carried slung over their shoulders.

Both men just walked through people, not even noticing. She wondered if the people felt anything.

She and Tommy moved around people, as if they were actually alive.

She had no idea where the two were headed.

But she had a hunch it wasn't anywhere classy.

Thirty-six

TOMMY FELT GOOD that they were following the two Brigade members. It felt good to be doing something, and even better to understand a little more about what they were fighting for.

In essence, he was a cop fighting for light and a good future, the bad guys wanted the world to be dark and nasty. Simple, he knew that, but for the moment, until they got a lot more explanation, it worked for him.

Good vs. bad. Got it. More than likely, as with anything, there were a thousand shades of gray between it all. He'd learn all that later.

One of the Brigade men merged with a guy getting into a taxi and the other Brigade man got into the cab as well.

Tommy pretended he had a communications link of some sort, like he used to have with the sheriff back in Buffalo Jump, and said simply into the air as they headed for an open cab. "K.J. stay with them. We'll follow along in a cab, but we might lose them."

"Got it," K.J.'s voice came back clearly. "They had the guy tell the driver to go to the airport."

"On our way," Tommy said.

Tommy climbed through the driver's door of a waiting cab and merged into the cab driver sitting behind the wheel, a single man named Parks from Indiana who was out trying to make a living in the sports book and driving cab in off hours. Tommy instantly knew the guy lived alone in a dive apartment out off the old Boulder Highway, dressed in suits and ties to go to what he called "the office" when in the MGM Grand sports book, but also liked wearing jeans and a t-shirt and driving cab and talking with people.

He had an ex-wife back in Indiana and a young daughter he saw every month when he flew back there and sent lots of money to and missed a great deal.

Parks had actually been doing pretty well at sports betting and had about a half million in a number of accounts. He really liked his life and driving cab, except for missing his daughter.

Tommy liked Parks and liked his attitude.

Jewel climbed into the front seat. Tommy got them moving toward the airport, using a fairly quick route that Parks knew and only took favorite customers. There was no way in the traffic to actually follow the other cab, so Tommy figured they might as well get there ahead of the Brigade men.

They rode in silence all the way to the airport and Tommy had Park just pull into the cab waiting area for pick-ups and left him with the feeling that it was too slow on The Strip so he had come out here to get a fare.

They slid out and both walked quickly toward the arrivals area.

They had just gotten there when K.J. said out of the air, "They are pulling up at the Southwest Airlines area."

"The Senator is coming in on Southwest tomorrow morning at seven," Jewel said. "I learned that from the information at the hotel desk."

Tommy just shook his head. "It looks like the fight for control of the Senator is going to be here, tonight, instead of in the poker room tomorrow night."

"K.J.," Jewel said into the air as they entered the terminal near the Southwest ticket counters. "On missions of this nature, how many of the Brigade do they normally send?"

"Two," K.J. said. "They honestly don't have that many soldiers, as the Brigade men like to think of themselves, around the world. As soon as you get settled with them in sight, I'll do some scouting, see if there are more in the area."

Tommy liked the sound of that a lot.

They moved over quickly to a couch area so that they could see the doors and sat down.

Tommy caught a glimpse of the men coming in the closest door and leaned over and hugged Jewel and kissed her, saying softly, "They are going to be close."

He kept his eyes in slits so that he could see around, but not look like he was doing anything but kissing Jewel, who was kissing him back in a very distracting way.

The two men with machine guns walked right past them, headed for the gates.

He pushed away and looked at her. "You weren't helping," he said, smiling.

"I was helping myself," she said, laughing, then turned to see where the poorly dressed men with guns were headed.

"Let's tail them," Tommy said, taking her hand and walking about sixty paces behind the two.

The Brigade men walked right through security, but Tommy felt that he and Jewel needed to act like live people, so he grabbed a couple ghost tickets from a nearby passenger, handed one to Jewel, and they went through security looking normal, but not waiting in any lines.

Tommy half expected the x-ray scanner to see him, but he didn't even cause a beep.

The two men went to a gate and sat down with their backs to a wall and out of the way of traffic.

"Let's find out if that's the Senator's gate for tomorrow," Jewel said as they strolled past the two.

Tommy nodded and Jewel went over to a woman working at a Southwest computer out of sight of the two Brigade men. Tommy watched as Jewel merged with the woman and within a minute had the flight information that the Senator was coming in from Denver and that was the gate assigned at the moment to that flight.

She left the woman after clearing the search and putting her back on the task she was working on.

"That's the Senator's gate," she said. "About nine hours from now."

K.J. appeared next to them. "Got them all wrapped up like little gifts under a Christmas tree?"

Jewel laughed and Tommy just shook his head. "We know where they are if that's what you mean."

"You police types are never any fun," K.J. said, pouting.

"Trust me," Jewel said, smiling at Tommy, "I can vouch for him being a lot of fun."

"On that fine sexual note," K.J. said, "I'm going to go scout for any other Brigade members in the area. Make sure we have this covered."

"And figure out how they knew where we were," Tommy said. That was the information he wanted more than anything else.

K.J. nodded and vanished.

"Now we wait," Jewel said.

There was a nearby bar and Mexican food restaurant, so they went in there and found a table in a place they couldn't see the two Brigade men, but would see if they left the gate area in a normal way.

Tommy was worried they could just go through a wall and come around behind them in some fashion, so as Jewel grabbed a basket of chips from a passing waiter and two glasses of ice water, Tommy kept watch.

And then together, they spent the next hour munching on chips and trying to make sure the two men didn't come at them in any way.

A very stressful hour.

It was just midnight. There was still eight hours left to wait.

It was going to be a very long night.

Thirty-seven

JEWEL WAS HAPPY that they had gotten something to eat, but at some point they were going to have to move since the restaurant closed at midnight. They would look out of place otherwise sitting in a close restaurant.

At one point Tommy had shaken his head and said simply, "We don't look like passengers. Keep guard."

He stood and quickly went to another couple sitting near the back of the restaurant and picked up the ghost versions of their bags. The woman had a small blue roll-around and the man had a leather briefcase.

Jewel was impressed. Something she had not thought of, but he was right. You almost never saw a person inside security without a carry-on bag or two.

He brought the bags back over and set them so that they could be seen from the main aisle of the terminal.

It was getting late enough that there just weren't many people around, which worried Jewel as well. It was a ton easier to hide in a crowd.

Suddenly K.J. appeared and sat in a third chair. "Luggage," he said, looking at their bags. "Nice thinking, but you could have had a little better taste than that ugly blue and the phony leather briefcase. You two were in Montana far too long, that much is clear."

Jewel, laughing, glanced down at the luggage and saw nothing at all wrong with either the small suitcase or the briefcase.

"So anything?" Tommy asked.

"No other Brigade soldiers closer than Los Angeles," K.J. said. "And I understand how they found you."

"How?" Jewel said.

"I forgot to tell you how to shelter yourself, so you two were broadcasting on all bands. Sorry, my bad, very bad."

"Broadcasting?" Tommy asked.

"Shelter ourselves?" Jewel asked.

"Are we broadcasting now?" Tommy asked, glancing in the direction of the two men with machine guns.

K.J. shook his head. "Been a while since I trained new recruits. All of us in this realm of real, but not real, this ghost realm, including Brigade members, sort of send out waves of faint energy through the air. Actually, live people do as well, but the waves don't get far from the body. The waves have been photographed, actually, on live people. They are called auras."

"Do these waves look like auras?" Jewel asked, "because I'm not seeing anything."

K.J. held up his hand for her to wait a moment. Then he said, "Again, my fault on this. I should have given this ability to you earlier. Anyone in this realm can see the aura waves others let off and find others. On missions, we block our own waves."

He then reached forward and touched Jewel on the forehead, then did the same for Tommy.

"See them now?" K.J. asked. "They are kind of pretty in an induced drug state sort of way."

Jewel instantly saw what K.J. was talking about. Around all three of them orange and yellow and blue and green waves sort of radiated away in all directions from each of them. But the waves were stopped by a large sphere about five feet away from them.

Wow, it was pretty. And very, very distracting.

She looked toward the Brigade men and could see black waves radiating from the area of the gate. No color, just all black.

"The sphere is our block," K.J. said. "I made it larger so you can see it. Another advantage besides looks and smarts and charm that we have over the Brigade soldiers is that we can block our signal waves and they cannot. We can always see them coming which helps a ton, let me tell you."

"And their auras are always black?" Jewel asked, stunned at what kind of person could just emit all black.

"Always," K.J. said, nodding. "Like a bad funeral without flowers."

"So how big are our the blocks normally?" Tommy asked.

"Skin tight," K.J. said. "I gave you both the ability to do it, so go ahead and try and I'll hold the larger block to keep from giving us away to our friends around the corner."

Jewel had no idea what K.J. was talking about.

Tommy clearly didn't understand either.

"No idea how to do that?" Jewel said.

"Just think the words aura skin tight," K.J. said.

Jewel did and the colors flowing from every inch of her body stopped instantly.

Tommy did the same.

"Now you two really look like live people," K.J. said. "Auras tucked in tight against your skin."

"So how come they didn't see us when they passed us in the airport? And in the buffet earlier." Tommy asked.

"I was blocking your waves," K.J. said. "I had a hunch that was how they found you in the hotel, but I had to make sure first. Again, my bad."

"So how long do they stay tight in like this?" Jewel asked.

"Until you release them," K.J. said, shrugging. "But honestly I see no reason to release them since you can then be seen by those idiots."

"How do we release them?" Tommy asked, "just in case we need to be seen.

K.J. looked puzzled, put the bubble around them again, and then said, "Just think that you want your auras open."

Jewel did that and again beautiful colors radiated off of her in all directions.

Tommy did the same and their colors mixed and blended in so many different places. She liked how they blended.

Jewel studied it for a moment, then thought about bringing her aura tight again and the colors from her body disappeared.

Tommy did the same.

K.J. nodded. "Quick learners as expected. Now look." He pointed out into the area of the gate.

The two Brigade men were clearly still there, and black waves filled the gate area like dirty waves of dark water.

"How far can that be seen?" Tommy asked.

K.J. shrugged. "A ways, which is how I knew there were no other Brigade members in this area."

"Look," Jewel said as the two people from whom Tommy had taken their ghost luggage walked past. She was stunned. She could, if she looked hard, see the auras of both people. The woman's aura was brown with only a few faint colors left. The man's was mostly black, with only shades of brown left.

She could see, without touching either person that they were unhappy and the man was working toward evil in some

form or another and clearly dragging his wife down with him.

"Wow," Tommy said softly as he stared at them.

A woman and a small boy about six were coming up the concourse. Jewel stared at them until she could see the colors that radiated off them. They had auras bright and colorful and active.

"Pretty amazing tool," K.J. said. "As time goes on, you'll learn how to use it on missions and other things. For example, see the woman's red area around her hips?"

Jewel stared hard and then nodded as the woman went past them.

"That is a sign she's fertile right now," K.J. said. "A signal to men to come a calling to keep the species reproducing in that old tried and true heterosexual way."

"So the various colors all mean something?" Tommy asked.

"I've been learning them for decades and I still don't know all of it," K.J. said. "But they mean a great deal. And black is evil, pure and simple."

Jewel glanced at the black waves radiating off the Brigade soldiers out of sight in the waiting area, then at the clock over the arrivals board.

Midnight. Another hour down.

Seven hours to go.

Thirty-eight

AFTER K.J. MADE sure they were all right, he said that they should call him if they had questions, he was going to bed. He said something about satin sheets and a fluffy panda to hug, but Tommy missed most of it, even though Jewel laughed.

They moved down the concourse a ways to a Japanese restaurant that seemed to allow people to sit in it all night, even though it was closed. They could still see the black waves radiating from the waiting area from their location.

They got some snacks from a vendor and then took turns napping for an hour, stretched out on the floor.

When Tommy awoke a little after five a.m. to give Jewel a moment to go to the

restroom and then get some more sleep, it dawned on him that they needed to take the fight to the Brigade men and do it before the senator arrived.

So when Jewel got back from the restroom after splashing water on her face, he called K.J. "Sorry to wake you, K.J. but need some advice on a plan."

Jewel frowned at him.

"Just a hair-brained idea," he said.

She smiled and kissed him.

A moment later K.J. appeared wearing one-piece flowered pajamas with feet. Tommy was surprised the feet didn't have bunnies on them. K.J. had a bright pink sleep mask pushed up on his forehead and a white teddy bear in one arm. And he looked like hell, his eyes barely a slit.

"Sorry again," Tommy said. "But people are starting to show up here and we have under two hours until the senator arrives."

K.J. said nothing, just nodded that Tommy should go on.

"You said you knocked out a Brigade man with a pan once?"

K.J. again nodded.

"So what happens if we go through that wall they are sitting against and hit them both with something hard, knock them out? Can we tie them up and make sure they can't bother us for the day?"

"Oh, I like that plan," Jewel said.

K.J. blinked, then said, "Let me go get dressed and brush my teeth. Night breath is never fun unless you have spent the night in wonderful and strange positions with a partner. And bunny here doesn't count. You two get something to eat for yourselves. I'll be back in thirty minutes."

He vanished.

They both grabbed their ghost luggage and headed toward a fast food restaurant that was just opening up. They both managed to grab cups of coffee and something that passed for a breakfast sandwich, then went back to the still-closed Japanese restaurant and sat down to eat.

As they were finishing, K.J. appeared and wrinkled his nose at their food. "Luckily you are already dead or that stuff would kill you."

K.J. looked freshly showered and was dressed in dark blue slacks, a pink shirt, and a light sports-coat-like jacket. He almost blended in. Almost.

"So can we do that?" Tommy asked. "I'm thinking we knock them out, tie them up, just before the senator's plane arrives."

"Is there something that can tie up a ghost?" Jewel asked.

K.J. nodded. "There is a ghost element to everything as you two have been learning. A ghost element in this realm is real to us, just as that food you ate was real. Bad, but real."

Tommy nodded. "So you like the idea?"

"I do," K.J. said. "But not sure you two can pull it off."

Tommy was shocked by that.

Jewel looked puzzled.

K.J. laughed. "You two are not the violent type. I'm not sure that even if you knew you couldn't hurt the two men for more than a day, you could swing something at a man's head hard enough to knock them out."

Tommy nodded. "I don't see us having a choice."

"I don't either," Jewel said. "We need to be free of those two to really make sure the senator isn't killed in that room with that girl."

"I agree," K.J. said. "But if either of you miss, they have machine guns remember? It has to be either them or you in a fight like that and you have to know it going in. One of you hesitates or doesn't swing hard enough and both of you will be waking up in a great deal of pain in a few days."

Tommy nodded and the three of them sat there in silence for a moment, thinking. Then Tommy decided to move to his next question.

"If we knock those two out of the picture," Tommy said, "would the Brigade send reinforcements? Would their bosses even know their two men were down?"

K.J. nodded. "They would know. And if they thought this assignment was important enough, and had someone close enough that was free, they would send two more, more than likely from LA."

"But they might not," Jewel said.

"And they might not have anyone free," Tommy said.

"They might not," K.J. nodded.

Again they sat in silence. That was worth a chance as far as Tommy was concerned.

Finally Tommy looked at Jewel. "You up for giving a guy a bad headache?"

She laughed. "I am."

"Then let's do it," Tommy said. His stomach twisted when he said that. They were risking the entire mission right here. But they had to get those two with their machine guns out of the way.

Jewel glanced at the clock at the top of the arrivals board outside where they were sitting. "Senator arrives in fifty minutes."

Tommy stood and went through the counter and into the back kitchen of the restaurant. There, hanging from hooks were two very large and very heavy skillet-like pans.

Tommy took both of them back out into the restaurant, making sure that the

two Brigade men were out of sight before handing a pan to Jewel. "Think you can swing that with some force."

Jewel hefted it and then nodded. "They won't know what hit them."

"And that's exactly what needs to happen," K.J. said. "Good luck. I'll go scout them out and make sure they are still against the wall. Watch for the black waves and follow them to their source through the wall."

Tommy nodded and he and Jewel stood as K.J. disappeared.

"You all right?" Tommy asked.

"Scared to death, but I'll be fine."

"Oh, good," Tommy said, smiling at her. "I was hoping I wasn't the only one scared."

"Deputies aren't supposed to be scared," she said as they headed for the wall that divided the men from the area they were in.

"Doctors are not supposed to be scared," he said.

"So much for those myths," she said, laughing.

"Yeah," he said, laughing with her.

But it didn't help the fear filling his stomach and clamping it tight around the breakfast sandwich and coffee he now wished he hadn't eaten.

Thirty-nine

JEWEL MANAGED TO keep her eyes open as they went through the wall and into a storage room for cleaners in the area between the two waiting areas. It had dim light and was full of cleaning carts. It smelled like bleach.

She could see the black waves coming through the wall directly in front of them. Two sets of waves about chest waist high.

"Both men are in position," K.J.'s voice said in a whisper from the air. "Both have their heads back, both are asleep. But better hurry, a couple is heading toward them and if they sit on them, the Brigade men will wake up."

"Ready," Tommy whispered.

Jewel nodded and made herself take a deep breath and grab the heavy pan with both hands.

Tommy moved over to the wall about three feet from the men and stuck his head through, then pulled it back. "Wall is only about five inches thick," he whispered. "We swing from here as hard as we can through the wall. Swing at the top of the waves about here."

He showed her where on the wall. Then he braced his feet.

She stood beside him and braced her feet as well.

She couldn't believe she was doing this, but she just made herself think of it as only an exercise. She forced herself to breathe and focus.

Breathe and focus on the spot just beyond the wall.

Tommy raised the pan over his head.

She did the same. It felt surprisingly heavy.

Focus.

"On the count of three," he whispered.

She nodded, staying focused on the point just beyond the edge of the wall, gripping the pan like it would fly out of her hands at any moment.

"One, two, three."

She swung the pan down as hard as she could at the same time Tommy did.

Her pan went right through the wall and hit something hard.

The impact stung her hands, and the impact vibrated up her arms, but she didn't drop the pan.

Tommy hit something hard as well.

The sound was a dull thud and crack.

They both instantly stepped through the wall and into the waiting area, pans raised like two mad cooks in a crowded kitchen.

Both men with bib overalls were slumped in their chairs, but the one she had hit was moaning.

Tommy stepped forward and smashed the huge, heavy pan into the side of his head, snapping it sideways with a loud thump.

Jewel was shocked.

On a live person, that was more than likely a death blow. K.J. had been right, if she had needed to see whom she was swinging at, she might not have been able to do it hard enough.

K.J. appeared and quickly pulled both men to the floor as the couple wearing Bermuda shorts and carrying cups of coffee took the two seats.

"There's some cord in the Mexican restaurant to guide people to the ordering area," Tommy said. "I'll get it."

He handed K.J. his pan and headed off.

K.J. handed the heavy pan to Jewel to hold and then got out some disinfectant in a small bottle and squeezed it all over his hands. "I hate touching those men. Just makes me feel dirty all over. Yuck."

Jewel just stood there, shocked that she had done what she had done.

There were good things about being a Ghost Agent, but also some bad stuff, and this was clearly one of those bad things.

She just kept staring at the two Brigade men knocked cold on the floor. Their black waves of aura still radiated off of them. Both still had their machine guns strapped over their shoulders. And they smelled like a backed-up sewer. She wondered when either of them had ever washed those bib coveralls, and if they wore anything under them.

She sure wasn't going to look.

Tommy came back with a bunch of the cord about a quarter inch thick and colored in bright reds and orange swirling colors.

He pulled one man's machine gun off and tossed it in a garbage can nearby. "Will that vanish in a few hours?"

"It will," K.J. said, nodding, still putting more disinfectant on his hands.

Jewel stood there with a heavy skillet in each hand and watched as Tommy pulled the other machine gun off the second man and tossed it into the trash as well.

For an instant she felt odd leaving weapons like that in the trash. Then she kicked herself saying that they were not real weapons in the real world. No kid was going to pick it up and use it by accident.

"Wow, these guys have an odor to them," Tommy said, making a face and turning his head to take a breath.

"These two are fairly clean ones," K.J. said, shuddering from some memory in the past.

Tommy expertly tied one wrist of one man, then wrapped it around the man's feet, tied it off, and then tied the other wrist. To Jewel the guy looked like a calf tied up at a rodeo with his hands and feet tied together behind his back.

Tommy cinched it tight, so tight Jewel wondered if it broke some of the guy's bones.

Then Tommy did the same to the other one.

"Perfect," K.J. said, handing Tommy the disinfectant, which Tommy gladly spread all over his hands.

"Now one more thing," K.J. said as Tommy finished and handed him back the small bottle.

K.J. went over to one of the Brigade men, and, making sure to not touch anything on the man, he pulled the guy toward the windows using the rope they were tied up with.

Jewel had no idea what he intended, but Tommy clearly understood and grabbed the other guy, also by the rope, and pulled him along toward the window.

Then when both men were near the wall that looked out over the tarmac twenty feet below, both K.J. and Tommy stood back.

"I give you the pleasure," K.J. said, bowing.

Tommy smiled and with one foot reached out and pushed the man through the wall.

Jewel came over and looked down at the tied up figure of the man smashed into the concrete below.

Tommy pushed the other Brigade man through the wall and he fell next to his partner.

The three of them stood there looking down until finally Jewel turned to Tommy. "That's going to really hurt when they come to."

Both Tommy and K.J. laughed as the attendant behind a desk announced the arrival of the senator's flight.

Forty

"YOU TWO ARE going to be very special agents," K.J. said as they stood waiting for the senator to get off the plane. "You've only been dead four days and you are already way ahead of most other agents."

"We have a good coach," Tommy said, smiling at K.J.

"Oh, trust me, sweet man with the wonderful smile," K.J. said, "I'm still not sure I would have been able to do what you two did to those two Brigade men. Brilliant idea, but beyond me."

"You said you hit one with a pan once," Jewel said a half second before Tommy could say anything.

"He was going to take over the body of my favorite chef to poison a customer and I just couldn't allow a master chef's reputation to be ruined like that. I had no choice. The Brigade soldier made me mad and I hit him three times before he stopped moving. He stayed down long enough to stop the poisoning plot. And I broke a nail on top of that. A horrid day all around."

Tommy just shook his head. He really, really liked K.J., but clearly the guy was from a different world completely.

At that moment the senator came out of the plane followed by two of his staff. He had a black garment bag over one shoulder. He had on a silk suit and no tie. He looked relaxed, yet ready to meet any press he might see.

Tommy instantly hated the look of the man.

Instantly.

But he had no idea why.

"Look at his aura," Jewel said softly, sounding shocked.

Then Tommy saw it. The aura was almost entirely black. Very few colors or light areas anywhere.

If black aura meant evil, this man was almost entirely evil.

"This doesn't seem right," Tommy said. "Let me find out what we are dealing with here."

He stepped over and as the senator passed, Tommy stepped inside the man.

And was instantly repulsed.

The senator had no morals at all. None.

And no remorse about anything.

He had even killed a man at one point in his life before entering politics, but had not been a suspect in the murder.

He didn't care about any laws as long as it made him richer and more powerful.

And he was a pedophile.

He had hurt dozens of young, underage girls in the last ten years, and he was looking forward to the one in his suite tonight.

Her name was Connie Benz and she was fourteen and from a local middle school. She loved politics and she had been told that she and three others from local schools were invited to talk with the senator for a school project.

She would be the only one and he was planning on raping her and then making sure she couldn't talk by threatening her parents. The senator, just for his own jollies, would totally destroy a young girl.

Tommy felt sick.

He stepped out of the senator and let the man move on.

Tommy staggered over to a spot out of traffic near the wall and stood there, bent over, breathing hard, trying to keep his breakfast down.

Jewel was at his side instantly. "Are you all right?"

Her wonderful touch helped calm him and after a moment he stood up straight and took one more deep breath.

Jewel had her arm around him, supporting him.

"That bad?" K.J. asked, looking very worried.

"Worse," Tommy said. "The man is a powerful pedophile who has gotten away with this numbers of times in the past. He has destroyed many young girl's lives."

"Oh, no," Jewel said, covering her mouth.

"Why would your bosses care if that piece of trash dies?" Tommy asked.

K.J. took a step back and looked white. "I honestly don't know, but I'm going to go find out. I'll meet you back at the Golden Nugget in the buffet as soon as I get some answers. This does not seem right."

"Damn right it doesn't," Tommy said, letting the anger in his voice show.

K.J. nodded, looking white, and then vanished.

He and Jewel stood there for another full minute, not talking, letting people walk by them as he slowly cleared out the images from the senator's mind.

Finally, he nodded. "The images are fading. But we need to change plans because I can't spend all day in that man's mind to play poker."

Jewel nodded. "We'll come up with something."

"Remember this name," he said to Jewel. "Connie Benz."

"That's the intended victim?"

Tommy nodded. He then gave Jewel the name of the girl's school and when she was supposed to arrive at the hotel.

"She will not be hurt tonight," Jewel said, her voice firmer than Tommy had heard it in their short time together.

He put his arm around her and hugged her. "Damned right she won't be. Now we are not just trying to save some piece of trash's reputation for some future event. Now we are saving a girl's life."

Tommy turned them toward the exit and they walked with the crowd, his arm over her shoulder.

And by the time they reached the fresh air near the taxi stand, he felt better, and the images from the senator's mind had faded.

Not enough that he would forget, but enough that they didn't make him sick anymore.

Forty-one

THIRTY MINUTES LATER they were serving themselves in the wonderful Golden Nugget buffet. The place smelled of bacon and eggs and wasn't that full, considering that most of the breakfast rush was past.

It had been a very long night and Jewel wasn't really happy that she had knocked a man senseless. But clearly at times this job was going to have to require her to do things she didn't want to do.

As long as it was rare, she was fine with that, if the cause was right.

Saving a pedophile's reputation was not a just reason, but saving a young girl's life and future was worth it. And she knew she would hit ten people with frying pans to do that.

She had pretty much finished her scrambled eggs and waffle when K.J. appeared and again slid in beside Jewel in the booth.

"The girl is the key," K.J. said. "She's very smart and going to be very powerful, I am told, if allowed to grow up in a normal fashion."

"So why the focus on the senator?" K.J. asked before Jewel could do it in an angry fashion.

"Because honestly," K.J. said, "it seems this predicting the future is much harder than it seems and isn't an exact science. Who knew?"

"You mean you didn't know that before now?" Jewel asked.

"Nope, I never questioned the goal," K.J. said, until now.

"So explain to us as much as you know," Tommy said.

"From what I was just told by Aeon himself," K.J. said, "they can see events and then paths from the events, like water being poured over a perfectly smooth surface. It can go anywhere in many streams."

"So events are the trigger," Jewel said. "But no real focus on the details of the event then?"

"Not until it gets closer it seems," K.J. said. "Since this event is to happen tonight, the implications of changes into the future can be a little more clearly seen. And it seems that the senator living or dying has no impact on the future, but the girl not being involved is the turning point."

"So what was going to kill the senator tonight?" Tommy asked.

"The girl," K.J. said. "She was going to stab him a few hundred times after he raped her and fell asleep."

Jewel wanted to be sick.

She pushed the remains of her breakfast away from her and just sat there.

Tommy was doing the same thing, nodding.

Jewel knew she needed to find this girl and stop her from getting anywhere near this hotel. There could be no chance that something might go wrong with this.

And they needed to stop the senator from ever ruining any more girls' lives. She had an idea about how to stop the girl

from coming here. But no idea how to stop the senator short of killing him. And that didn't feel right.

All three of them sat there for a few minutes, saying nothing, letting the sounds and talking of the live patrons flow around them.

Then tommy looked up at her. "Remember what we did to those two men in the diner in Buffalo Jump?"

"You mean stopping them and having someone tie them up?" she asked, having no idea where he was going with this.

"No, the part about making them feel pain."

Jewel nodded, slowly starting to understand where Tommy was going with this.

"Is there any way," Tommy asked, "to make a person feel pain if they had a sexual thought or inclination?"

Jewel nodded and sat back, doing her best to remember her classes on the nerves and the brain. After a moment she nodded. "I'm going to need to test it."

She motioned for Tommy to come with her.

"Stand guard for us," Tommy said to K.J. and he nodded, looking puzzled.

She and Tommy both climbed inside a middle-aged man two booths over. She instantly knew his name was Hank and his wife's name was Bobbie and they had been married for thirty-five years since high school. He loved her and she clearly loved him, but their sex life had pretty much vanished. Right now he was excited about getting to the slot machines.

She said to Tommy, "Can you hear me?" Even though they were both inside another person, she felt like that might be easier if he could hear her.

"I can," his words came back strong and surprised.

"Get small and follow me into dear Hank's brain here," she said.

She felt like she was in a bad science fiction movie, moving up through Stan's neck and into his head. She then described to Tommy in as clear a non-medical language as she could an area of Hank's brain.

"I see it," he said.

"I'm going to try to change Hank's thinking," Jewel said, "that Bobbie is looking hot and he wants to make mad love to her before hitting the slot machines."

"And that needs to be focused into that area?"

"It does," she said. "I'm going to make Hank here think of intense desire while in Vegas for Bobbie."

She focused at the area of Hank's mind, commanding over and over that he find Bobbie a sex goddess.

Suddenly thoughts of Bobbie naked poured through Hank's mind, memories, lustful moments of Bobbie riding Hank like he was a bucking bull in a bar.

Thirty years of sexual images poured to the surface of Hank's mind and he found himself dropping the fork and panting slightly

"Oh, my," Tommy said, laughing. "Let's get out of here."

They both left as Bobbie looked worriedly at Hank. "Are you all right, dear?"

"Just thinking you are really hot-looking right now," Hank said. "Remember that time in the back of the Chrysler?"

Bobbie blushed and said, "Hush."

"How about we head back to the room after breakfast and see if we can pretend we're in that back seat again."

"I don't know," Bobbie said.

"Let me see if I can help the situation along a little," Tommy said.

He vanished inside of Bobbie.

"How about we pretend we are in that tent on the desert, remember the tent?" Hank said. "We could pile up the blankets and pretend it's a tent."

Suddenly Bobbie smiled and looked at Hank as Tommy appeared out of her. "You done with that breakfast yet?"

"Totally done," Hank said, tossing his napkin onto the table and moving over and kissing Bobbie like they were on a first date.

And she kissed him back.

"So what was the point of all that?" K.J. asked as she and Tommy slid into the booth, both laughing.

"I'm going to plant in the senator's mind thoughts that will cause extreme pain," Tommy said, smiling at K.J., "every time the senator even thinks of ever having sex again. With anyone."

"And you could put it in his mind that if he even thinks about a young girl or boy," Jewel said, smiling at Tommy, "his penis will feel like it's on fire. You could even make him believe his penis is always dripping pus, even though it wouldn't be."

"Perfect," K.J. said, laughing. "Remind me to never let you two in my mind."

"Sorry you have to go back into the senator's mind again," Jewel said, looking at Tommy.

He nodded. "I don't mind to do something like this."

Then Jewel turned to K.J. "Can you tell if other Brigade members have arrived in town."

"I can," K.J. said. "And you two are shielded perfectly so they would never find you again if they did show up."

"Just keep watch," Jewel said.

"It's nine in the morning," K.J. said. "We have eight hours, since the senator is supposed to be found dead with the girl around six, and she is supposed to have the meeting with him at five."

"I've got a plan," Jewel said, "and I think we need to get moving on it to make sure the event doesn't come close to happening."

There was no way on this earth, or in this ghost realm, that she was going to let that girl get near the senator in that suite.

Period.

Forty-two

ONE HOUR LATER, Tommy walked into a meeting in a fancy ballroom in the convention area of the Golden Nugget. The center was on the second and third floors in the older wing of the hotel, but the place looked completely remodeled with deep carpets, high ceilings, lots of mirrors and glittering walls, and roman-like pillars along halls.

The meeting the senator was sitting in had nine people, four women, five men, around a large oak table with deep leather chairs. A ring of people sat in chairs against the wall behind each person at the table, clearly assistants taking notes.

Tommy really didn't want to go into the man's head again, but at this point, he had no choice if they were going to save young girls' lives. He had to stop this monster.

Jewel had headed to the middle school to find Connie Benz. Jewel was going to climb inside her. K.J. was going to signal Tommy when Jewel was securely in place with Connie.

Tommy stood out of the way, listening but not caring as a couple of the people in the meeting droned on about something.

Suddenly K.J. appeared near Tommy.

"Jewel is in place with Connie. Not sure how she's going to handle being with a middle school young girl."

"She used to be one," Tommy said, smiling. "She should do fine."

"And there are two Brigade soldiers heading this way from LA," K.J. said. "They will be here in two hours."

Tommy took a deep breath. "This had better be long done by then."

"Agree," K.J. said. "Good luck in that cesspool of a mind."

"Thanks," Tommy said, taking a deep breath and heading for the senator.

He merged into him and again found himself almost too disgusted to think. K.J had been right, this was like wading into a cesspool.

And as far as this meeting was concerned, the only important thing to the Senator was who could pay him the most under the table.

Tommy went into the senator's mind and then focused on the area Jewel had shown him in Hank's brain.

Tommy focused the idea that any sexual thought would cause extreme pain in his groin.

Stinging pain.

And then he focused the idea that with even the slightest bit of sexual thought about anyone, his penis would feel like it was dripping hot, acid pus far worse than any urinary tract infection.

Tommy found that the senator had had two of those, and took those thoughts and magnified them, over and over.

And just looking at a young girl made it even worse.

He put the image in the senator's mind that just by looking at a young woman, pus would drip down his legs and stain his pants.

After five minutes, Tommy felt like he had the images and feelings planted firmly, but he needed to test it just a little.

He made the senator look at one of the woman sitting at the table.

Extreme pain doubled the senator over and he coughed, trying to catch his breath.

That stopped the meeting as the senator's aides ran to his side and the man next to the senator offered him a glass of water from the table.

Tommy watched as the pain cleared and the senator nodded. "I'm fine."

He sat sipping on the water, worried about what had just happened to him.

Tommy went back to work, giving the senator the idea that he needed to go to the middle school to talk with students in one hour. The same middle school Connie Benz, his intended victim was at.

Jewel's idea was that instead of the senator cancelling the meeting, or having Connie get sick and not be able to go, it would be better to watch the senator get sick. That way the young girl would have a reason why a powerful senator didn't meet with her and others her age, even though there were to be no others.

She would be disappointed, but she would take the positive from it that she had been picked, not ever knowing how close she had come to having her entire life destroyed by a monster.

So Tommy planted the seeds of the coming meeting.

Then Tommy left the senator's mind and went into the mind of the young man who clearly was his assistant.

The guy's name was Fig and he was gay and hated the senator, but had ambitions in Washington. He was a good guy who had looked the other way a few too many times. He had no idea the senator

was a pedophile and might have killed the senator himself if he discovered.

Tommy planted in his mind that the senator had the don't-miss appointment at the school to drop in and talk with Connie Benz's class in one hour.

Then Tommy left and moved over beside K.J.

"You all right?" K.J. asked.

Tommy nodded. He would be better as soon as a bunch of the senator's memories faded.

"We need to test this again," Tommy said. "We can't let this pedophile near kids unless he is fully under control."

"Agree," K.J. said. "That first test was damn funny if you ask me."

"The pain was very, very real to the senator."

"Good," K.J. said. Then he pointed to a very young assistant to one side of the room in a short skirt. "How about I have her flash her underwear at the senator, see what happens."

Tommy nodded. "I'd love to watch this from the outside."

K.J. walked around the table and then blended into the young girl. After a moment she shifted so that her legs were facing the senator.

And then, as he looked up at her as he was taking a drink of water, she opened her legs for just a little too long before crossing them.

The reaction was spectacular as far as Tommy was concerned. And he wished Jewel were here to see it.

The senator spit water all over the table, grabbed his crotch and shouted and screamed in pain.

That brought everyone in the room to their feet and backing away.

The senator's two assistants grabbed him by the arms and moved him, bent over and holding his crotch, toward the door quickly.

K.J. appeared beside Tommy, watching as the senator left. "Looks like you have just made the rest of the senator's life a very painful and sex-less experience."

Tommy just nodded. It was the least he could do to that monster.

Pain.

Lots and lots of pain was exactly what the senator deserved, considering the pain he had inflicted on young girls over the years.

Forty-three

JEWEL HAD DECIDED that staying inside Connie Benz's head for too long was just too dangerous to Connie. Jewel was afraid she might plant a stray thought or emotion that would change Connie's life.

Besides, she remembered being a young teenage girl just out of puberty. She didn't want to go back there. So she had dipped into Connie's head for a few minutes, then got out.

She stood near the back wall of the classroom, listening and watching the reactions of the kids in the room to the lesson. Some were bored and paying no attention at all to the math lesson, others were taking notes. Connie, who had on a bright blue skirt, a white blouse, and matching blue shoes was taking notes.

Jewel had no idea that in very few years, Connie was going to be stunning looking, with pure white skin, long brown hair, and a blossoming figure.

For the short few minutes that Jewel had been inside Connie's head, she saw just how excited she was that the senator had invited her to the special meeting. Her parents were going to go with her and wait in the buffet until the meeting was over.

From everything Connie and her parents had been told, two teachers and six students would be meeting with the senator from different schools around the town to ask him questions about being a senator and about living a life in politics.

On the surface it sounded wonderful for a selected group of young kids. Connie and her parents had no idea that a true evil monster was lurking, waiting for her.

Jewel had seen her share of abused children when working in Seattle. It was never pretty or easy. And every one of them had torn her heart out.

One of the older doctors noticed how distraught Jewel had been about one young girl pulled from an abusive household and brought to the hospital for treatment of injuries. The doctor had said to Jewel. "It never gets easier. And you never grow hardened to it, unlike some things around here."

"Good," was all Jewel could say.

After almost an hour of watching, K.J. appeared beside Jewel.

"How did it go?" she asked.

K.J. smiled. "Spectacular. Tommy will tell you all about it later. Right now I have two things to tell you."

Jewel turned to look at K.J., now suddenly worried.

"Two more Brigade men are on their way from LA and will be here in just over an hour."

She didn't like the sound of that at all.

"The second thing is that the senator is on his way here. About ten minutes out. From what I understand about what

Tommy did to the senator, he'll be in the hospital by the time he leaves here."

"I like the sounds of that," Jewel said. "Where's Tommy?"

"Riding with the senator and his assistants, making sure they keep this appointment," K.J. said. "I'm going back to help him now."

K.J. vanished.

Jewel stood, making herself breathe evenly, clearing her mind of as many worries and thoughts as she could.

Then she moved over and went back inside Connie Benz, making herself very small and only seeing and hearing and thinking what Connie thought.

Two minutes later there was a commotion at the door and the principal of the school, a balding man of about fifty in a button-down brown sweater walked in, followed by the senator and his two aides.

The senator was keeping his eye on the principal while the principal went on about how honored they were for the senator to be there.

Jewel could tell that Connie was so excited, she could hardly breathe. A real US senator was standing in their class-room.

Finally the introduction was over and the senator, with a smile in his pasty-white faced turned to look at the class.

Jewel kept her mind contained, not letting any thought leak out to the young girl she was inside.

The senator looked at a couple of the kids. Then he started to speak as his face got whiter and whiter.

Jewel stepped quickly out of Connie. She was in no danger now.

"Over here," Tommy said.

He and K.J. were standing in the back of the room. She moved over to stand beside Tommy and hold his hand.

"Watch this," Tommy said.

Then the senator just stopped speaking.

The room was deathly silent as every child waited for the senator to start talking again.

He looked around at the classroom full of children, and then bent over and screamed, before grabbing his crotch and passing out on the floor.

"Call 911," one of the assistants said.

"Everyone, file out the back door of the classroom please," the teacher's voice came in strong and commanding over the commotion.

The children did as they were told and Connie was with them.

"We need to watch her for the rest of the day," Jewel said. "Just to make sure."

"Agree," Tommy said, smiling and laughing.

"So besides what we talked about," Jewel said, facing Tommy, "what else did you do to the senator?"

Tommy laughed. "You mean besides the extreme pain in the groin and feeling like he has the world's worst urinary tract infection that is dripping pus every time he thinks about sex?"

"Yeah?" she asked. "What more did you do?"

"Made it so that every time he looked at anyone under eighteen, period, boy or girl, he would see a skeleton face."

"So he was looking at a classroom of skeleton faces?" K.J. asked.

Tommy nodded.

"I really love you two," K.J. said before breaking into laughter so hard, Jewel was afraid the poor little guy would hurt himself.

Jewel loved that Tommy had thought of that. Perfect and wonderful, just what a monster deserved for the rest of his life.

She moved over and kissed Tommy. "I like how you think."

"And I like what that kiss does to me," Tommy said, giving her that smile that could melt her in half before kissing her back.

"You heterosexuals make it clear why the population is overcrowded," K.J. said, shaking his head. "I'm going to go talk with Aeon, see if this event, this mission is over."

"We'll keep an eye on Connie," Jewel said. "Just in case."

K.J. nodded and vanished.

In the front of the now empty classroom, the senator was moaning and holding his crotch. And from what Jewel could tell, he had peed himself.

Outside, the sirens of an ambulance could be heard. Jewel just hoped the senator got some really attractive and sexy nurses.

It would serve the bastard right.

Forty-four

JEWEL AND TOMMY stuck with Connie for the next hour, standing in the back of a classroom as a teacher discussed with the kids what had happened, that senators were human as well, and that they fell ill just as everyone did at times.

Tommy was glad the teacher was putting it that way, making leaders real people to this group of kids. A good lesson to have.

Jewel ducked inside of Connie just for a moment, then reported back to him that Connie was all right, just disappointed.

"This will be a great memory of the day the senator passed out in her school," Jewel said.

Tommy was glad to hear that.

"All clear and your first mission is a complete success," K.J. said, popping in. "The bosses above me are impressed."

"Glad to hear that," Tommy said. For the first time since his death, he let himself relax a little.

"What about the other two Brigade soldiers?" Jewel asked a fraction of a second before Tommy could get the question out.

"They just went out to the airport," K.J. said, "loaded up their two men, and headed back to LA."

"So this area is clear of Brigade for now?" Tommy asked, relieved.

"Totally clear," K.J. said. "And now, if you two will excuse me, I have a party tonight I want to throw. A black tie hot tub party. I love those. You can only get into the hot tub if you are wearing only a black tie and nothing else. Delicious fun."

Tommy just shook his head and then a fraction of an instant before K.J. vanished, he asked, "Wait! What's next for us?"

K.J. shook his head. "I would imagine, from the look in Jewel's eyes there, that it will be some of those really gross things you heterosexuals do without clothes on."

"There will be a lot of that," Jewel said, laughing as Tommy sort of stammered. "But I think Tommy was asking about our next mission."

"Darned if I know," K.J. said. "You'll know when I know."

"Normally, how long between missions," Tommy asked.

"Might be tomorrow, might be in three months," K.J. said. "You two just keep figuring out what you can do, keep practicing, and I'll be in touch when the time comes."

He vanished.

Tommy took Jewel's hand and they headed out of the school, strolling comfortably toward the nearby road where there was a stoplight and they could jump into a car for a ride back into the heart of town. The day was growing hot and it was just barely noon.

"So what are we going to do now," Tommy asked.

"Besides sex?" Jewel asked, laughing.

"I expect lots of that," he said, smiling. "But yes, any ideas about what we should do while waiting around?"

"I do," she said. "We need to think about finding a permanent place to live. We both like to cook and I have a hunch we're going to get tired of buffet and restaurant food for every meal."

"Really good point," he said. "That's going to take some thought on how to go about doing that."

"You have any desire to go back to Montana?" she asked.

The question surprised him and he took a few steps to think about it before saying, "Not now. Maybe going back to visit down the road. But I like it here, to be honest."

"So do I," Jewel said, squeezing his hand.

"So you want to stay tonight on the strip or downtown?" Tommy asked.

"I'm kind of fond of that nifty Golden Nugget buffet," she said. "And I want to explore that downtown and Fremont Street area."

"Sounds like a start until we figure out how to get a more permanent place of our own," Tommy said. "And next time we see K.J. we need to ask him if we can

communicate directly with live people and let them see us."

Jewel again squeezed his hand. "Good thinking. But I have one more thought for today."

"Oh, oh," Tommy said. "I've only known you for five days and I already know that means trouble."

She laughed. "I think we should go visit the senator in the hospital."

That surprised Tommy. Of all the things she might have suggested, that wasn't one he expected.

"Why's that?" he asked.

"I'm just thinking that we don't let him recover at all," she said. "Connie was a very sweet girl and he would have destroyed her completely. Especially if she had stabbed and killed him as one future showed."

Tommy remembered the other young girls that man had destroyed from the senator's memory and nodded. "K.J. did say we should practice."

Jewel laughed. "He did, didn't he?"

"I'm a cop, you're a doctor. Aren't we supposed to be saving lives instead of torturing monsters?"

Jewel squeezed his hand. "We stop this monster, make sure he never has another sexual thought, saving lives is exactly what we are doing."

Tommy had to completely agree with that.

Thirty minutes later, Tommy watched as a young nurse with a perfect figure walked into the senator's room. He knew Jewel was inside of her.

The nurse bent over to check something attached to the senator, letting the top button on her blouse fall open just a little to show some white lace on her bra.

The senator had his eyes closed.

"Anything I can do for you, senator?" the young nurse asked in a very sultry voice.

The senator shook his head and opened his eyes and looked at her and at her slightly open blouse.

The scream of agony as the senator grabbed his crotch and rolled out of the bed could be heard two floors away.

~

The First Seven Issues
from all your favorite booksellers
in trade paper and electronic editions.

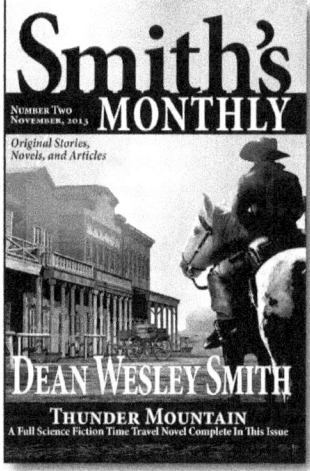

A subscription to *Smith's Monthly* saves you money and ensures you receive a monthly dose of diverse reading from *USA Today* bestselling author Dean Wesley Smith. Subscriptions are available in electronic and trade paper formats and begin with the very next volume. Subscribe today at www.SmithsMonthly.com. And if you missed one of these previously published issues, they're available from your favorite bookstore or online retailer.

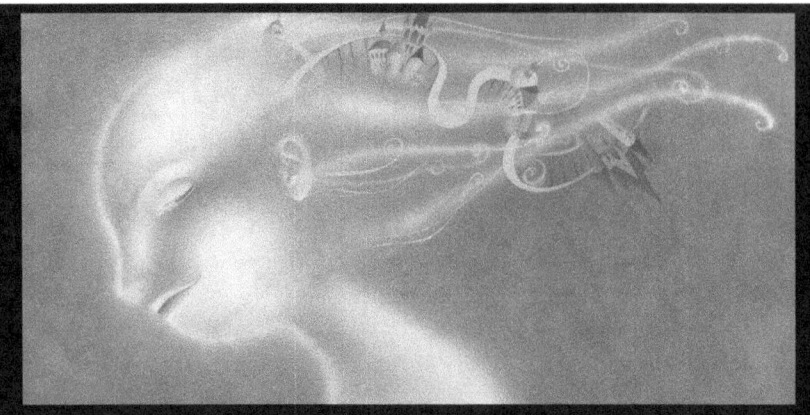

Poems by DEAN WESLEY SMITH

Jukebox Memories

My past whirlpools
on a disc of notes
composed in a faraway time.
Smells...
from sounds...
from Speakers...
her memory.

I stare as my memory moves
across the room
and retreats
BACK...
Back...
back...
into the past.

I hope they don't punch that key again.

www.ingramcontent.com/pod-product-compliance
Lightning Source LLC
Chambersburg PA
CBHW081150170626
46813CB00009B/3142